LAZY EYE

Donna Daley-Clarke

Scribner

First published in Great Britain by Scribner, 2005
An imprint of Simon and Schuster UK Ltd
A Viacom Company

Scribner and design are trademarks of Macmillan Library Reference USA, Inc.,
used under licence by Simon and Schuster, the publisher of this work.

1 3 5 7 9 10 8 6 4 2

Simon & Schuster UK Ltd
Africa House
64–78 Kingsway
London WC2B 6AH

www.simonsays.co.uk

Simon & Schuster Australia
Sydney

A CIP catalogue record for this book is available from the British Library

ISBN: 0–7432–5980–7
EAN: 9780743259804

Typeset in Granjon by M Rules
Printed and bound in Great Britain by Mackays of Chatham plc

For my grandmother, Ellen Virginia Sutton
(10 May 1926 – 22 February 1980),
with love and gratitude.

Thanks to Ben Ball, Camilla Hornby and Rochelle Venables for allowing the characters from my head to live between the covers of this book.

Thanks to Candida Clark, Jeremy Gavron and Michèle Roberts for writerly support and guidance beyond the call of duty.

Thanks to my siblings for childhood games, attentiveness at story-time, midnight feasts and inspiration.

Thanks to Sola Makinde and Melanie Daley for believing in me always.

I have crossed an ocean
I have lost my tongue
from the root of the old one,
a new one has sprung
                    Grace Nichols, *Epilogue*

Behold, this dreamer cometh.
                    Genesis 37:19

Geoffhurst

Flat 7d

Instead of cats and pilchards from flat 7b the hallway smells of the instant-headache perfume worn by women who get on number 38 buses at West End stops. I shut the street door behind me and take the stairs two at a time, slowing down when I get to the last four because a white girl is sitting on the floor, leaning her back against my bedsit door with a box of half-eaten pizza beside her. Her legs, crossed at the ankle, are blacked out by tights. She is my age, or thereabouts – twenty max, pretending to be older, playing dress-up with a 'day at the office' outfit. I drop my sports bag, spread my legs and evenly distribute my weight, but it's hard to strike a pose with stale sweat from the game on my body. I ignore the urge to lift my arms and sniff my armpits, folding them in front of my chest instead. She stops shuffling my post to pick pepperoni off a wedge of pizza.

'Can I help you?' I ask, aiming for polite but intimidating, mimicking my least favourite store detective, the one who is always up my arse, pretending to assist me. She spreads a paper tissue that says Frankies down one side on her lap and drops a crust on to it. She licks three of her fingers, rubs her hands up and down her short woollen skirt and stands up.

'Nicola Stephens.' She names her newspaper and extends her hand, dropping it slowly to her side after a few seconds, transforming rejection, as if her offer was a stretch all along. She rests her head on one side. 'Your mum . . .' She pulls a sad face like a daytime telly presenter switching to world disasters after recipe of the week.

'Excuse me,' I pick up my sports bag, and take a step towards my door. She scuttles to one side.

'Sonny Johnson, your dad. He's due for release.' His name, outside of my head, called by a stranger, makes me flinch. I try to absorb the tagging of his name to mine, but it's as if I'm reading racist graffiti on a bus shelter and have just spotted my name in amongst the insults.

'I'm offering you a chance to tell your story.'

From the pile of identical newspapers I stockpiled nine years back, the only one I didn't leave pre-shredded outside flat 7b for Nutty Shirley's cat trays comes back to me: the winners of the bouncing baby contest on one side of the page, a head-and-shoulders shot of my father on the other. He has the square dimpled jaw I have tried to convince myself belongs only to Clint Eastwood and me. I'm reminded that evil isn't always ugly. It should be – so we can all know what we are up against. The contents of the article have warped with time, leaving one readable word: sorry. Time arcs behind me and backflips; Saturday mornings with the Hulk, sucking Coca Cola cubes until the roof of my mouth bled, chewing black-jacks until my gums were as black as my arse. *Sorry.* A word I use if I step on somebody's toe or leave a watermark on Auntie Harriet's oak table.

I snatch my post from her hand.

'Nah I'll pass.' She has left oily fingerprints on a brown envelope. I try opening my door, but I can't find the keyhole and the metal keeps scratching.

'It's a big story for us. You're looking at a five figure sum.'

An ignition turns over and the engine of a sleek black Saab 900 purrs inside my head. I touch the cream leather seats and smell the walnut wood interior.

'*You're* looking at concussion if you don't move,' I tell her as my key connects, turns, and lets me in.

♠

I sit on the breakfast bar with my feet on the back of the sofa, listening, hoping to hear footsteps walking away on the other side of the door. I check the soles of my trainers. They're clean but I kick them off anyway, spin on my bottom and dangle my legs in the kitchenette. On the wall above the fridge is a photo of a girl in a hairy coat on the platform of Liverpool Street Station; boxes and a rectangular suitcase hide her feet. She stands next to a ticket collector; the zigzag ribbons in her cornrowed hair are level with the peak of his cap. She runs from the top to the bottom of the photo like a streak of golden syrup. Like a baby after fifteen rounds of peek-a-boo, my reaction refuses to lessen, because something should be done – a letter to the Queen, a reordering of the universe, a petition on Downing Street, a judicial review for people like me, to give us more time, so I coulda known her then, when she was a girl, before she was my mother.

I have other pictures. They're with Auntie Harriet for safekeeping. It's for the best. The past, the future, they need protecting. You owe it to yourself to pay attention to the new memories you're creating. Listen up. Focus. Tomorrow is yesterday soon enough and you don't want to be relying on photographs of dead people. They're tricky and need careful handling. Don't get maudlin, staring at them for long stretches every anniversary. Now and then is better, and even then go easy. Don't exceed five minutes or before you know it your recollections get duller but the photographs get sharper, then they erase your memories, and when they're gone you're fucked because memories don't have negatives. The pattern of a loved one's hair blowing through an open window is vulnerable to fading. The journey of a smile can vanish overnight.

I listen to all the sounds that make up peace and quiet. Just when the calm gets too loud Nutty Shirley shakes a box of cat biscuits and taps the side of a cat food can with a knife. *Here kitty-kitty* she calls, in the kind voice she only uses for animals.

The TV nudges my right hip as I shift positions. I turn it on without the volume and stare at the screen. The muteness demands my attention. I see angry miners. Creatures from *The Black Lagoon* with a third eye on their foreheads. They carry signs; speak in sign language. *Traitor. Scab.* The sky above their placards is dirty. Cut to Maggie Thatcher sitting at a desk with flowers on it. She wears a blue blouse tied at the neck in a bow. She shakes her head from side to side and smiles. She has un-movable hair.

The Saab 900 haunts me. I close my eyes, scared to open them in case there are dollar signs on my eyeballs. Then I remember Mum starching and ironing the clothes she gave to the Red Cross and the Live Aid concert where despite all the starving Ethiopians most of that crowd looked pretty pleased with themselves. I could be chari-table – paint the walls of my bedsit yellow to hide the damp before giving it to someone less fortunate. This would be a perfect gaff for a cripple. He could make himself a cup of tea in the breakfast bar without getting out of bed.

The air turns thick and lonely. To slice it up I change the TV channel and raise the volume. *Coronation Street* music wails out. Stan and Hilda are missing from their home and new people are there instead. It doesn't throw me. I remember the dimensions of rooms, the sizes of windows. People get fatter and older but interiors are pretty much fixed. Buildings – they're more stable than people.

Coronation Street is Auntie Harriet's favourite programme. She came to England round about when it started. She's missed eleven episodes since 1961 and knows stuff, like Ken Barlow's mother died when she was electrocuted by a hairdryer. She talks about the characters as if they're real people. Dolores (Auntie Dolores to me because *a near friend is better than a far relative*), she came to visit in a leopardskin coat with a collar that stood up under her chin. *Elsie's got one of those*, Auntie Harriet said. And when her next-door neighbour had women's-troubles-down-below I heard her say, *Rita Fairclough suffered with the exact same thing*. I tell her to go on *Mastermind*. She thinks I'm joking. *Look at my face*, I say, *am I smiling?* But she says it's for people who have been to university and done serious studies, which is how they can have Western Europe from AD 400–800 or the life and works of a dead composer as specialist subjects. Besides, it's a bit like *Coronation Street*; they're not keen on black faces. *They're keen on the licence money though*, I tell her.

If we had a normal family and Les Dennis could apply words like 'parents' to me I'd apply for *Family Fortunes*. I would put up with lame suntan jokes and not mind when he asked what my mum fed me on and what the weather was like 'up there'. Getting on the show is easy; you only have to write them a letter. If you are selected you have to stop being yourself and start conforming fast. Just think like the man in the street for thirty minutes and know the top answer when a hundred people are asked a question like, *Name something you can put your foot in*. You can't be smart or funny. Pressing the buzzer and saying *your mouth* or *an awkward situation, Les*, that won't win you a family car or a holiday in the Seychelles. Socks, slippers, shoes; they're the sorts of answers Les is looking for. You have to be average, run-of-the-mill, which I'm not, but Susie is my sister and Jason's my best friend from longtime, so I know how ordinary people think.

The pane of glass in the street door rattles as it slams. I go to put the kettle on and then I lean on the rotting window ledge and look out at the weed-choked garden until the glass panes smear from the boiling water.

I wonder what Auntie Harriet would say if I phoned her and instead of, *Yes I'll be there for Sunday dinner*, I told her I feel like an old biddy on *The Antiques Roadshow* who has just been told the ugly jumble-sale painting in the attic is worth half a million? *Geoffhurst boy,* she'll say, *you don't know jack.* And because she is *sick to the back teeth of listening to rubbish*, and *only interested in sensible conversations* because of all the crap she's heard over the years, she might hang up after that. But I do know. I haven't forgotten. The summer of '76 stands out like a splash of red in a black and white movie. It was hot enough to wonder if government scientists were doing a weather experiment – inventing a fifth season or cranking up the sunshine to kick-start the soap industry. Old people drying up and fading away. Broken-down buses steaming in rush-hour traffic. Cracked clay at the bottom of the River Lea.

I sit on my bed, shift my mug of tea into the other hand and press the button for BBC2. A city-type talks. His words sticking and unsticking. He was a tea trader before he was knocked off his bike when he wasn't wearing a helmet. Now he has head injuries and can't tell how near or far objects are, so he doesn't know where to place his hands when he picks things up. I feel bad for him, being sort of handicapped myself I notice things; like they treat the disabled like shit and when they can't say the old word any more, no matter how much saliva they swallow, they bring in a new one. Negro, coloured, black, I know what I'm talking about. Water on the brain has drained away, the deaf are no longer dumb and I haven't seen a collection box for the Spastic Society since I don't know when. They didn't find a new word for my condition. See I have a lazy eye.

If I were talking to you now I'd be looking right at you but after a while my right eye would wander off, turn out. It looks like an advantage, as if I can see remotest right, almost around corners, like a frog or a rabbit, excepting I can't and it isn't, because people treat you differently when there is something wrong with you. *There's no flies on you*, the woman in the post office says when I catch her short-changing me when I cash my giro. She's not wrong. I'm the observant type – a lifetime of overcompensation. So I'd sussed Mr Typhoo wasn't right in the head before he spoke. I'd clocked the rich-white-boy wool suit – black, cut just short of tight. He cares about threads. So explain the navy socks. Turns out he doesn't know his wife's name or how many kids he has. An information message for brain-injured people flashes and is gone. Fuck knows how the people with the scrambled brains are supposed to get down the number when there wasn't enough time for a normal person to remember where he put his pen. Poor bastard. I'd be happy to swap, because he wants to remember, and I can't forget.

♠

The light from the television flashes around the room. It's getting chilly so I pull the top bedcovers over myself without getting into bed, not wanting to soil my sheets with my stinking self. I start thinking on crazy people who slacken on their hygiene and sort of understand, because at times of stress there is more comfort in smelling yourself than you might expect.

My stomach growls. I haven't eaten since way before football and I had Jason on my team and worked harder to make sure we won, made sure the need for a scapegoat was eliminated. I picked J second. I've done that since Langley Junior Mixed. Choosing him first risks bum chum taunts, J feels patronized, and I miss out on guys who can play for real. Today he bottled on a dead cert, passed the ball straight back to me without even sizing up the situation, made me wish I'd picked him third. I could've afforded to – he's the worst player and the only white boy so he was hardly going to be snapped up. He has no confidence in his body's ability to perform. *You should have a bit more faith in yourself*, I told him after the game. *So should you*, he replied.

Jason getting lippy is my own fault. I made the mistake of telling him I was tired of liming on street corners in the summer, daytime TV in the winter. Sick of jobs where after six weeks of written warnings and appraisals with a deputy-section-supervisor in a shit-fabric suit who drew up *way forward* plans, I ended up punching my way to freedom. I was thinking about going into advertising I said – being part of a creative services department. I held it down, but the corners of his mouth twitched so I knew he was pleased. He started testing me to see if I was serious. I had it covered. *Apparently qualifications are not a must. You bring originality and an interest in popular culture and it's not unknown for them to train you on the job*. He wanted me to know that trainee posts don't pay much at the beginning. But like I said, *The dole isn't exactly raking it in*.

Jason has a habit of saying the wrong thing for the right reason, so even when he makes me so angry I lose the power of speech and want to roar and toss him through a window, I hold back until the surge of blood in my ears is a regular stream and I can speak again. That's the time, if I wanted, I could have told him how knackered I was from the effort it took to make up for having someone on my team who lacked the confidence to judge an egg without resorting to an egg-timer.

I do a food inventory without moving – an onion, a Swiss roll, margarine, half a carton of chicken chow mien and milk that doesn't smell bad even though the sell-by date passed two days ago. I could use thick chips and curry sauce from Mrs Wong's, but it's spitting outside and that can be the beginning of stiff rain, and who knows how long I'll have to wait for the chips – long enough for the sky to start rumbling and for black rain to leave everything it touches spoilt and miserable. I rename the cold leftovers Japanese Noodle

Salad (a girl trick I learnt from watching my sister get more pleasure from cheese on toast when she spreads a tissue on her lap, uses a knife and fork and calls it Welsh rarebit), and tuck in, careful not to let my fork touch the foil container, because then it tastes metallic and imagination can take you only so far.

A piece of shredded chicken gets stuck between my two front teeth. I pick at my gum-line with my thumbnail trying to pull the trapped food forward but it's lodged. Memories step out of the shadows innocently asking for a time check before mugging me.

I'm ten years old. My possessions include a broken milk tooth, a very long toe-nail clipping and an *Incredible Hulk* comic that will one day earn me serious money.

I use the corner of a double-glazing flyer to push it through, poke it with the tip of my tongue. I can't leave it alone. Special fried rice from now on. They moved playtime to 2.15 when the sun had stopped blaring, but at 3.30 when school was out, we were still popping blisters on white girls' arms. Fuck Mrs Wong. It's still there niggling. It won't go away.

In the mirror above the kitchen sink I peel my lips back and prise mushed chicken away from the gap with an opened safety pin. When I've picked it clean I smile at myself – not from satisfaction. This is the smile I give to kids when their body weight is being suspended from one lengthening arm, or when they're being shamed or slapped in public places, immediately before I go out of my way to bend down and whisper 'bully' in their mother's shell-like. It's a smile of recognition when all other eyes are studying the sky, or searching for dropped coins for the bus fare home. My lips spread automatically in such circumstances, so I'm not surprised to see the reassurance smile, because if I didn't know better, I'd say the face looking back at me is more than a little scared.

Expect: *v.* reckon on; anticipate; look for; suppose

We learn more up to the age of five than we do for the rest of our lives. I don't disagree with that entirely. It's true that from then on in learning deteriorates into book lessons from adults saying the same things over and over until you remember what someone else taught them. By the time I was four and a half I was reading *We Like to Help* in the Ladybird series and I could tie my laces in double bows, so I was no sluggard. But me? I learnt the most during my tenth summer.

There are old black folks who think there is such a thing as *too much* learning; some don't go a bundle on *too much* thinking either. Auntie Harriet was extra anti-thinking, even by old people standards. *Think too long, you're gonna think wrong*, she used to warn.

I won an *Oxford School Dictionary* that summer. Nineteen seventy-six, I'm sure about that. They gave it me for coming first in the long jump. I remember cussing because Mr Clifford, my PE teacher, said the prize would be *useful* so I had in mind running shoes, or a stopwatch. It was one of Sir's jokes. He liked torturing us boys, not enough for you to get mad and start smashing stuff up, no, just a little, so you had to admit after you cooled down that yeah, that was funny. *See* there were days when I'd thought on a word long enough for the sense to shrink to nothing, and then I'd go to the dictionary and check how a word started out before the grown-ups got a hold of it.

Sir was right, the prize *was* useful, but not in the way I expected.

The unexpectedness that summer began before the dictionary, with the realization that weathermen and other grown-ups, the people in charge of the world, could get so much so wrong. The heat made the tops of my legs rub together, my head move in and out. I forgot where the outside of my body was so I kept getting bruises from doorframes and table corners. Dibby teachers on playground duty closed their milky eyelids and showed the underside of their wrists to the sun, as their charges – damp stinky kids called *Sunbeam* when we were good and told to *turn the telly off and enjoy the sunshine* – kept playing, convinced of the goodness of the sun, running in midday heat, tar pulling away at our feet like a toffee strip, as we dodged our own vomit that baked into pease-pudding countries, forming a map of the world.

I did a swap about then. A boy called CJ or BK or two other initials instead of a name gave me what I thought were two *Spiderman* comics but one was *The Incredible Hulk* and after a while Hulk filled up my head until I had to stop me squaring up to my mum and saying, **DON'T MAKE ME ANGRY. YOU WON'T LIKE ME WHEN I'M ANGRY.**

After two terms of sucking up and one term of being reserve milk monitor, Shelley Stewart finally got to be the real thing, and then they scrapped monitors because the milk kept curdling before eleven o'clock break. They moved playtime to 2.15 when the sun had stopped blaring, but at 3.30 when school was out, we were still popping blisters on white girls' arms. I drank so much water my wee looked like cream soda, and I could piss my whole name against the wall and underline it, without running out. The kids who cycled from Sycamore Street were darker on their left sides where the sun hit them on their way home. Flies flew at half-mast. Dogs stopped chasing cats.

When I was ten and three-quarters I had myself down as inventive. No word of a lie, I invented the ice-cream float before Wimpy. I'm not saying I didn't make mistakes. Inventors have off days. God made a summer like a too far orange that ends up red. But I made an invention I've never topped. It marched out of my head and lasted all summer long.

Geoffhurst. Jason. Tony. Peter. We were The Four Aces. Although most of the time we were three.

♠

It was the last quarter of English and the classroom smelt of vomit and bleach because a first year had been heat sick in the lesson before us, so I kept thinking of swimming although I was banned for not leaving the pool when the lifeguard told us blue bands to get out.

I sat at a desk near the back of the classroom, my elbow resting on the windowsill, arm half inside half out, listening to the tune of the ice-cream van melting into traffic. I must have been sitting next to Jason.

I moved with lots of people, but me and J, we were the tightest. If I said different at the time it's because I'm no nancy-boy and I didn't want to sweet him to his face. I hold my hands up to duffing him up now and then. I was Bruce Banner turning into the Incredible Hulk. A black haze covered my brain. **I'M CHANGING! I CAN NO LONGER HELP IT . . . NO LONGER CONTROL MYSELF!**

I've split J's lip. Twice. Once, I knocked him unconscious for seven minutes. Miss had to use the special key to open both sides of the school gates for the ambulance to come through. They checked him for concussion and everything. His mum came up the school, shouting the odds, calling my name and others meant for me, but Jason wouldn't grass me up. He stuck to the accident in the playground story and all the other kids kept shtoom. One time, I cut his upper eyelid with a left hook. Now he has a scar in his eyebrow where hairs won't grow. It'll be that way for ever, and I'm not proud of that.

I couldn't concentrate. My thoughts kept evaporating. I've never been able to think all the way through if I have a bodily need, and I was thirsty. The subject was 'our house' and we were supposed to write about the people who lived there before us, an impossible task because we collected our keys from the council office. I could have written 'They took the cupboards off the kitchen walls and made fires with the wood and for a long time all our clothes smelt of burning', but I figured that was my business. I stretched my hand in the air and waved it. I might have had an important question, or the answer to one, but Miss must have known I didn't have either because she wouldn't catch my eye.

'Miss *please* can I go to the water fountain?' She carried on reading over Tia Maria's shoulder.

'The answer remains the same,' she said patting Tia Maria's back. I was being denied water because she didn't believe I really wanted it, and if I had two regular eyes I wouldn't be licking the crust forming on my bottom lip. Through the window a two-tier waterfall gushed over the hopscotch markings. Palm trees were springing up between the railings. The leaves were dark green and feathery and there were clusters of coconuts at the top.

Miss Middleton snatched my paper away and read from the page. '*I live in the flats with my mum and dad and sister*. And?' The back of Fred's head nodded with silent laughter. Freaky Freddie wore size 15 shoes and got his uniform from a special shop, and but for him I would have been the tallest boy in the school. She sighed. I turned my head towards the open window to escape her sour breath. 'Do these flats have a name?'

I was Geoffhurst and I lived in The Flats. Letters that gave a number followed by 'The Flats' as the first line of the address arrived no problem. It was like asking the Queen, *What palace?* I turned back to face her. My outer vision caught movement around the ceiling. A vulture circled the light fittings.

'You're heading for detention,' she said. I shrugged. Her attempts to bore or shame me to death had failed so now she was going to cut off my water supply and watch me shrivel. Without water I was unlikely to survive until after school anyway. I licked my arm. Salt. I thought about apartheid and Nelson Mandela, and how it wasn't worth sticking to a rule if it killed you.

I had my pen on the paper waiting for the second sentence to show up when the idea of the gang came to me – the name – what we could achieve – the Ace of Spades sticking out of the pocket of my Farrah's. My new gang was strutting through my thoughts on its way to an adventure like a Saturday morning picture short.

I looked sideways at Jason picking sunburnt skin off his neck – my second in command – the Ace of Hearts.

Jason fought like a featherweight who hadn't noticed his opponent was a heavyweight. His arms spun, he got dizzy and lost his balance. **BAH! WEAK HELPLESS CREATURE.** I worked with him, a few jabs and some combinations I thought might help. He got better with the other kids in the playground but forgot all the lessons when he fought me. When I wanted to do Jason in I'd find something he did that I knew he couldn't stop, like when he cracked his knuckles when he was nervous or when he clicked his tongue on the top of his mouth from boredom, and I'd warn him, 'You're pissing me off J. One more time, just one more time.' And when he did it again, as I knew he would, I'd go 'Right you asked for it.' But we both knew he never. It wasn't a regular thing and not once was it planned. 'Not premeditated.' Even the courts know that makes you less bad. I didn't do it often and I would like to say I felt terrible, but the truth is I felt better – as if I'd chucked up every last chunk of carroty vomit that had been building for weeks. It was like a game of tag and after I'd caught Jason I was just glad someone else was 'it'. I'd promise myself it was the last time, but a few weeks later I'd hear Jason clicking his tongue **ARGHH! I'M CHANGING! I CAN NO LONGER HELP IT . . . NO LONGER CONTROL MYSELF!** and the sickness would push up in my throat, like a breakfast kipper when you were just about to tuck into plum crumble.

I would like to know why I hurt him so much because the truth is this: every year until I was seven, when Mum told us to do our Santa list and my sister was halfway down the page writing Tiny Tears, or the name of some other dumb-arse dolly that copied a real baby doing irritating stuff like crying or wetting itself for the hundredth time, I would write just two words: *a brother*. I stopped writing that on my list the September I met Jason.

There wasn't any spit left in my mouth and my head was expanding and shrinking. I wondered what would happen to Miss Middleton if I fell into a coma. She wasn't getting any younger and like Dad said, *Jobs weren't ten a penny*. I coughed. It would be best all round if I was allowed a drink. Squinting slightly I smiled.

'Miss, I thought you should know my eyes are drying out and I can't see properly. About that drink of water . . .'

Misunderstand: *v.* (p.t. misunderstood), not understand rightly; identify wrongly

I have an overactive imagination. Let's be straight: that's a putdown, another way of calling me a liar. It stems from not being able to look someone straight in the eye. First impressions count and once they've made up their mind I'm not to be trusted, they keep watching until they catch me in the sort of everyday lie we all tell to get by. *See, I told you*, they say. But I'm with them to a point, because truth be known, I am good at making things up, though I don't always follow through. The Four Aces could easily have stayed at the ideas stage. I owe Liam on a few scores. It was down to him that the gang got going for starters.

Liam smelt like he wet the bed wearing his school clothes, jumped up, grabbed his satchel and came to class. He was a pissy little white boy who never threw a punch, but he gave me my best-ever fighting lesson when I was already a boss fighter. (Not *that* good actually, but life is about appearance and looking like the thing you are supposed to be is usually enough to carry you through.)

Mr Clifford, our PE teacher, had gone into hospital (to have his feet smashed in and reset because of bunions), so we had a substitute teacher who wore a flowery skirt and had unfriendly tits that refused to sit next to each other.

'This is your second week without a kit,' Miss said to Liam. He put his chin into his chest. Snot smudged his shirt. He didn't answer.

'Miss, he can't do PE because he's poor and pissy,' I said, swaying against a rope, squeaking my plimsoles as I dragged my feet across the floor.

Liam never had a PE kit or a tin of beans for harvest festival. It wasn't fair, her showing him up like that. Stuart started laughing and the rest of the class followed. I got a detention for defending Pisspot, another example of not being believed, of people taking me wrong. That same day a blonde girl looked at me sideways when I said a nice thing to her in the dinner queue. It's my lazy eye.

On her third week Miss came in with a new PE kit for Liam; a snow-before-the-traffic top and grey shorts with a crease in the front. When he got changed all that newness made the rest of him look grubbier and I saw he was scarred in all the places his clothes usually covered. I went through the list of diseases my mum went on about. It wasn't foot and mouth. (I couldn't see his feet, but his mouth wasn't scabby.) I settled on some kind of pox: smallpox, chicken pox, or some bigger, life-threatening pox come back from the olden days. I didn't fancy another detention so I kept my lip buttoned. I left it to someone else to ask about the marks on Pisspot's arms and legs but nobody did. Miss looked at him in his new kit and her unhappiness ran along the parallel bars and leapt over the horse to reach me. I couldn't shake the sadness. It stuck around all day like smoke on my clothes when I sat upstairs on the bus.

♠

I didn't go straight home after school. I walked through the park. I recognized some of the trees from our trip to Epping Forest a few weeks ago, the day after we slept at Auntie Blossom's because Dad had received some disappointing news to do with him being a famous footballer and playing on TV someday soon. I knew he hadn't taken it well because Mum kept adjusting her Lady Penelope glasses and wouldn't talk, just kept throwing stones in the leg-of-mutton pond.

The park was the longest way home, but I was after breasts with lots of stuffing and it was a good place to see tits – pulled high in slings that tied at the neck, pushed forward, shoved up towards female faces, swinging loose, littering the park like conkers in October. I made family comparisons. My sister's tits were gobstopper hard. Even so I begged for a feel in exchange for her turn on the washing-up rota, but once she knew how keen I was – though I tried to pretend I wasn't – she got silly and wanted me to be making her bed and all sorts. My mum's were like flat bike tyres; the nipples gazed down at the floor in a never-ending search for a puncture repair kit.

I hoped tits would be like the Raleigh Chopper that leant against my brain until I got it, and then it was no big deal and I was able to think about football again.

I stopped at a standpipe near the bus stop. There were three people waiting in line. They might not have wanted a drink. Sometimes I didn't. I drank because the standpipe was new and it made me feel like I was in an American movie. When my turn came I angled my head. Water rushed on to my face. I swallowed hard, killing my thirst because I wasn't going to spend my pocket money on lollies or drinks. When my throat closed I gargled and rubbed water into my face and head. I licked my arm inside the crease of my elbow. I could taste dirt but no salt. My hair and shirt were dry by the time I got to the Paki shop. Instead of a Space 1999 and a Coke, I bought four Consulates for Peter who only smoked menthols. I wanted to ask him to join my gang. I was going to offer him the Ace of Clubs, and I figured he could tell me about Liam.

The council had turned a blind eye and let Peter take over a garage near Charley Park. In exchange Peter had ordered other kids to go easy on the graffiti and stop burning out the other garages. Peter used his garage as a den. He slept there sometimes when he was getting on his mum's tits or when his stepdad did his head in. I knocked five times, three short two long. An eye appeared behind the spyhole. He unbolted the door. I stood back out of the way.

'Geoffhurst – my main man.' His greeting gave me hope. Perhaps we were tighter than I thought. 'Come in.'

Peter was sat on a milk crate bouncing the top half of his body in jerky circles to the dub track from the radio-cassette jumping on the floor. 'What's up?' he shouted over the bass. I shrugged. His feet were rested on a beer crate that he kicked towards me. I sat on it.

'Pull a can,' ordered Peter. I plunged my hand into a bucket of melting ice and wet fag butts and pulled out a Tab. There was a four-inch gap under the door for air to circulate and a school fan tossed warm air around. I untied my shirt from around my waist and used it to mop sweat from my face. The fan stopped. Peter kicked it but it was kaput, so he opened the garage door. There were sweat patches under the arms of his black Cecil Gee shirt. My trousers felt damp around the crotch. He tilted his head and blew smoke rings that moved in and out like jellyfish.

I was thinking how great it would be *to be* Peter, but without the ginger hair and freckles. Mr and Mrs Walters took a risk. It could have resulted in a girl with wavy hair and chocolate eyes. They ended up with a boy with a ginger afro. Some black–white combinations were too dangerous. Simple as. I'd been at the back of the ugly queue. It was as if I'd been drawn as Clint Eastwood but coloured in with a Muhammad Ali paint set.

'What's going down?' Peter turned the music low, then threw a butt into the bucket of water; it sizzled and died.

'I'm starting up a gang.' He burped. 'The Four Aces.' His breath smelt of orange and singed toothpaste. I unzipped my pencil case and gave him the cigarettes. 'You could be the leader . . . Jason's going to have to be a member so if . . .'

'All right, but don't be up in my face. You see me when you see me, yeah?' He tucked two cigarettes behind each ear. I felt the same as when I found money on the pavement and knew the happiness wouldn't run out soon because there would be 'spending it' happiness and 'having the thing I spent the money on' happiness. I raised my can into the air. Peter raised his.

Then I told him about Liam and the new PE teacher. He didn't answer straightaway. I watched his Adam's apple move up and down as he finished the rest of his Fanta. He let out sad, weary air, 50 per cent yawn and 50 per cent sigh, and then he crushed the can with one hand. 'It's this way,' he said. His afro made a clean curved line that blocked out Donna Summer's tiny tits in the poster behind him. 'Those marks on Pisspot's arms and legs. You think they're chicken pox scars. Right?'

'Right.' I dropped my head until I was looking at my thighs. I patted my afro into shape with both hands in the middle and front where it was highest.

The tape stopped. I could hear a motorbike revving up far away, or a nearby bee buzzing.

'Wrong. They're where his old man puts out his fags.' I nodded, sure he was right. I remembered a conversation I'd had with Mr Clifford. *Is it normal for a man to make his wife scream and moan?* I'd asked. He'd smiled. *Perfectly*, he'd said, but something about that conversation left me unconvinced.

Peter smoked another cigarette. I finished my drink, then I crushed the can with one hand but I must have done it wrong because it hurt.

♠

Somehow word got out. After that PE session some of the boys – but not me – stopped calling him Pisspot and he became Ashtray.

Only teachers and dinner ladies spoke to Pisspot directly, so I never thanked him for showing me there were other mums and dads fighting like superheroes – flying, tumbling through the air, splattering on walls. And some of those parents made their kids join in.

Gang: *n*. set of workmen, slaves or prisoners; band of persons acting together, esp. for criminal purposes

♠ Ace of Spades Geoffhurst Johnson
Geoffhurst started up The Four Aces. He is a talented footballer. His skill with marbles is legendary. He will one day be a great long jumper. Lucky he doesn't wear leather jakets or he would be mistakan for Shaft, although he is also James Bondish because he is cool and deadly. Girls, boys, teachers, mums, dads, everyone is charmed by him. ~~He has an amazing cents of humer hewmer hyumor.~~ He is a <u>very</u> funny guy.

♦ Ace of Diamonds Tony Kostaraciou
Tony is in the gang even though the fownding member did not want him there. He is rich because his dad owns a chip shop. He can aford to go to the sweetshop before and after school. He reckons he has a post office savings book if we ever need it and he can give us free saveloys on Tuesdays. Tony has a very fat head.

♣ Ace of Clubs Peter Walters
Peter is nearer to thirteen than he is to twelve. He does not come to all the meetings because of his age. He is in a class with yunger children because he is sposed to be stupid. He

noes most of the things grownups don't want you to noe about. He is good with locks. ~~He says he is a consolet consultunt~~.

♥ Ace of Hearts Jason Regan
Jason was fareley voted in but not everyone wanted him joining because he is sensitive.

♠

If I hadn't been on the ball Tony Kostaraciou would have stolen Jason's birthright. I was in Charley Park, the only park I ever knew with nothing green – not a tree for miles around, nothing to hide behind. (You would always be found in Charley Park, unless you were really inventive and wore grey clothes for camouflage and laid flat on the garage roofs.) It was stinking hot. It smelt like all the everyday smells had been put in an oven and the door was being opened near your face. I moved my head slowly from left to right listening to the ice-cream van tinkling: Antonio was about five minutes northwest. I checked my pockets – 12½p, four marbles and an out-of-date Red Bus Rover ticket. I cheered myself up by remembering that Antonio was stingy with the hundreds and thousands, his cornets were on the small side, and at 30p each the true cost was 1½p a lick.

I untied my shirt from my waist and used it to wipe sweat from my face and armpits. I tied it back and started carving a spade into the wooden baby swings, which isn't as mean as it sounds because the rust from the swing chains came away on your hands and I never saw a baby in Charley Park. It wasn't a place for kids. I couldn't get a curve on the spade with my penknife and the others hadn't turned up yet so I took a marble out of my pocket.

I liked to practise for when I got a game, though I hardly ever did because to say I *played* marbles was like saying Dad or Pele *played* football, and I bet they had trouble finding mates for a kick around at break time. I wouldn't have played me either. It was the price I paid for being a master player and owner of an indestructible double marble with a blue twist that, on summer days, blended into the sky when I flicked it from the drain cover next to the headmaster's windows and sent it spinning through the air, bending past the boys' toilets to land near the school gates where the girls skipped.

I was rolling Bluey between my palms when Tony, Peter and Jason turned up, all sporting bare chests in nut colours. Jason was the colour of the papery bit around a peanut that can stick in your throat if you're not careful. Tony had gone straight to Brazil.

'I'll be the Ace of Hearts,' he said, with fatheaded rudeness. No *What's happening*, no handshake – nothing. I squared up to him, putting my chin as close to his face as his belly allowed. I'd seen their heads stuck together like deformed babies sharing one brain, so I knew they'd been talking.

'I don't *think* so,' I said. Peter wanted Tony in our gang. *Turning ideas into reality costs*, he said. That was fair enough, but not everything had a price and the Ace of Hearts was not for sale.

Not that Jason was helping any.

'Don't worry I'll take diamonds,' he said, using the pussy voice I told him a hundred times to drop because it let other kids know they could fight him and win.

I carried on eyeballing Tony, wondering if I could take on a guy twice my width. Let him fear me! Let 'em all fear me! Maybe they got reason to! 'Cause they're only humans.

'Children, children, *please*,' said Peter, sitting on the roundabout. Tony looked away first.

I'll show them. I'll show the whole crummy world.

'It's too hot to fight over a card. If it means that much to you . . .' said Tony wimping out, breathing cheese-and-onion-crisp words over me. I relaxed my shoulders down and headed towards Jason, who had his feet on the armrests of a baby swing and was bending his knees, working up speed. The ground was dusty and cracked. Jason slowed down and dragged himself to a standstill with his heels and then he snatched the Ace of Hearts card from my hand. He didn't look all that grateful, considering. He picked up his can of Fab from the floor and after looking inside for flies he offered it me. I killed it and smiled.

'Geoffhurst!' He shook the dregs I left.

'Sorry J, I thought you were done.'

Peter was spread out on the big roundabout – the one you couldn't push on your own before dinner without getting light-headed. We all went and copied him, lying flat on our own triangular slice to look up at the sky. I was a perfect fit; the heels of my Converse trainers at the edge of the wood. I didn't *ever* want to outgrow the roundabout. I flicked a ladybird off my eyebrow. We moved in a slow circle. The sky had no clouds; it was like an upside-down sea from another country, and for once I was as small on the outside as I felt on the inside, less than .005. Not big enough to affect the number next to me. I could smell warmed-up nappies from the bins and glue from the crisp bags on the ground. Tony had to go home to eat the pies from the shop that didn't sell the night before and Peter had some business to attend to, but me and J stayed there going round and round watching the world swing past slow, but much too fast, and I remembered that I was seven not long ago but now I was almost eleven. The sky kept slotting in past the edges of my vision, never stopping because there was that much blue. When we came to a standstill neither of us wanted to push and I didn't have the energy to bust J's arse, and I was trying to stop all that anyway, so we stayed there looking up and I don't know about Jason, but I might have been happy not to move or grow another inch. So we waited until the last leg of the relay when the sun passed the baton to the moon.

Play: *v.* amuse oneself; engage in games, gambling, acting, etc.; take part in

To have fun at playtime you only had to know if you were a boy or a girl, the day of the week and what colour you were. Some kids had a rough time in the playground, but it's like our headmaster used to say, *Life will always be difficult for those children who don't pay attention.*

Mondays were when Doreen Watson, unable to accept Diana Ross had gone solo, auditioned other soul head girls who wanted to be Supremes while the white girls who weren't playing it and kiss-chase fought to be the blonde one in Abba. On Tuesdays we played marbles, jacks and hopscotch, Wednesdays netball, Thursdays and Fridays football. Girls jumped rope every frigging day, so although I don't remember what day it was, I can still hear the skipping songs from the day The Four Aces met for the last time.

♠

We had been building a reputation on a patch that stretched from Charley Park to the ABC cinema. Whenever we committed a crime we left a card on the library shelf in place of the book we stole or sticking out of the rows of Topics in the corner shop. There were only four aces in the pack, so we spent a lot of money on decks of cards.

We were sheltering from the sun in the bike sheds, wet to the waist, recovering from the excitement of being spectators when Craig tried to strangle Gordon with his tie for calling him a

Sonovabeech, which Stuart had told Gordon was German for a tackle from behind. Fights were breaking out most playtimes over stuff we would have been cracking up over a few months earlier when our brains weren't overheating and our thoughts were cooler.

'If we used all fifty-two cards we'd save money. Why don't we change our name to *The Cards*?' We pretended not to have heard Tony Kostaraciou because it was kinder that way and besides it was too hot to shame him. I wiped my forehead with my arm. Auntie Harriet was right, rich people were mean. *That's how they stay rich – sitting in their big cold houses wearing four jumpers with the heating down low – serving one chop and seven peas, all shared out on to the plates, and to hell with the hungry somebody dropping by.*

'I'm bored,' said Tony offering Jason cheese puffs but holding the bag halfway down so J couldn't take too many. I wiped dribble off the top of Tony's Tizer bottle and took a greedy glug before passing it to Peter, hoping he would do the same. Natalie was jumping and the rope swingers were counting her in – *Mississippi one*, *Mississippi two*. Her legs disappeared under her skirt and came back down again. The heat made me itch, but whenever I scratched a ladybird shell or a flying ant crushed under my nails. I flicked an insect wing at Tony, who had started chewing on a pink iced finger. The edges of his hair were pasted to his face. I couldn't help noticing he didn't have lips and without lips there wasn't a mouth, just a hole, a cake-hole in his big fat face.

Ippa, dippa, dation, my operation.

Jason was laying on his back with bike wheels either side of his ears.

'Suppose Shelley, Yvonne and Natalie were the last three girls playing kiss-chase, who would you go after?'

'Tony Kostaraciou,' said Peter. The place laughter came from was dried out. I half smiled and turned to look at Tony to see how he would deal with his latest insult; sweat trickled down the sides of his face. He stopped pressing his wet forefinger on to the crumbs in his cake bag.

'Why don't we rob the tuck shop?' he said.

It was a great idea, a chance to test Peter's padlock lessons. I felt mad with Jason for not having thought of it.

'Tuesday would be best, that's when they do crisp deliveries,' Tony said, excited by his one bright idea since infant school.

'Nah, Wednesday would be better,' I said, picking any other day because I didn't want Tony thinking he was running things.

'There's a staff meeting on Friday afternoon, we'll do it then,' said Peter without taking his eyes away from the girls skipping.

I imagined owning a whole box of Crunchies, enough for a summer of easy food; no cutting and chewing or searching for bones and other dangers. I could relax my mouth over chocolate until the honeycomb softened – live on it and leave my mother's food until after the heat wave, when her meals – with bones and hidden chillies to find and herbs to pick out – wouldn't wear me out before they filled me up.

'We can store the boxes in Peter's garage. If that's okay with you?' said Jason, turning to Peter and licking drips from the corner of his mouth.

'Yeah, but transportation is a problem with boxes,' said Peter pulling at his chin. The girls on each end holding the rope slowed down to count a new skipper in. *Mississippi one*, *Mississippi two*. Peter turned to watch them. *Made you look, made you stare, made the barber cut your hair. Cut it long, cut it short, cut it with a knife and fork.* 'We can empty the boxes into bags in the boys' toilets,' he said without turning back to us. 'They're on the lookout for *boxes* so they won't suspect boys with bags.'

'It's like changing getaway cars.' Sweat ran into Tony's shiny eyes. 'Brilliant,' he said shaking his head.

'We can flush the boxes down the toilets,' Jason suggested.

'If we put the bags on our handlebars we can cycle to the garages—' I said.

'Where we stash the gear,' said Tony, belly-flopping all over my sentence.

Mississippi one. Mississippi two.

My boyfriend gave me an apple. My boyfriend gave me a pear.

Miss shook the brass bell three times and the volume in the playground came down, but the skippers kept on. The rope smacked the floor. *I gave him back his apple. I gave him back his pear. I gave him back his kiss on the lips and threw him down the stairs.*

We all got up. Peter was in front of me, on his way to an extra reading class on account of his back-to-front Ss. I noticed the freckles on the back of his neck were joining up. It seemed wrong, him being in the class for thick kids. I didn't know if he understood Pythagoras, but for everything not on the blackboard – for the important things – Peter knew the answers before we had properly understood the question.

J was waffling on. I don't remember what he was saying. I was sure our crime would go down in school history. Perhaps a kid whose dad had six shops would hear about us and beg to be the Ace of Diamonds. I was walking towards an hour of medieval history but I didn't care because we were The Four Aces and we had a master plan.

♠

I went to Jason's for my tea. When you like a person for long enough you end up having to eat their food. With my one, good eye, I couldn't always see what everyone else saw – but I saw J's mum, I saw her clearly. I didn't like her. She didn't like me. We both liked Jason. *Make an effort*, he said. I looked away. *There's a wonder of nature at my house*. I shrugged and tried not to appear sceptical. *I have tit pictures of pretty women*, he said.

♠

'I would have done something special for tea if Jason had told me we were having company,' said Jason's mum, spooning an orange worm-cast of spaghetti on to a plate that she passed to me.

'I told you five hundred times,' said Jason.

'Help yourself to cheese Geoffhurst,' she said.

'Thanks Mrs err . . . Thanks.'

Jason returned to the table, with a jug of squash, mouthing *Jenny* over the top of his mum's head, as if I'd forgotten her name. But it didn't feel right calling grown-ups by their first names. I couldn't call her Mrs because she had lovers instead of husbands and you can't call a person *Jason's mum* to their face.

I looked up from my plate. She had canary yellow hair brushed into the air at the sides of her face like she was blowing through the corners of her mouth. A kid had painted the sky on her eyelids.

'Bread?' She passed me the first two floors of a block of lazily buttered bread with dry edges.

'No, you're all right,' I said, raising my palms, thinking her tits were probably fake, like Auntie Harriet's roast potatoes; all golden crispy angles on the outside, hollow inside.

'Geoffhurst, I'm sure your mum does a very different sort of tea but make yourself at home. As I keep telling Jason, as far as you're concerned, I'm colourblind.' I shovelled spaghetti into my mouth and swallowed hard.

Jason opened the double-page spread, closed it quickly then opened it again, in the teasing way Yvonne Green did with her knickers when we played show me yours and I'll show you mine. There were eight pairs of tits – just like he promised, although a staple hid one nipple. He had lied; the women weren't pretty, they were beautiful – necks like upside-down beer glasses, shaved heads, wide noses and no lipstick. Before I saw them I would have said that pretty was the square root of beautiful.

'What d'ya think?' said Jason, pulling the knuckle of his little finger until it cracked.

'Yeah, safe.' The girl with a stapled nipple had no stuffing in her breasts. She carried a baby on a sticking-out hip. I thought of Theresa-Downstairs on her balcony, sunbathing next to the cat litter tray on a blue-striped deckchair – her titties spread out like two fried eggs with overdone yolks. She must have got them on Tuesday or Thursday. I couldn't be exact, but what I did know was, she didn't have them the Saturday before.

'Did I tell you about the potato from the vegetable rack?' Jason was on his knees with one arm sliding back and forth under his mattress.

I was on my back on Jason's bed reading (an early *Hulk* comic: Rick Jones becomes the only human to know the true identity of the Hulk when Bruce Banner rescues him from an explosion. As pay-back for his life Rick, the skinny white kid, makes it his job to minimize the damage the monster is capable of).

'Shut up J.'

'*No really*, it's shaped like a willy with balls and everything.'

I put down the comic to try a hamstring stretch Mr Clifford taught me.

Jason put the potato on the bed by my side; I held my thigh against my ribs with a locked right arm but I sneaked a peep at the potato, just in case it did have balls. I looked over at J for an explanation. He was sitting curled up on the floor, holding his head with his hands.

'What's up Jason?' I asked in my softest voice. He didn't say anything but I knew he'd heard. He could be a bit sensitive so I let him be and lay back on the bed, turning the lumpy vegetable all ways trying to see what Jason saw. I wondered if J had given me the wrong potato, and I was just about to pull up the mattress and slide my hand around when he said, 'They're fighting. I hate it when they fight.' I felt he was asking for my help but I didn't know what to do so I crept out of the room and let him be.

Now, I hadn't heard a thing, so I started to listen. I couldn't hear actual words but J's mum started talking on a low level and ended up high. The man's words were hard and crunchy like walking on busted beer bottles. They took polite turns. Plates didn't smash; furniture didn't snap; bones didn't crack. No one screamed. Body parts stayed with their owners. No one flew.

Jason still had his hands over his ears but I went and sat on the stairs to listen as they volleyed bad words 'whore', 'bastard', back and forwards, 'tramp', 'liar'. J's mum was starting to push ahead with two-handed slam shots. 'Lousy-fuck.' 'Piss-artist.' Then the door banged shut and I crept back to J.

I wanted to ask if his mum would let us watch *The Bionic Woman* at 7 p.m. but it didn't seem right. I searched out my gentle voice again.

'It's over J, don't worry.' I went to rub his back but it came out more like a pat.

Jason's mum put her yellow wings around the door.

'Just wanted to remind you both, there's a Battenberg going begging.'

When we were downstairs eating cake I couldn't stop from doing the kind of deep thinking Auntie Harriet had warned me against. It affected my digestion. The crumbs kept getting stuck in my throat and making me cough, because the way my parents fought was yet another difference between us, like my hair growing out and his growing down.

Accident: *n.* unexpected happening; unintentional act; mishap, disaster; *a.* accidental

THE BODY OF A BRUTE THE SOUL OF A MAN, said the opening header. In less than five pictures he was roaring and tossing humans in the air.

My door pushed open. Mum stood in the doorway. She raised the palms of two pink washing-up gloves into the air.

'Well?' she said. I was supposed to be cleaning the inside of my bedroom window after school, even though I could see out and sunlight saw in. It was the sort of job Mum made up, which was why she didn't have time to invent cars or superheroes. I put the comic down. 'You can do it when you come back – we're going shopping.'

'Can I stay?'

'Yes, of course.' I settled back down. When I looked up she hadn't moved. 'Your dad has helped with the shopping by giving me budgeting tips and a lecture on best sources of protein, unfortunately he can't help carry home the weekly shop. But I can see you're busy too,' she said, getting louder and faster. 'So I'll let you get back to sitting on your backside reading comics.' And then she shrieked, 'The chauffeur will carry the bags or I'll ask them for home delivery, shall I?' and then she slammed my door.

DON'T MAKE ME ANGRY; YOU WON'T LIKE ME WHEN I'M ANGRY.

♠

Clouds muzzled the sun but the heat got you all the same. It was hot, but if you tried to fry an egg on the bonnet of Mr McIntyre's car it would have just run down the edges and made a mess, because despite what it said on *John Craven's Newsround*, it wasn't hot enough for that. Me and Susie were helping mum carry the shopping home from Tesco. I was. Susie dragged her behind as if she had the weight of *real* shopping to carry and not a box of Sugar Puffs in one hand and Weetabix in the other. My load was so great my bags had two other plastic carriers inside them to stop the tinned tomatoes and pilchards and frozen burgers from tearing through on to the street. My chest was closing because of the exhaust fumes. Flying ants were sticking on my face. I tried to use the situation positively – doing an upper arm workout by keeping my elbows tucked into my waist and my lower arms pushing back. When I passed Tony's dad's chip shop I raised the shopping in front of me, my arms at forward right angles.

'Mum, Geoffhurst isn't carrying the bags properly.'

'I am.' A yellow Triumph TR6 with the soft top down drove past, gleaming like a buttercup in a field of cement.

'There's a car wash ban, prick!' someone shouted. The car took a left past the traffic lights. I was wondering what my first car would be when I noticed the edgy 50p-piece tits usually only seen in black and white movies. They belonged to Mrs Davies and I knew she was gonna stop and chat. Mum called her *sometimeish*. She didn't always want to talk to us, but today, with the insects and heavy shopping and heat, she was crossing to our side of the road, even though the green man wasn't flashing. She rushed towards us carrying a basket of vegetables.

'Hindy how are you? Hello Geoffhurst,' she said, offering me a white paper bag. I pulled out a pear drop with another stuck to its side. I popped them both in my mouth. 'You'll never guess. James passed his entrance exams. He's off to St Augustine's!'

'Never!'

'C'mon Mum,' Susie wailed, walking on ahead.

'Just a minute,' Mum said, pushing one of her silver bracelets up her arm and shooting Susie a 'have manners' look.

'Bottle green stripe on black background. *And a tie.*' Truth is, we knew before Mr Davies. Yesterday morning Mum shushed us after hearing Mrs Davies' letterbox smacking. *James we did it. We passed. We're going to St Augustine's.* Then she came over all religious, *Oh My God, oh my God*, she said, over and over like she was taking a beating, or it was Saturday afternoons and she and Mr Davies were having their weekly sexing up when James was at his trumpet lesson and Theresa went ice-skating.

'Must rush, I still need to find nutmeg for my stroganoff.' And she was gone before I could put the bags down for a rest.

'Where's Susie?' Mum asked turning in a circle. I looked over my shoulder but Susie wasn't on the pavement. She was breaking rule three of the Green Cross Code; stepping out between two parked cars, crossing the road swinging her shopping bags. If she had looked both ways she would have seen the white van approaching. It screeched towards her. Mum spun round to face the sound of burning rubber. She dropped her bags and flew through the sky, landing in the road, where she volleyed Susie with both hands, butting hard enough to lift my sister into the air.

People in the street watched. A scream. A woman with triangle tits and no bra covered her eyes. The white van heading for Susie trembled to a stop in front of Mum. I watched her legs fold down. The driver of the van got out and so did a woman passenger.

'I could have killed that child,' he said, as if he had woken to pee in the night and he was sleeptalking.

'It was an accident,' the woman said, placing her hand on his chest. Mum sat on the floor like a striker on the six o'clock news. A blue Escort jerked to a standstill behind the white van, forcing the car behind it to stop too. Traffic hiccupped along the high street in both directions.

'I could have killed that child.' The man from the white van repeated his line as if he hadn't said it the first time. The woman hugged him round the neck but he stayed upright.

Two cars on opposite sides of the road were tuned in to the same radio station. The Real Thing sang *Oh bab-y Oh bab-y* through open windows. A driver dropped his head on to the steering wheel. The horn held its note, and then stopped. Fat Brenda came out of the crowd with little fat Joe and they wobbled over to help Susie up. There was dirt on the seat of Susie's green hot pants, and when she turned around the skin was grated off her knees and gravel stuck in her raw flesh like currants in an Eccles cake. She was doing the type of crying that increased the size of her head. *You to me are everything,* sang The Real Thing.

The shopping next to my feet couldn't go back in the bag – snot from the smashed eggs ran out of it, and a block of raspberry ripple ice cream leaked on the pavement next to a dented can of peeled plum tomatoes.

I didn't dare look at the white van. I imagined caved-in metal, a dented front grille, a bill for damages, and Dad fuming because he'd have to pay for the repairs when *money doesn't grow on trees*. It didn't cross my mind that Mum would receive little more than surface scratches. I didn't fret about her. Real harm didn't befall heroes. My heart was as steady as when I watched Flash Gordon dangling from an unravelling rope over a cliff edge, when, with my eyes on the screen, I blindly poked red liquorice threads into my sherbet dab. Flash, Mum, they couldn't be harmed – we needed them both for next week. Anyway, like Auntie Harriet said, *What don't kill you makes you strong,* and by that reckoning Mum had been building up strength for some time.

After the accident I kept imagining life without Susie – I had cold blood and goose-pimpled arms, and the world smelt like the rancid slime on maggot-ridden meat. For a while I tried to share my knowledge. I wanted her to know all the stuff I nearly didn't have the chance to tell her – like don't eat pears after sucking pear drops, you will be disappointed because they use too much essence in those sweets, and multiplying a taste a hundred times stops it tasting like the original thing.

Surveillance: *n*. supervision; close watch, esp. on suspected person

Susie almost dying worked in our favour. Mum was still feeling protective when I caught a cold four days later. She let me stay home from school and Susie went to stay in Auntie Harriet's germ-free environment. The top of my head felt clogged with dirty chip oil. I kept walking round the kitchen looking for the buzzing; kicking the fridge before remembering it was *inside* my head. I couldn't smell a thing, not even my own farts if I made a tent with the sheet to trap the stink.

I lay on top of my bed, naked except for my underpants. I hated the sun for being overgenerous the way I hated Tony Kostaraciou on Tuesdays when I ate free saveloy and chips from his shop. I was sweating enough for the pillows and sheets to feel damp whenever I changed positions. I had used up all my energy kneeling up at the window, watching the comings and goings. Our flat (opposite the dustbins) was perfect for surveillance and if the filth weren't such dimwits they'd have asked to use my bedroom as a stakeout to clock the estate's activities. Instead they spent their time watching cars, when you'd have thought they'd have known – not all villains drove, but *everyone* had rubbish.

I poured myself a glass of warm Lucozade and put the bottle back on Dad's domino table by my bed next to all the other things keeping me alive; two tins of vanilla Nutrament, a jar of Vicks Vapour Rub and a bottle of iron blood tonic. I was reading the comic where

Hulk had been banished to outer space. The Hulk left all the yapping to the people around him. Superman, the Silver Surfer, most of them talked you to death, not Hulk. He was above the New York skyline holding a man round the waist with one hand. On the ground were two plebs in hard hats, one was *firing ammunition* but the other had sussed the situation and was pointing at Hulk but looking at the reader. **LOOK!! NOTHING CAN STOP HIM NOW! HE CAN FLY!!**

I had got to the bit where Thunderbolt Ross was holding a meeting to plan the capture of Hulk.

'Geoffhurst, the telephone wants you. Come quick. *Your* sister is running up *my* sister's bill. Talk fast.'

'Coming.' I picked my pyjamas off the floor, put them on and pulled my dressing gown off the hook on the back of the door and ran down the corridor tying the cord as I went.

I picked up the receiver from the telephone table. Mum stopped painting her toenails pig-liver red when I came in. She walked on her heels from the sofa to where I sat at the smoked-glass dining table. She placed the back of her cool hand on my forehead and neck and shook her head as she did up the two top buttons on my pyjama top. I smiled at her even though she was strangling me.

Susie started singing. She always sang when she was trying to make me jealous.

'Hiya Susie.' I wanted to tell her to come home, that Dad's bad mood had turned inwards not outwards.

'I had pizza for dinner yesterday. Uncle Leighton drives me to school *and* Auntie Harriet says I can stay on for the holidays *and* I can have a new doll *and* we're going swimming tomorrow.' But I knew life at Auntie Harriet's was no picnic. The whole family sat at a table to eat together. Anthony had to ask to *please pass the potatoes* even though he could reach them by stretching his arm out. And if you finished your meal you had to sit there watching Slow Joe Uncle Leighton overchewing his food with his mouth open.

'Yeah, don't worry; it sounds worse than it is. It's only a cold.' Mum was butterfly-kissing my head. I waved my free arm hard enough to show I was no sissy but not so hard that she'd stop.

'Uncle Leighton's taking us to Whipsnade Zoo.'

'No really, the doctor says I'll be fine in a few days.'

'I can have anything I want here. I can have—'

'Yeah I know, I miss you too Sister dear,' I said, and then I hung up.

'Geoffhurst, when my toes are dry I'll bring you a can of something nice.' I knew it would be soup. White soup happened a lot when I was sick – cream of celery – cream of chicken – mushroom. I went to bed to escape hot white liquids and pretended to be asleep and in the end I was, which is the thing I've noticed about pretending – it can easily lead to reality.

♠

When I woke it was night, but not that dark because a big white football of a moon was throwing off light. I was lying in my sweat on a tangled sheet, my body still paralysed with sleep. I could hear the sanded-down voice Dad used with Mum when we were supposed to be sleeping. There was an echo and the sound of water turning over. They were bathing together. I hadn't shared a bath lately, not even back to back, not since Susie decided she wanted to keep her tits to herself. I imagined them: Mum liked using the stuff Auntie Harriet gave her – the home-made bath powders and the yellow candles. She probably had a glass of cold wine from the blue bottle with a nun on the front. He liked cigarettes and didn't mind the tap end. Their knees stuck up in the air and joined in a wigwam. Dad's voice echoed the way mine did the time I was exploring a cave on a school trip and called Miss something that may well have been true, but was also a rude word.

'When the governor told me to go and warm up I didn't feel bad for the other fellar – too busy feeling sweet with myself. Twenty-two months sitting on the bench and now I was being called. They called the match a *friendly*.' He laughed. 'When I tell you how swell up I feel.' I thought about the water shortage and the government man on telly saying if we didn't cut water use by half we'd be on rations until at least Christmas, and Mum shouting at us if we pulled the chain after peeing and using washing-up water for the plants on the balcony, and the brick in the toilet cistern, and here they were sneaking baths. It seemed a bit two-faced.

'I came out of the dugout, started jogging around the touchline.' My eyelids flicked open. A match struck three times before it flared. Someone shifted. Water lapped then settled. It went quiet. The plastic from a new box of cigarettes ruffled. 'They were making animal noises, scratching under their arms, hooting, and they had food throwing. Peanuts. Bananas. They were pointing their two fingers at me and chanting, *Pull the trigger shoot the nigger*. Banana skins on the pitch. My feet felt like bricks. My mind told me to finish it before they finished me. I walked back into the dugout. I wanted to run but I walked.' Dad sounded scared. It was an interesting idea, Dad as the scared and not the scarer. He kept on with more sentences. Mum must've been using the look that worked like Wonderwoman's truth lasso. She used it on me sometimes, and I always spilt.

'I couldn't feel my feet. I don't think I'm going back . . .' He paused for a long time. I kept waiting for him to finish off the sentence. I don't think I'm going back . . . *next week*. Or . . . *until I get new football boots*, but he didn't say either. I remembered him telling me, *You're only a failure when you stop trying*.

'Hush.'

'We can't eat dreams,' he said. I wondered if the people calling Dad names were from the National Front.

'There's always Trebor. Leighton said whenever you're ready.'

The NF held meetings in the Swan. Jason's mum was a cleaner there. He tackled her about working in an NF pub but she told him not to talk out of his arse, she needed the money, and did he want to go on the geography field trip or not? According to J's mum the landlord was a bit previous. The Union Jack at the front of the pub was down to him being early for the silver jubilee celebrations. J said he thought she was telling the truth; *Remember he had his Christmas lights up in November?* And I nodded because you can't tell another man his mum's talking bollocks without fighting and I was trying to stop doing him in.

Peter Walters thought the National Front was just a bunch of tossers with bad clothes sense, but I wasn't so sure. Dad called me in to watch the six o'clock news the week the NF killed a little Paki kid in Southall. *You see. I tell you*, Dad kept saying, jumping up from his chair then sitting down again. I felt bad for the mum because they stabbed her kid and left him by himself, and if I were him I'd have been crying out for her and she looked like a mashed-up cracker, as if she knew he must've been bleeding and calling, bleeding and calling and all the time he was dying she was probably doing mum jobs like cooking tea or ironing.

I wished Susie wasn't at Auntie Harriet's. I wanted to wake her. Slap her face and when she woke up confused I'd tell her, *Calm down, it's all right you were having a nightmare. I'm here.* Then I'd hug her until she fell asleep. Instead I tried to remember my favourite things like the nun says to do in *The Sound of Music*. I was lingering on walnut whip tits when I heard water being sucked down the plughole, gallons of water. More than the five inches we were allowed. They padded into their bedroom and closed the door.

I stared at the night sky so hard my right eye gave up and the moon wobbled like a china plate suspended from a string in a school play. I was trying to imagine how it might be if Dad stopped being a promising footballer and got a job at the sweet factory. I couldn't get past the Black Bomber giving up. Everyone said he was going to be *something*. What if it turned out he was nothing? Nothing? Wonderwoman had married Clark Kent and when he wasn't being Superman he made a convincing Roy of the Rovers.

He was wrong about dreams and that made me suspect he might have been wrong about other things. It wasn't so long ago that they were combing my hair, laying out clothes for me to wear, bathing me. Now they were asking me to make decisions left and right. *What secondary school did I want to go to? What did I want for dinner? What colour jumper did I prefer?* But the worst part of growing up was thinking for myself and realizing that what Mum and Dad and Auntie Harriet said wasn't the truth – it was just what they thought, and what was in their heads might be different to what was in mine. Dreams were essential foodstuffs – bread and butter and eggs and if the adults didn't write the list and provide the money and bring home the shopping what was I supposed to do when I was still too young to go out and get my own?

They were whispering. Quiet or angry talk could flip suddenly into them sexing each other up. I pulled the sheet over my head and tried to go to sleep before the sexing began. I heard a train approaching in the distance, gathering speed, coming closer, faster and faster, powering along, grinding the tracks until it was speeding, rushing and screeching towards a tunnel where it was muffled. It screamed on the other side, and then it was gone and all I could hear was blood pulsing in my eardrums.

Serious: *adj*. thoughtful, not frivolous or joking; important, esp. because of possible danger; requiring earnest thought or application; sincere

'What do you think you're doing?'

SO YOU DARE TO QUESTION THE HULK?!

The soles of my trainers squeaked to a standstill on the waxed floor. I lowered the crisp box until I could see over the top. Shelley Stewart stood there, her back to Mrs Lane's corridor art, the tips of four fingers of one hand covered with a sticky label. Under her arm was a piece of black card.

OUT OF MY WAY INSECT! There was no time for bribes or lies. Lowering the box to chest level, I raised one hand and drew a slow line with my forefinger, across my throat, from one ear to the other.

Shelley's bottom lip shook. When I ran off I heard dried pasta and peas from her collage drop to the floor.

♠

Water snaked from the entrance to the boys' toilet into the play-ground. I quickened my pace. Inside, two inches of bog water covered the concrete floor. Four of the six cubicle doors were swinging open. I heard familiar crying coming from behind one of the closed doors. I would've looked under the saloon-door gap but my feet were already wet and I didn't want to spoil my trousers. Instead I pulled my body weight over the top of the door, the way Mr

Clifford taught me to do for upper body strength. A soggy Tony Kostaraciou was crying. He looked up at me.

'They won't flush away,' he said, and then sobbed. 'They won't flush away.'

'Yeah you said.'

'Shall I call the caretaker about the blocked toilet?' asked a first year at ground level.

'Butt out,' I said, jumping down. 'Wait. Put the chocolate from this box into these bags. Do it quick and I'll make it worth your while – five, no – ten bars.' I shoved Trebor factory bags into his eager hands. I kicked the swinging door where most of the water seemed to be coming from. Squashed in the toilet bowl was the whole side of a crisp box. 'Get your fat arse in here. We need to unblock this toilet.' Tony filled up the doorway. There were dark patches under his arms and he was shuddering like a party jelly. 'Calm yourself down man.' I squashed back into the left-hand corner to give him room. Tony pulled a wet piece of cardboard out of the toilet. 'I said tear the boxes into *small* pieces.' I pulled a folded side of a crisp box out of the bowl. 'Small!' Tony started blubbing like a girl. 'Pull yourself together. Where's Peter?' I asked, frantically tearing wet cardboard.

'Flat tyre, he couldn't make it.' Tony's dozy fingers came to a halt. 'Geoffhurst,' he said. I wanted to ignore him but I couldn't risk more tears. I tried to keep my voice low and even, but with the heat and being crammed between the toilet bowl and Tony's bloated belly I was being robbed of air.

'What now?'

'We're in *so much* trouble.' My cardboard pieces were smaller than they needed to be, but I made them smaller still.

♠

Me, J and Tony Kostaraciou sat in the headmaster's office waiting for him to come back from an important meeting and decide our future. Jason had lost his shirt. There were lines of dirt and sweat on his chest. He had melted chocolate on his face and was crying like he had hiccups; quiet for a while, then little breathless sobs. Tony Kostaraciou was melting like a Kwik Save pork sausage on a barbecue. I was soaked through. My shirt clung to me. I thought I had caught a disease from the toilet because my tongue had dots on it; I could feel the roughness against my teeth. There was a painting of an onion by some kid on the wall. To take my mind off my troubles I imagined it was *my* vegetable picture and if the headmaster liked it enough to put it up in his office, then he might like me a bit too.

Sir came in frowning. We all sat up straight. He took off his jacket, hung it on a hook and sat behind his desk; he pressed his hands together like he was going to pray. My throat felt suddenly dry, almost crispy.

'Please Sir,' I asked with Oliver Twist politeness. 'Can I get a drink of water?'

'Water. Water. *You* are asking for water?' First I thought he was a bit deaf, then I realized he meant only good kids were allowed drinks. I was tempted to say, *Yes water, you know H2O, wet stuff, comes from taps.* But I could hear Mum. *Give it a rest*, she said. *No one likes a smart Alec.*

'I know *exactly* what you boys have done. There were witnesses.' Yeah, well waddya know? I wished I had been nicer to Shelley Stewart. 'And even if there were no witnesses, you were foolish enough to leave three cards behind.' He pointed at Jason, 'Hearts,' he said and then he jabbed at me, 'Spades.' Tony didn't look up to claim his title. 'Diamonds.'

We were stupid, but stupid was another word for reckless or unwise, and so was brave – other kids would remember our bravery.

I smiled. 'If I were you, I'd wipe that smirk off your face Geoffhurst. This isn't funny; it's serious, pathetic and possibly criminal. I'm sure your parents will agree with me.' When Sir said *parents* Jason stopped crying and wept like Jesus in the Bible when he knew he was going to have to die. The Ace of Hearts and the Ace of Diamonds touched along the top widths – a slight movement could cause a collapse. The Ace of Spades lay on its side strengthening the foundations. The Ace of Hearts shook. I nudged Jason.

'Get a grip J, get a grip,' I whispered, but he couldn't hear because of his bawling.

The Ace of Diamonds wobbled.

'I'll admit everything. I'll pay for it all. We don't need to involve our families. I have four Premium Bonds and a post office savings book. Have mercy on me. Please don't call my dad,' said Tony. I watched the cards flutter and tumble.

'What do you have to say for yourself?' Sir asked me. I couldn't help it; I took a soggy Ace of Spades out of my trousers pocket and laid it on the table. I pulled my chair a few inches away from Sir's desk, crossed my legs at the knee and raised one eyebrow, imagining I was James Bond. I expected him to look at me like I looked at Mr Clifford when he did things that were bad but funny. The head-master's forehead creased and then he sighed. He opened his briefcase and took out a diary. He pulled a piece of paper with phone numbers on from the pages. He picked up the phone, pushed his index finger into the zero, pulled down sharply and began to dial. The crying in the room got louder.

'Why do you do it?' Sir asked. Our parents were being called. I thought of Dad who was born in a small house in a small village on a small island. He left behind proper sunshine and a place called Mango Gully where you could sit in a ditch and eat fallen fruits until your belly cramped, you got the shits and your arms were covered in juice to the elbows, but that didn't matter because you could wash off in the sea. I remembered how he hotfooted because everyone butted in his business. He ended up in The Flats; where even people in the blocks furthest away do the triple jump to interfere in your life. I thought of Mum who wore sunglasses on cloudy days, headscarves and long coats on sunny days, and the sound of her swallowing her screams, and the way she stroked my forehead when I couldn't sleep, and how she pushed the knots of cramp out of my legs with her thumbs, and I wished I hadn't done it.

Sir was asking all of us, but he didn't expect a response, so it was to none of us really which was just as well as I couldn't find an answer that stood up on its own. Lock practice. The heat. Difficult food at home.

Principle: *n.* basic general truth; guiding rule for behaviour; moral grounds

Bed was the best place for me. I went without argument. I thought of the convicts on death row and all the early nights they must've had. I wanted to escape Mum's disappointed face and I thought it'd be best if I were out of Dad's reach when he came home. He was unlikely to wake me to beat me. In films where the killer sees their victim asleep they stand over them, maybe touch their hair, but they are safe until the next time. I couldn't sleep. I listened to car doors slamming and hissing from the blue Triumph Stag Errol had been fixing since February that still needed water for every trip.

Outside my window exhaust fumes stood up soldier still. There was a game of rounders and some of the mums were joining in, including Big Fat Brenda from the corner block, which would have been a laugh, but I don't always want to laugh even if things are funny, so I didn't go to the window, but I'd cracked it a couple inches, small enough to stop bluebottles buzzing in. A wound-up fly bounced off the glass. I listened to cutlery on plates, laughter and all different types of music fuse together. Mostly I listened to Mum bad-mouthing me to Auntie Blossom. She lived on the fourth floor like us, but in the next block, so the rooms at hers were the same as ours but the other way around.

'Girl, you should bring him to church, let the pastor lay hands on him, pray for his soul,' Auntie Blossom said leaning out of her bedroom window to talk to Mum who was in her chatting position; bum on the coal-bunker, feet on the edge of the kitchen sink, so her legs made an upside-down V and the side of her body faced the kitchen window.

'I don't know why . . .' she sucked words and smoke together, facing the yellowing kitchen ceiling, '. . . he does these things,' blowing the rest of the sentence through the open window. Her blackening lungs and possible cancer felt like my fault.

'I told you, you should have christened him.'

'The headmaster says he is one of those children who needs a firm hand.'

'Spare the rod and spoil the child,' she said. I wanted to interrupt their conversation to explain the headmaster meant taking away treats and not allowing after-school TV. He wasn't talking about beating me. 'Hold up. Two ticks. I'm turning the fire off under these ox tails and I'm coming over.' Auntie Blossom wasn't family but that didn't stop her eggsing up in my business. I called her Auntie because Mum said I should, as *a near friend was better than a far relative.* We'd spend the night there when Dad's mood blackened until the lemon walls of the hallway darkened and only lightened up after he and Mum had time alone to talk.

Auntie Blossom bought too much of everything on purpose to save money. She had a giant biscuit barrel full of economy custard creams. She didn't have kids so it was down to Susie and me to eat them. They got softer every time we went to stay. They were still wrist deep and I knew she wouldn't refill the barrel with fresh biscuits until we reached the bottom. Mum said she got stuff cheap because she worked on the tills at Kwik Save, although if you asked what her job was she'd say, *I'm in the Lord's Army*, and salute you.

The latch on the front door was clicked up ready for Auntie Blossom's arrival. In a couple of minutes she'd be at ours. I hoped she wouldn't hold my head with both hands and conjure up the Holy Spirit. She gripped too hard. I was wondering how to make myself sick. My door knocked three times and Auntie Blossom burst into my bedroom.

'Come in,' I said, because she already *was* in, and I wanted her to feel embarrassed about not waiting for an invitation. My eyes were fixed on the ceiling. Outside music from the ice-cream van slowed and the driver who hardly ever had raspberry sauce stopped on Antonio's patch.

'I hear you busy fighting for the devil.'

'No Auntie, I'm not.' Little fat Joe was screaming for ice-cream money and other kids joined in. Coins and ice-poles rained past the window, bounced off concrete.

'I hear you is a *thief*. They have a special place in hell because of the abundance of sinning – all the cheating and lying that goes with your new occupation. If I were you I'd get off my back and on to my knees.'

'Yes Auntie,' I said without flexing a leg muscle or taking my eyes away from the ceiling.

♠

I could hear Auntie Harriet's voice. She was in our kitchen, so was Auntie Blossom. Usually they bad-mouthed each other to Mum. Now they were going to have to talk to each other. I tried not to feel good about bringing them together by remembering I had done a bad thing. Auntie Blossom started praying for me. Auntie Harriet wouldn't like that. She didn't believe there were answers in the bottoms of glasses or up in heaven. I was on Auntie Blossom's side on that one. It was nice to think when the last whistle blew there was another chance for goal scoring in extra time. Auntie Blossom was querying why Auntie Harriet was drinking tea in hot weather. *It cools you down*, Auntie Harriet snapped back, *ask the Turks*. I kept forgetting I was *for it* and thinking everyday thoughts until I remembered what I'd done and then my stomach felt like I'd been at the top of the big wheel and dropped down too quickly.

Auntie Harriet loved me, *You are my one nephew.* But I'd upset her sister and she knew her first and loved her more, which I sort of understood, even though I'd known my sister for ever and I loved cherry Cabanas more than her when I'd only tasted them fourteen weeks ago.

Auntie Harriet is dangerous – you might even call her crazy. I think that's because she's no shaper. You'd never catch her looking like a square but being a triangle. Mum said she wasn't crazy, it was because she had principles and cared more about people than she did money or things. Dad said – well, he acted strange around her, the way I did with girls I was really into if they weren't the girls everyone else thought I was supposed to like, not that he pulled her hair or pretended she smelt, he just, well he was the one who called her crazy. *Play nicely or I'll stop the car and fling it out the window*, she said to me and Anthony when we were off to the cinema. And when he ignored her she threw Anthony's Six Million Dollar Man out of the car window and kept driving. That was in January and I know she'd queued for an hour in the cold three weeks earlier for that toy because I was with her. *If a piece of plastic is going to stop you acting loving, it can go*, she said. Principles.

My doorknob turned slowly – like in films when a murderer comes in when a lady is on her own, in her white nightie. My bedroom door squeaked open and Auntie Harriet walked in and sat on the end of my bed. I pulled my legs in and sat up with my knees tucked under my chin. Auntie Harriet crossed her fat black-pudding legs. She had cotton shoes with strings that tied halfway up her shins – reminded me of Spartacus. She looked at me for the longest time, then she shook her head slowly.

'You're messing with my sister's head again. Exactly how much grief are the men in your family planning on giving her?' I knew a trick question when I heard one; I wasn't trying to calculate an amount, I just wanted to explain.

'Auntie Harriet I—'

'Shut up. Don't *Auntie Harriet* me with your butter mouth.' Her lips and eyes disappeared.

SHUT UP? NOBODY TELLS THE HULK!

'Little Big Man, I seen you and your posse slinking around like grey-bellied rats, carrying on with your foolishness, but we both know you are no tea leaf, so if you can please to stop acting like one.' She uses just the right combination of boosting and battering. That's why she doesn't have to beat Anthony. She has a way of smashing you up without raising a finger.

'Listen good, Mr Hard Ears,' she said grabbing my ear.

'Ow, you're hurting me,' I moved my head in the direction of the twist like Starsky driving into a skid.

'So sue me. Listen. No more trouble; study your books and keep this clean,' she said letting go of my ear to tap the side of her nose. Susie and Anthony giggled on the other side of the door. **THE HULK HAS NO FRIENDS.**

'Another thing. One grey hair on my sister's head and you're going to have to take me on. Do I make myself clear?' Then she said loudly in a spaced-out way, even though she hadn't left a gap for me to answer the last time, 'DO – I – MAKE – MYSELF – CLEAR?'

'Yes Auntie Harriet,' I said, because she had.

♠

I was still *for it* but I needed to think. There was a possibility I would be offered a choice and I didn't want to be too scared to help myself. Any dithering and Dad would call Susie for *my slipper* or *my belt*.

Susie could outrun Speedy Gonzalez and couldn't be relied on to lose her way, or take pigeon steps, or develop short-sightedness. The slipper seemed like the soft option but it brought him up close enough to see if I cried too soon – or not soon enough, then he'd dump the slipper and use his hands. The belt was okay as long as I got the soft end and the blows only lasted as long as my lesson. I still had buckle-marks from WHAT'S. DONE. IN. THE. DARK. WILL. APP-EAR. IN. THE. LIGHT. Eleven syllables was an exception. Most of his teachings were shorter. He rotated wisdom. Under the circumstances I was expecting seven strikes – TWO. BULLS. CAN'T. REIGN. IN. ONE. PEN.

I dreamt I was Clint Eastwood.

Ah-ah, I know what you're thinking punk. You're thinking did he fire six shots or only five. And to tell you the truth I've forgotten myself in all this excitement. But being this is a .44 magnum – the most powerful handgun in the world and will blow your head clean off – you've got to ask yourself a question: Do I feel lucky? Well, do ya punk!

Dad calls my bluff and laughs. Big mistake. I blow him away. He falls in a river. Water splashes soak me through.

When I woke up my bed was wet; with a cold pissy patch that spread to my back. That was the trouble with hot weather, you ended up drinking much too late at night.

Dead: *adj.* breathless, deceased, gone, lifeless; cold

I now know it was the same day Dad went to see Uncle Leighton about a job at the Trebor sweet factory, and the count for black footballers playing league in the whole country went down from fifty to forty-nine. When he put his dirty footy gear in the bagwash it was for the last time. I'm not saying I would have acted differently; just that I didn't know is all.

♠

A week had passed since my suspension and though technically the summer holidays had started, it didn't feel like it because I wasn't allowed out to play and there hadn't been a proper end to school – no final assembly or school disco. I missed the things I thought I didn't like: the smell of the first-aid room, the brass bell at playtime, Jason's whining.

I was on my way back from Melvin's flat. Since the heat wave he'd been selling ice. He lived in the furthest away block on the top floor. He cut hair cheaper than the barber's and when there was a wedding in the community hall youths took up the top floor stairwells waiting their turn. He sold cans of meat with missing labels and tubes of glue from a suitcase under his bed. His sister was a spastic who liked water. Melvin was in third-year secondary and since leaving primary he'd been saving for a swimming pool. We had a laugh behind his back wondering where the pool was going to go. (On the roof of his block? Ha ha.) But Melvin didn't joke when it came to making money. Sometimes I pretended to lose a few pence when I went shopping for Mum. *All right, give me what you've got,* most people said, and I'd spend the difference on rhubarb and custard chews. I didn't do that with Melvin just in case he came through with the pool.

I carried the slab of ice wrapped in the plastic bag Mum sent me with. The flats were full of bodies that needed covering up. I passed an old lady with overfamiliar upper-arm flaps that waved at me although I'd never met her. I passed a pink beer gut. I couldn't wait for winter, for rollnecks and trousers. The sun was boring a headache into my forehead. Sun-loving cats tiptoed in the shadows of buildings. I hugged the melting ice, walking towards my block as quickly as the heat allowed. Water dripped on to my sandals and trickled between my toes. I kept tripping because I couldn't see my feet over the ice and the tarmac had exploded with mini earthquakes that stuck up out of the ground. When I reached my porch it was top-of-the-fridge cold. I rested on a stair for a minute, licking the ice, glad to be in the shade. I went upstairs. Our front door was already open so I kicked it wider and walked in.

'I've got the ice Mum,' I shouted as I walked up the hallway, nearly falling over Dad's work bag. It was early for him to be home. It was football training in the morning and a cash-in-hand job on a labouring site until it got dark this week. He was sitting at the kitchen table. The top button of his jeans was undone. His chest was bare but he still had boots on. He was leaning back in the chair with his hands folded behind his head. His boots bothered me, building-site boots, white with cement. He usually left them in the hallway and when he forgot Mum reminded him. They were unsuitable footwear for inside the flat on a hot day, unless he was looking to argue, and Mum was stuck on a peaceful evening. The room looked almost right but tiny details were wrong like a picture where you had to spot the mistakes from another *almost* identical one. Mum was cleaning the cooker with lemon Jif. I wondered why he was home so early. The room had a pretend citrus smell.

'Hi Dad.' I put the ice in the freezer. A *green* bluebottle circled over crockery in the washing-up bowl. I added that to the mistakes in picture B.

'Geoffhurst.'

'Yes Dad.' I wiped my face with the bottom of my T-shirt.

'So, you is a bad man now?' I looked at Mum for clues, for help. She was polishing the window ledge, rubbing the duster deep into the paintwork. Apart from sneaking to the phone box on two occasions to call Jason (and I was sure I hadn't been seen) I'd been behaving like John-boy Walton for days.

'No Dad.'

'Are the teachers telling lie pon you? You never steal the people's tings and get catch?' He was shaking his head as if a terrible injustice might have been done.

I'd thought I was safe. More than a week had passed and I had supposed Mum hadn't told him or if she had, he was leaving the punishment to her, and he was happy with her decision not to let me play out. By law, you could only be punished for a crime once. Mr Clifford had explained double jeopardy when I made the same mistake with timing on the triple jump twice. Dad was sweating on his nose. If he knew about the robbery *before*, beating me now was illegal. His mouth was moving. I was deciding between the slipper and the belt. My sweat smelt cheesy.

'Bring your marbles.'

'The slipper,' I said, then I realized what *he'd* said.

'Fetch them come,' he said, moving his mouth but not the rest of his face. My feet unstuck. I went to my room trembling and pulled my box of marbles, the whole three-year collection, out from under my bed. A dust-ball hung off the corner of the shoe-box. Marbles bashed against each other each time I shook. I wondered how long he was going to confiscate them for. I wanted them back before I started secondary school. I had my sports skills and my good looks but my marbles singled me out – won me friends and fans with a flick of my thumbnail. I felt sick. I put my head out of my bedroom window. The bins smelt high. I was tempted to drop the box, have it crash-land to safety on the strip of grass below.

Mum wasn't in the room when I came back. I didn't want what was about to happen to take place without any witnesses.

'Close the door Son.' I pressed against the door with my back. It closed in slow motion. The tap when the door slotted into the frame sounded like a nail being hit with a hammer under water. My heart jolted. Maybe he was going to throw my marbles down the chute and I mightn't be able to get them out of the downstairs dustbin before the bin men came because I was grounded. A part of my life could roll into the path of cars. I saw piles of powdered blue glass – Bluey's ashes.

Dad snatched the box and emptied the marbles on to the floor. My yellow and brown tiger's eye rolled under the fridge, winking at me from a safe place. The plain green marble that won me a *Thor* comic hid behind a chair leg. Bluey ran along the skirting. I was willing it to the other end of the room when the heel of Dad's size 14s came crashing down. He shifted his heel left and right as if he was outing a cigarette. He lifted his foot. I couldn't cry. I wanted to be dead.

I drive on to the pitch at Hackney Marshes on a Sunday morning.

I am dressed in leather. I have a gun with a silencer. I shoot him. Just before he dies I raise my helmet. Watching his face is like flicking through an old-time cartoon book of emotions.

When I opened my eyes Bluey was still alive. Fee fi fo fum. Dad was stomping and sniffing out marbles. He found a red marble, one of three identical triplets. He tried to separate them for ever. He was charging around the tiny kitchen turning this way and that, stamping on marbles in a glass-eyed rage, dancing like a giant Rumpelstiltskin, intent on turning the kitchen floor into a cemetery. Spoons and cups jumped on the draining board.

'I'm here trying to teach you something.' For the first time, I questioned his lessons, his qualifications for teaching me, for teaching my mother. I wondered about *This is for your benefit not mine. This is hurting me more than it's hurting you.* His eyes shone, like a tramp high on Special Brew, like he was on the football field pulverizing the defence. I looked at him, my lazy eye perfectly focused – right matching left. He was Rumpelstiltskin. Not one person in the kingdom could guess his name. Nobody knew who he was except me. A kaleidoscope of fragments settled and I saw him perfectly. He turned away. I wanted him to face me, admit he was *enjoying* being angry and mean and destructive because it lifted him high above his life. It was like me doing in Jason, or bunking in to Saturday morning pictures, or chopping the legs off spiders or smashing windows. *Doing bad things felt good.* I was nearly eleven and I knew that about me, and he was the Black Bomber and he didn't know it about him. Power surged through me stretching my T-shirt over my expanding chest.

'You looking at me like you want to take me on, like you hate me.' Why shouldn't I hate you? Why shouldn't I hate all of mankind? 'Is there some girl at school you're trying to impress with this bad behaviour?'

'Is there a girl *you're* trying to impress with *your* bad behaviour?'
I said.

And then the lights went out.

When I came round I could taste blood in my mouth and a harmonica was playing spaghetti Western music two blocks away. A horse neighed and rose up on its hind legs before its hooves crashed down. I had stopped wanting to be dead. I was alive and wanted to stay that way. *Eat your greens and you'll grow up big and strong like your Father*, but I never believed her and I'd been right. It was *less* than the truth because I'd be bigger and stronger and he'd be growing older and weaker and if I wanted I could kick away his walking stick and smash his skull in with the hooked end and there'd be nothing he could do.

If anyone was doing any dying, it wasn't going to be me.

A smell of pretend lemons and bleach got stronger and then I smelt onions too and I knew Mum was holding me. She shook me. *What happened?* she asked. My eyelids fluttered. Her face jumped up and down like a TV picture with no vertical hold. And then someone must've slapped the top of the box because suddenly she had one face. My lazy eye whirled away, wouldn't look at her, so I trained both eyes above her head and the next time she asked what happened I told her about the woman Dad was trying to impress. The woman he acted strange around because he liked her when he wasn't supposed to.

I told Mum about Dad and Auntie Harriet.

Back then I couldn't have laid hands on my father in anger – no strangling or stabbing. My arms were glued to their sides – by Auntie Blossom and the King James Bible *honour thy mother and thy father* – by Auntie Harriet who had once been to the funeral of a child who'd hit its mother and the kid's right arm, still raised in the air, had to be broken and then folded inwards to fit in the coffin. But I could have managed damage from a distance. I could. If I had a .44 magnum I would have torn the skin on my arms to lift the gun higher than my head – up. Up. Up. Left of centre, level with his heart, and without laying a finger on him I'd have avenged the attempted death of my marbles and taken him out with   one   clean   shot.

Starve: *v.* (cause to) die or suffer acutely from lack or shortage of food

I blamed the heat for withering my taste buds. It was similar weather when I was little and Dad force-fed me six-o-clock news footage of dead people to encourage me to eat. He weaned me on African stick-men with tennis ball joints, shrivelled skin the same colour as mine and uncombed hair like the peppercorns I grew after a week away at boys' camp. Years later I could conjure up those pictures and eat until I sneezed food through my nose, in case more cold mashed potato than my body could stand would stop babies dying with flies in their eyes.

Without telly I would have thought children only died of starvation in the olden days, in the cold, when they couldn't get enough money from sweeping chimneys and had to live in the workhouse with strangers who were stingy with the gruel. Starving in the sunshine seemed impossible. The way Mum and Auntie Harriet told it, in tropical places where there was *real* sun, you could suck an orange dry, dash the pips over your shoulder on the way home from school, and the next morning pick oranges for your lunch box from the orchard that sprang up.

Sausages with onion gravy, shepherd's pie with a splash of ketchup, spicy chicken wings with potato salad, nothing could tempt me. I ate so little Auntie Harriet made me drink bitter bush tea with twigs still in it to help me shit. I didn't hear from my stomach all summer long – not a grumble. My hunger switch melted away and much later, when it was cold enough to see my breath and I could feel my ribs through my duffel coat, I stopped looking.

♠

The breeze through the window dried the sweat on the right-hand side of my face. I listened to James downstairs playing the trumpet. He was sad about something; the notes wailed out in a blues version of 'The Golden Cockerel'. A man with his shirt buttoned to the neck, sporting a gold-leafed Bible, walked up the stairwell into Auntie Blossom's flat. In the block furthest away, the woman living in the flat under Melvin's was throwing ripped shirts and trousers out of the window on to the grass strip at the front of the block where dogs went to crap.

'Why don't you read one of your comic books?'

'Nah, I'm okay Mum.' I listened to excited voices from the prayer meeting being held at Auntie Blossom's. *Praise the Lord . . . Give Him the glory . . . Hallelujah.* The posters stuck on her window had changed. *When you are DOWN to nothing, God is UP to something* was gone, so was *Thank God for Jesus*, but the glass at the bottom was pushed to the top and I couldn't make out what the new posters said. I stretched my legs full-length pressing my toes harder on to the sink, my buttocks on to the coal bunker to stabilize myself. Blocking my lazy eye with my hand I peered out of the window until I made out the words, *If you're not close to God guess who moved?* And by its side, *Real men love Jesus.*

I don't feel no way tired, Auntie Blossom sang, and the prayer group joined in. *Nobody told me the road would be easy, but I don't believe He'd bring me this far then leave me.*

Mum stopped rubbing meat with half a lime turned inside out to pick up onion peel. Her legs folded down so far I thought she deserved an extra set of knees halfway up her thighs. She peeled the type of yam that starts out white but marbles grey after cooking.

'Mind you don't fall out. I don't have time to visit casualty. Your father has worked that job for a whole week and we're having his favourite dinner tonight. Now chop up some garlic for me.' I got down from the window seat. She stopped massaging seasoned flour into fleshy pork chops to pass me a knife. I peeled the skin off the garlic and pierced it with the tip of the knife. Liquid bubbled up. Her dress was wet at her shoulder blades where it stuck to her body and her skin glistened like the lawns in Hackney Downs if you go there really early in the morning because you can't bear to hear grown-ups fighting because you don't know who to root for, there's no referee and the word for someone who calls the police or social services is 'grass'.

♠

We ate in the kitchen at the little table made bigger by pulling the side flaps out. We fitted – just. Susie with her back to the cooker, the dial for the left-hand back burner between her shoulder blades. Mum under the window by the sink. Dad opposite her, wedged against the tall cupboard with the cereal boxes and spaghetti jar inside. I had my back to the hallway. There was a fan whirring next to the bread bin, blowing the leaves of the flower in the vase on the cooker. A tulip or daffodil or rose.

Dad was grunting like a shot-putter. He mashed yam with the length of his fork, then speared three butterbeans. A sweat bead ran off the end of his nose and into his gravy.

'Will I be allowed pocket money now you have a job?' Susie asked cutting the creamy band of fat off her pork chop.

'He *had a job before*. He was a footballer, remember?' I said, not quite believing it was over, wondering what instrument measured 'working twice as hard as everyone else', and if there wasn't one, how did you know when you got there? And how long you were supposed to stay before giving up?

'*I know*. I meant a proper job with wages.'

'Your father wants to eat. Let him be.'

'This is good,' Dad said, slurping sluggish onions, his face close to the plate. False. Once I started doubting him I couldn't stop. I found white lies, untruths, fat fibs and falsehoods. He was at it all the time, could hardly tell the truth ever.

'What do you do at the factory?'

'Susie!'

'I put the flavour in the sweets. They all start off as different coloured sugar. If I mess up, the cough candies could end up tasting of lemon sherbet.'

Talent + Hard work = Success. He practised every day. He didn't eat sweets. He worked out all his moves before the ball came to make sure he touched it no more than twice. He could score off his left foot or his right. *Naturally gifted*, they said. It was to do with him being big and having to play football in a little country where the streets were narrow and living in a small house with other people all around, so he had to do all the things he wanted in not much space. It taught him control.

The sums didn't add up.

I scooped the soft things from my plate on to my fork, reminding myself that I was able to force my body to do all sorts of things it didn't want to do – swim a length underwater, for example. I started shovelling and swallowing, shovelling and swallowing.

'Mum, Geoffhurst is being a disgusting pig.'

'Son, take time,' Mum said, pushing the palm of her hand against my forehead until I broke contact with the fork. I looked at my plate. There was a big enough dent in the food to stop. I reached for the jug of white drink and then drew my hand back.

'It's not soursop juice is it?' I figured only a fool would drink it knowingly. The clue was in the name.

'It's punch,' Mum said. I picked up my heavy crystal glass and took a gulp. Condensed milk and stout swelled in my throat.

'I need water.' Mum took a plastic cup off the draining board at her side, turned on the tap, filled it three-quarters full and passed it to me without leaving her seat.

I drank without breathing, returning the cup for a refill and drinking again until the food and drink inside me diluted.

'It's not so bad. Plenty rest. I leave the football bench for the factory bench. Always sitting,' Dad said, then he laughed and curved his mouth upwards but there was no happiness in him. Mum stabbed another pork chop and dropped it on his plate.

'Yes man!' he said. But he wasn't into the food much either. There were no piles of chewed-up bone on his plate and I sussed he was doing the underwater swimming trick too.

♠

He rubbed the middle of his chest in a clockwise circle with the top of his fist. I waited. He put his fork down. I ran my tongue over the inside of my lip where the skin was still raised. He was a quitter and a coward. I didn't want to admire anything about him but I couldn't take my eyes off him. He opened his mouth and a belch came out that took a full nine seconds to die away. I'd asked around, there were no other dads who could do that.

♠

Pork chops, onion gravy, butter beans, white yam and peach slices in syrup with Carnation milk.

If I'd known the last meal with my family was going to *be* my last meal with my family I would have behaved different – looked up from my plate at my mother – kept my elbows away from my sister – chewed before I swallowed – used my back teeth to grind, the tip of my tongue to taste. I would have said *thank you* for the vegetables she scrubbed and the chops she fried crispy brown in ninety-seven degree heat. I would have scraped my plate and licked gravy from my knife, and when I'd finished eating my knife and fork would have been pressed neatly together to read two minutes to twelve. And if I couldn't have managed any of the above, I would at least have eaten my dinner.

Look: *v.* use eyes; gaze, stare; **looker:** *coll.* attractive female

Every guy thinks his mum is beautiful. Jason did. So what if he had shit in his eyes – I understood. My favourite ice cream is rum and raisin, but if I have one on a Tuesday don't offer it me again before Friday. *Everything*, even the things I love, bore me if they happen too often. But one time I looked at my mum's face and never wanted to see another as long as I lived. I used to catch Dad staring at her, so I thought it was the same way with him. But over the years I've examined the last picture taken of them a thousand times looking for clues. And the most I can find is: he wasn't looking. He was watching.

♠

Susie flung Auntie Harriet's front door wide open. Green glittered on the space between her eyelashes and eyebrows.

'Did you miss me?' she said. I shrugged, watching my reflection in her lips. I wanted to punish her for being away but figured Dad would do it for me. I smiled, waiting for him to clock her make-up. Instead, he gripped her at the waist raising her off the floor in an impressive straight-armed lift.

'How's my princess?' he asked, kissing her on a small surface of clean skin. Mum joined in the slobbering.

'Susie, what's happening?' I said, turning my head on my way to find the birthday boy before she answered.

In the kitchen I pulled four toothpicks piled with small food from out of a grapefruit and took a can of drink out of the fridge. I followed the smell of burning through the open kitchen door and into the backyard. The garden was half the size of a five-a-side pitch with two fruit trees at the far end and a shed pushed up near the back fence. Anthony was leant against the naked chest of Uncle Leighton on the lounger. They were sun-buffed like brown school shoes on a Sunday night. The barbecue was smoking but no one took any notice.

'How's the birthday boy?'

'Hot,' he said, one hand sheltering his eyes from the sun, the other trailing in a pot of crisping orange flowers.

'Geoffhurst, how's tricks?' asked Uncle Leighton. I figured Anthony hadn't opened his presents.

Uncle Leighton mistook things you needed to live – clothes, shoes and schoolbooks – for presents. Last year there were tears and Uncle Leighton was gripping the box of thick-soled Clark's lace-ups. *Space hopper?* he asked, holding the squashed shoebox out in front of him. *What does it* **do**? It was so sad and funny at the same time I couldn't swallow the cake without three glasses of fizzy orange. I didn't laugh because adults aren't amused when you spurt drink from your nose.

I wandered over to the shed and opened the door. The net curtains at the windows made it feel like a little house. A chair, a blow-heater, a kettle, a radio, a green-and-red checked blanket, some tapes and a biscuit tin on the shelf next to a tool kit.

'Keep your nose out,' Uncle Leighton warned.

Auntie Harriet swung into the garden carrying a plate of silver fishes floating on waves of lettuce. She'd gouged their eyes out and stuck cocktail onions into the sockets. She lifted a checked cloth on the table under the kitchen window and placed the plate on top of a larger tray of crushed ice before covering the food back over. In the four-second gap my lazy eye took in a plate of jammy dodgers and a hard-dough loaf from Nyam, the West Indian bakery, where customers, about to buy a bun or wax off a salt-fish patty, dropped jokes that creased me up so bad it didn't matter that the queues stretched into the street and I only wanted one fried dumpling.

'Happy birthday,' I said, handing Anthony my present. 'That's from me. Mum and Dad got you something else. Susie got you nothing.' I shrugged.

'Except this,' she said, prancing into the garden with a present bigger than her head, wrapped in girl's paper with a matching bow and a nametag. 'Happy birthday Cuz.'

'Thanks,' said Anthony, all excited, taking the big present first in a bad-mannered way, ignoring his cards, which was where a polite child would have started, reading the words out loud, pretending not to get excited about the pound note inside, before working up to the best presents. My back prickled with heat. It was my sister's fault. It was the thing I didn't like about girls like Susie: their hand up too quickly with the right answer, brushing their teeth after sweets and remembering summer birthdays in spring so they could save up. (Girls *always* save – check out the toes of their shoes.) And girls like Susie couldn't ease back; hide their brains and goodness now and then, so boys could feel *they* were nice people who got it right sometimes too.

'It's the Sonny and Hindy Show,' said Uncle Leighton. Mum and Dad stood near the kitchen door facing on to the pear tree. She wore an iced-biscuit-pink halterneck, legs, and the eyelashes that slept in a box on her dressing table. Dad had one arm wrapped round her shoulders, the other held on to the top of the doorframe. He rocked back and forward. Mum's thumb hung off a belt loop on his denim jeans and she rocked gently in time with him. We all watched them ogling each other like grown-ups on television just before they suck face. I wasn't sure they were being polite. I wished there were someone older than them to break it up, to say, *I don't care which one of you started it, but you can stop it right now*.

'Anthony get your uncle a cold beer,' Uncle Leighton said, pushing Anthony off his lap and on to his feet. 'Hindy, beautiful as ever.'

See. Beautiful. He said that.

'What's cooking?' Dad asked Uncle Leighton, clasping the back of his neck close enough to touch chests before they released each other, springing apart. Auntie Harriet went inside and came back out holding a tray of drinks.

'How was the dancing lesson?' Mum asked Susie.

'The teacher won't let me do legs until I get the arms right. I've been stuck on arms for four weeks now. What sort of dancing stops you moving your feet?' Susie asked, pointing her toes, making an arc with her arms and then spinning in a circle.

'Maybe the teacher was doing you a favour,' I said, rolling my eyes, counting balloons pinned in the branches of the pear tree.

'Maybe you should shut your . . . Mum tell Geoffhurst.'

'I told you pumpkin, all that height you have,' Auntie Harriet said. 'She knows you have potential. That's why she's working you the hardest.'

'That's my girl,' Dad said.

'Those are your mother's legs,' Auntie Harriet said.

'Here's another possibility. *Maybe she can't dance!*' I said.

'Harriet,' Dad said.

'Sonny,' Auntie Harriet replied without looking at him. They greeted each other as if they were taking turns to call the school register. Then she hugged Mum or Mum hugged her. It was a difficult call with those two. Auntie Harriet passed me a glass of cloudy ginger beer. I took a throat-scratching slug. She went inside to refill the jug.

'Two twos,' said Dad and he went off as if he'd forgotten something inside the house.

I banged my empty glass down and breathed out noisily.

Anthony came back and held up two cans of beer.

'Where's Uncle Sonny?'

♠

'Anthony fetch the camera,' said Uncle Leighton, taking a Red Stripe beer from him and passing it to Dad. Auntie Harriet started singing in the jaw-stretching way kids did on *Songs of Praise* when the camera swung in their direction.

'All into the living room,' said Uncle Leighton. I liked outside better. The pear tree's teardrop fruit, and the tubs of herbs all around let me imagine I was in one of the countries off holiday programmes where the hills were mauve.

'Why not out here?' Susie asked cutting an outfit from the back page of *Bunty*, folding the paper tabs from a dress around a cut-out dolly.

'Too much sun. We'll end up with red eye in the pictures,' Uncle Leighton said. Mum slapped then brushed her arm. Fat from the sausages dripped on to the coals. Fire sparked then died.

'Your uncle said all inside for a photo.' Dad jerked his thumb towards the house.

Susie pushed through the kitchen door ahead of me, elbowing me in the waist.

'Ladies first,' I said, standing back and rubbing my side.

We lined up against the living-room wall. I dried my forehead with the back of my hand. Uncle Leighton told us to link arms and smile, 'say cheese'. Susie picked sleep-sand from the corner of my eye, pulled her dress at the hem, and tucked hair behind her ears.

♠

She is getting ready: to leave her shelf of white plastic dollies dressed for white plastic places. She lowers her chin, preparing to somersault into adulthood faster than Tessie Tumbles.

Cheese.

Auntie Harriet's killer afro – thick with a double share of iron, patted into the shape of a Madonna's halo painted by a well-rotted Italian – can't be contained by a four-by-seven. It mushrooms out of the picture. Her arms are crossed around Anthony's neck. There must be a dozen silver bangles – the same size as her earrings – on each arm. Her feet are spaced level with her hips, cowboy stable, the way mine are when I'm on the tube at rush hour and there's nowhere to hold on. She's centred, grounded, less likely to be heading for a fall, closer to the floor. Short.

Short people act hard done by, they're overlooked for the best jobs, short-changed when it comes to getting laid, blah, blah, blah. You wouldn't think so to hear them droning on but they're better off than tall people. They walk the streets safely because there's nothing to be gained from bashing them in. We let them stand in front of us at concerts, squeeze up to the railings for better views of the fireworks. They suffer less with back problems and their hearts don't have to pump blood very far so they live longer.

Mum didn't stand a chance. Miss High and Mighty, her head in the clouds; one set of knees; towering above the axes at ground level waiting to cut her down to size. Things might've turned out different if they had been the same height, if Auntie Harriet had got the eight and a quarter inches Mum owed her.

Anthony's arms hang low. The face of his digital watch is Yorkie thick. His other arm droops down to Auntie Harriet's wrists. There are crumbs on his cheeks. His eyes have the Bostik shine of unopened presents. *Mother and son.* Mum is looking down on Auntie Harriet. *Sisters. Twins.* He – Mr Sonny Sylvester Johnson, biological father, the Masquerader, sporting Joe 90 shades and denim bell-bottoms – is next to Mum. I can just see his eyes, but even if I couldn't, the angle of his head with his carefully shaved cheek to camera shows he is looking at her. Watching? Mum is happy. Happy-sad – happy-scared. Happiness – dabbed on her wrists, sprayed behind her ears, for special occasions.

I am between Mum and Susie – who smelt like the cherry lip gloss slicked over her mouth. The Polaroid, a four-by-seven with a matt finish, has curled-up corners. I look skinny – thought I was broader. A dumb kid – thought I knew everything; Peter Walters, me and *The Oxford School Dictionary*, all bases covered. Handsome. My left eye is looking at Uncle Leighton. My right is turned towards Susie. A cross-eyed bastard, always looking the wrong way. For fuck's sake turn your head around, *watch him*. I'm boss-eyed. Cock-eyed. Nobody's to blame. It's not hereditary or anything. It just happens. I wore the patch the doctor gave me; stumbled half-blind through the skewed shrinking stinking world, but it didn't help. It's not my fault. My right eye – it's cast. I can't make out what's coming. *See, I have a lazy eye.*

'Move in a bit,' said Uncle Leighton. Our heads moved to the centre. *We are a family.*

Dad is pulling Mum towards him, away from us. *They are husband and wife*. Their heads touch ear to ear. Susie leans on me. *We are brother and sister. Lean on me Susie, I won't let you down*. Siblings on the edge; pushed aside; up against the thin white borders of a snap. Between us and Mum are the brown and yellow swirls of the wallpaper pattern.

End: *v.* abolish, close, terminate, destroy, kill, finish

I couldn't get a handle on Alice, but the Mad Hatter – the waist-coat – big watch on a chain? He slays me. *Start at the beginning and keep going until you get to the end.* But I can see a movie and it's so obvious what's going to happen it might as well be over, or I catch the parting of the curtains, and I stay put past the credits and treat it like the beginning, imagining the other story that comes after. Ends and beginnings. They're the same thing.

♠

Knocking woke me. Tap – a stranger at the window not sure of the reception. Tap. Tap – stuff your bed with pillows and come out to play.

I slept with my head under the covers (Susie does too – it's a family thing) but I heard it through the sheet. I thought it was Ken from 134. He walked the flats at night until three in the morning. One night after Auntie Harriet closed *The Lion, the Witch and the Wardrobe* we heard Ken walking around. According to Auntie Harriet someone had stolen some of his hair, made a slit in the back of a rabbit's neck, pushed the hair into the hole and sewn the fur back up. *He can never stop walking until they kill the rabbit* is what she said.

All I know is Ken didn't bother anyone as long as he got plenty of exercise. Because of the fast walking his mum got the shoemaker to put metal clips on his heels to stop his shoes wearing out and make her pension go further, but I reckon she took comfort from being able to hear him clicking nearby. Anyways, the noise wasn't down to Crazy Ken. It was rain. No bolts of lightning, just gentle tapping against the glass of the top window – here and there, reminding itself how it was done, making up its mind whether to bother.

I'd forgotten what it sounded like. Hadn't *really* been sure it'd be back. The whole country was waiting for rain and here it was – like some dad who had run out on his kids and they'd been missing school because the mum had no money for uniform and the cat was dead from starvation so there were mice and the gas and electric and telephone had all been cut off and the smallest kid is going bow-legged from lack of vegetables and the mum comes home from turning tricks for the first time, and there he is sitting in his chair reading the paper. *Put the kettle on*, he says. And there are no special presents for everyone from a faraway place. He hasn't been on the run from criminals who tore out his fingernails and threatened to kill his wife and kids if he didn't co-operate. He didn't bump his head and forget his address.

I pulled back the sheet. Between the pitter-patter of rain outside I heard something break and angry voices.

'For the last time where were you?' I didn't hear Dad reply and then another dish or a glass broke. 'You disappeared. Where were you?'

My lazy eye hadn't woken up but my left eye took up the slack until sleep fell away. **SLOWLY, PONDEROUSLY, FROM OUT OF THE WRECKAGE.** I got out of bed and stood in the same spot gaining my balance, swaying in my underpants, scratching my balls, trying to work out where the crashing was coming from.

'Nobody told me. They didn't need to. I've seen the way she looks at you,' she screeched. Dad started laughing.

I opened my bedroom door and stood in the hallway facing light and noise from the kitchen. My left arm tingled with pins and needles where I'd slept on it turned under.

A plate frisbeed left to right past the kitchen doorway before smashing. Another whizzed and shattered.

'Why not? You did in nineteen sixty-four,' she said, corking Dad's laughter so all I could hear was rain racing to reach the ground.

There were no people in the picture until Dad came from the left, naked except for his tight red briefs, batting dishes away like they were flies. **MY THROAT GROWS TIGHT! MY HEAD IS THROBBING.** From the right a flexed foot with liver-red toes thrust forward and connected with his balls. He moaned and bent over double. She ran across the screen and returned with a green stool. Crash. She backed away holding the seat, two of the four legs now jagged stumps. She had the look on her face they have in films when they've done their worst and realize it isn't enough. He came back at her, fist balled up and held high. **ARGHH.** They were out of view. I wanted to go into the kitchen and stop him. You will hurt her no more! But my feet wouldn't move. She was back in the frame, holding the seat like a shield to bounce blows away from her.

He looked at the blood on his hands where his fists had been pounding the broken stool legs.

'Bitch!' He kept trying to wrench the stool seat away, but she clung on. My feet were stuck. Spiderman had me in a tight web. I tried picturing what was in the hallway behind me, empty bottles to exchange for cash at the corner shop, an everyday thing to turn into a weapon, but there was just a long stretch of nothing.

Suddenly she let go of the stool and he fell backwards. The glass in the kitchen window snapped and fell four floors where it smashed to smithereens. I imagined him doing a back somersault through the shattered window, splattering on the pavement. The world seemed to stand still, trembling on the brink of infinity.

By now Auntie Blossom would've run to the telephone table, dialled 999. I listened for the sound of sirens and screeching brakes from the Bizzies on their way to draw a chalk-line around his body. There was a metal taste in my mouth. My tongue stuck to my teeth.

The Dutch-pot sat on the back ring of the cooker like a stage prop. Then he flew out from the left. There was blood sticky in the back of his hair, the sound of a chicken wing snapping off the Sunday roast chicken. She whimpered. He had to run out of steam sooner or later, and when he did . . . with my strength . . . my power . . . the world would be mine.

The lino looked like Sobell's ice rink when the big boys came off. His feet were cut. Blood between his toes. Skating on red ice. He dragged her by the hair. She slid past on her bottom, dragging broken cups and plates with her. Fingerprints of blood spread out like eagle's wings across the chest of her Stars and Stripes nightshirt. Then I couldn't see her. There was just his back muscles shivering like he'd held a barbell too long and the sound of gurgling and hissing. Silence. Long seconds passed before I saw him walk like a blind man into their bedroom.

I walked towards the kitchen to begin getting back to normal. This was when I rescued the remains of ornaments we'd brought back from school trips: tubes of coloured sand from the Isle of Wight, paperweights from Margate. When the kettle boiled, I would make tea with five sugars, put three chocolate bourbons on the saucer, if Susie hadn't scoffed the lot. Sweet things and brandy were good for nerves Auntie Blossom said (but it wasn't Christmas so brandy was out, besides I couldn't swear for strong drinks making you feel better but chocolate biscuits worked for me more often than not). Then I'd open the Quality Street tin in the cupboard where the shoe polish was and take out the TCP and cotton wool and after I fixed up my mum I'd sweep up cracked glass and busted china. The nightmare is over!

Wind tossed the lace nets through the windowpane. Mum lay on the floor surrounded by broken things and torn slices of bloody Mothers Pride. I pulled her nightshirt down to cover her knickers. I couldn't understand why she hadn't moved. I wanted to run her a bath with a capful of Dettol – smelling of recovery and allrightnowness. Hurry her along – remind her of the way things were supposed to go. Then I realized it was my fault. I'd come in at the wrong time, before the end.

LOOK WHAT MEN HAVE DONE TO ME!

Outside the sky groaned. Wind huffed and puffed and blew through the flat. I sat down next to Mum, lifted her head on to my lap. Her hair was soft against my legs and sparkled with chips of glass. I listened to rain whooshing down as clouds, slashed with a blade, burst open. There were sharp things cutting into my bum and the backs of my legs, and the longer I sat the deeper they pressed. I cleared the floor around Mum with the side of my hand. Rain streaked Melvin's block until I couldn't tell where the floors were and the world outside turned the colour of lead pencils. I picked glass from her hair. Rain ranted and raged, kicked spray in one direction, then turned around the other way and punched through the kitchen window. Then it streamed down – like a white-haired man who was crying for the first time – and I might have joined in if the biology teacher hadn't told me how much of my body was made of water. I didn't want Mum to wake up to a pile of my bones and clothes on the lino. The air cooled. I covered her shoulder with a bloodied tea towel. I waited for her to get up, but she was caught in her magic lasso forged from the girdle of Aphrodite, unable to break free, unable to spin and keep spinning until she was beautiful again, to throw her lasso around his neck and choke him until he told the truth, said how sorry he was for being bad and straight up, for real, *he loved her*.

Her head got heavier. I waited.

Harriet

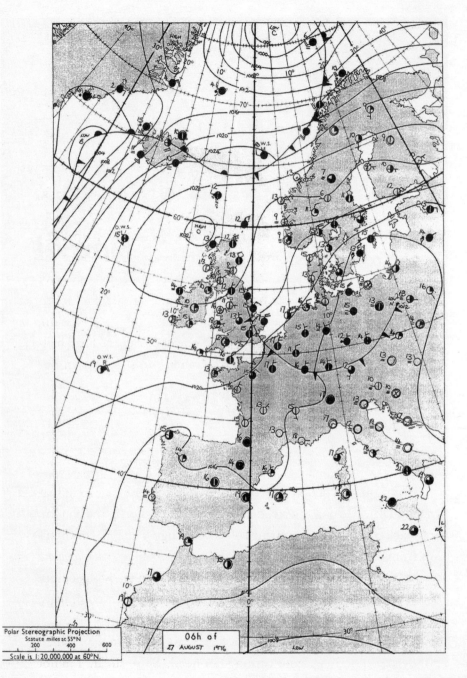

Polar Stereographic Projection
Statute miles at 55°N
200   400   600

Scale is 1: 20,000,000 at 60°N.

06h of
27 AUGUST 1976

A fair amount of sunshine: May 1960

The sea is a mad grey dog frothing at the mouth. I keep well back, don't let it catch me. Hindy copies the crazy English children, burying her toes into pebbles, waiting for foam to gobble them up. She's trying to look warm so Fardder don't make her come out of the water. There are pimples on her arms but she still glows orangy-pink like day dawning over Breakneck Point. If Fardder catch her trembling in the sea he will feel cold for her and that will vex'im, although he won't hold vexation long. None of us can hold bad feeling against Hindy. I *try* but it's hard when the sun rises in her forehead.

'It's cold,' I say, hugging myself and stamping my feet over and over on the same spot. 'Let's go back.'

'Soon come,' Hindy says, turning away from the waves towards me.

Turn right and planks of wood on stilts stand ankle deep in seawater. Halfway along the wooden path, and on and on to the bottom, are shacks both sides, and strings of carnival lights loop in children's Ws from the top of one building to the next. *Love me tender, love me true*, Elvis sings. People walk out on to the platform with long empty hands and come back with carrot-orange fish in see-through bags, pink candyfloss and dried-up coconuts fit for pigs.

'What's candyfloss made of?' I ask. I'm about to ask again when Hindy says quietly without turning her head, 'Spun sugar.' I'm not sure if I hear her answer from inside myself, or outside. I don't want a sweet thing to remind me of my sister's hair but it does. When we used to play *little white girls* she could flick, toss and shake without a towel on her head. She's the only coloured girl I know who can *brush* her hair. She takes after Mooma's side. *High yella*, Mooma's friends call her, for she's light-skinned and follows Great Grandma Myrtle who was the colour of an Ethiopian apple. I sweat and tug and rake, watching Hindy brush her hair 100 times with the silver-backed brush Grandma Evadnee didn't give me. (There was a mirror to match and she didn't give me that either, not because Hindy was prettier with more need of a mirror, but because she didn't want to break up a set.)

I twirl my finger round the end of one of my plaits wondering how old I got to be before Mooma lets me cold straighten my hair blow-in-the-wind smooth. Hindy is holding the skirt of her dress bunched up against her thighs like there might be ackee shells or pea skins in her lap; it makes her legs seem longer.

Hindy and I started out far, but not *so* far apart in height, then when we were six and a half she flew up overnight like a coconut tree, and now she is tall, tall, tall. Press the stick down hard on her head and the mark on the wall is still over six feet. If there had been a fair share at birth eight and a quarter of her inches would have come my way. At thirteen, she is mostly leg. Fardder says when we were born he remembered a tribe in Burma called Padung – giraffe women. I asked Grandma Evadnee about the giraffe women and she didn't know about that, but she did tell me there is a people in Mali saying the world started with a drop of milk and the sky was low down one time and man could eat it but man turned greedy and the sky moved out of reach. I asked Mooma about the giraffe women and the milk and the sky. She rolled her eyes and said, *Don't pay them no mind*. The eye-rolling is one of the reasons Grandma Evadnee didn't waste her knowledge on my mooma, and why she was waiting for a certain somebody to born with two black moles on her shoulder, moles full up of water that itch on storm days. Looking at Hindy's legs stretching out of the sea it seems Fardder was right about Padung.

'Next time Fardder gets a bonus we should ask for a different something,' I say stroking my cheek that in England feels cool and rubbery like a peeled boiled egg. A wave curls up and licks Hindy's shin. She bites her bottom lip and closes her eyes.

Someone screams and laughs in the same long breath.

'We'll ask for the funfair. I heard them have dodgems and ghost rides and sausages in tall buns,' I say, turning back to the fair to watch golden horses rise up in the saddle and fall back down. 'Think they'll let us go by ourselves?' I can hear Fardder already. *You mean Kelco Cochrane 'by yourself'? The same 'by 'imself' youth those six white low lives left dead on the pavement last year and up to now nobody catch them. That's the kind of 'by yourself' you girls asking for?*

Hindy opens her eyes. 'Ask? Let us. May I? Am I allowed? You *push* people into refusal. Sometimes you have to take what you want,' she says kicking the sea.

A donkey trots past, a *grey* donkey, the colour of washed stones, carrying two jump-up children and shitting on the way. I didn't know you could ache for colour. I pine for flat-ironed pink clouds and Grandma Evadnee in equal parts. I long for red, red dirt.

I look up the slope behind me. I don't have a strong head for measurements or figure work so I can't say how far in feet or yards, but a couple minutes' walk uphill is a wall. In front of the wall rows of grown-ups sit in flimsy chairs. Parked behind, on the pavement, above the wall, looking down on the beach is a raggedy white hut with peeling paint. *Whelks and Cockles* it says across the front. Next to that is a hut with open shutters. A fat woman with rings on every finger passes out cups of tea with two plastic-wrapped biscuits on each saucer. Mint green china is all over. The adults not holding cups and saucers in their hands have them by the side of their canvas chairs. It's like Grandma Evadnee said when I asked her about England, *tea, tea, tea*.

'I don't see Mooma and Fardder,' I say, but my words don't carry, they sit open-winged on the wind.

They call beach *seaside* in England but side the sea is stones only – no sand or trees. I close my eyes; feel my sand-burnt feet hitting the sea. *Feesh, feesh*, shouts the dreadlocks with thick white teeth walking along the seashore with a rope around his neck holding a driftwood tray of pink goggle-eyed snapper and bearded goatfish.

'Indyanarriet, come 'ere quick time.' You can call Fardder an easy man on some counts, but not when it comes to the things we do that let the race down, hold us back, the things that have nothing to do with the white man. Timekeeping is one and rudeness is another, and there, *Mooma* (*manners maketh man*) and Fardder (*Don't play into their hands*) are in agreement. When Fardder calls we must be in his sight by the time his tongue clicks at the end of our name. If I am busy I act as if I can't hear 'im. Fardder can take deafness, prefers it to rudeness.

'Indyanarriet.'

I never tire of the sound of our name. I don't mind my half being behind hers. It's her birthright. She came first, slipping out and into her name. I was hidden behind, mistook for fluid, pushing against a nerve near Mooma's spine, and her back never felt righted again. Grandma Evadnee said my birth wrong-footed Fardder. It took 'im two weeks to recover from the shock of being robbed of a son twice, and after Mooma stopped cooking for 'im when he wanted to call me Marcus, then stopped washing his clothes when he switched to Mosiah, he called me Harriet because she might not have been easy on the eye, but she led the slaves outta captivity. And when Mooma started cooking and cleaning again because Harriet sounded pretty when you said it after Hindy and she long ago had praise for her capital Hs making it her favoured letter to write down, I got my name.

Air sucks saltwater from the sea.

'What, you can't hear Fardder calling?' I ask, knowing she heard and isn't ready. Two children been making waves, shuffling towards Hindy like light-footed crabs. The younger of the two, a toddler, is close enough to touch her, but Hindy going on like she don't see 'im, even though he's burning up the beach with his red hair. The little boy stretches out a white round-dough hand towards Hindy.

'Let's build a sand castle,' says his sister, swinging a yellow bucket with a spade in it. But it's not digging he's looking to do.

'Hair,' he orders. Hindy collapses her legs down and crouches. Her skirt darkens, wetting-up in the sea. The boy touches her hair. His hand springs away. He tries again, this time holding on, pulling gently. He stands up steady, so his sister lets 'im free but stands guard. The baby babbles, seasoning his speech with a few recognizable words.

Scissors – paper – stone is a game we played back home, holding our hands behind our backs and choosing two fingers or a fist or a flat hand to bring upfront fast. Since I've been in England I play another game inside my head. Beauty – colour – money. Fardder has a friend; his blood is mix up with a white man in the 1800s who made and lost a fortune from limes, but 'im dark still. Rockefeller buy 'imself a house in a good area, surrounded by shut-mouth white people. 'Im don't seem to have coloured worries at all and is bullfrog ugly, so money tops colour and beauty, but beauty beats colour and Hindy was all set for the Miss Petroleum title if we hadn't come to foreign. Call her exotic if you will, because that is when colour so far doesn't count against a person it comes all the way round and starts

counting *for*. She is coloured and talk fast like all of we, no matter –
the seat next to her always gets taken on buses. Hindy is the kind of
'different' people move towards.

A fully dressed woman shoots past me; running into the sea like
she catch a fire; her flame-coloured hair a frozen wave. She steps
over the baby ignorant to the down-growing she has just caused 'im.

'Naughty,' she says pulling the baby away from Hindy, but he
won't let go and my sister's neck is bent, her head dragging towards
the baby and his mooma. Hindy unlocks his fingers to free them
both. The baby screams, his face a squashed custard apple. The
woman doesn't look at my sister. She treats Hindy like a door her
baby has caught his fingers in.

'Dirty.' She holds his hand in front of his face. Clutching the baby
to her chest she marches away, ignoring her daughter running to
keep up by her side. Hindy cuts her eyes and breathes in as if she is
pulling up bad word to fling after the woman, even though our
mooma says we mustn't cuss ignorant people, and that includes the
teacher who calls us *you people* and Raymond Godfrey who looks
under my desk and laughs if I have taken off my shoe to set my toes
free or 'im look up my skirt searching for my tail. *They will get used
to us, and until they do turn the other cheek*.

Hindy walks towards the shore and stops. The sea yo-yos in and
out, baring her feet then cloaking her ankles and shins in noisy foam.

'Tell me how Grandma Evadnee dealt with people she didn't
like.' Hindy is twisting her toes, sinking something into washed
pebbles. When she moves her foot a mashed sea sponge or small
animal's brain disappears under the seabed, sucked out of view. I'm
not minded to use Grandma Evadnee's teachings as plasters to stop
homesickness flowing, the way Fardder uses cow-heel soup or
coconut dumplings.

'Not liking don't come into it,' I say. I bite the inside of my right cheek and press my lips together tasting salt. Hindy knows I promised Mooma to leave my backwards ways behind me, try to rise above my raising and concentrate on book-learning at school so I can be a typist and work in an office. (We don't know Hindy's future but all agree her strong long fingers are piano, not typing, fingers.) She knows the lesson in pride God sent Mooma that forced her to accept the money Fardder's mooma saved from selling the yams given her by her son to eat but she went and sold them at market for years and years, and sold a ring besides, one never seen on her hand, and nobody could account for how she came by it, to make the fare for an adult and a child so the family didn't have to broke up and we could all come to England and improve ourselves. She was sitting on the edge of the same turquoise bedspread when Mooma took her open Bible off her satin pillowslip and made me repeat back to her, *To everything there is a season, and a time to every purpose under the heavens: a time to get and a time to lose, a time to keep and a time to cast away* . . .

In truth, it isn't respect for Mooma locking my jaw. I am tempted to hold back to protect Hindy because it is the person asking who must bear the consequences. But I'm thinking of the way that woman said 'dirty' was the same way Mooma said 'hot' when she blew on our green banana porridge. And those lessons last long, long, long, because even now at my big age I catch myself blowing out fast and saying *hot* when I scald myself.

I look at Hindy bowed in on her self. She can be red-eye over the things Grandma Evadnee taught me. It didn't bother her none at the beginning. She kicked the ground around the bull tongue bush and paid no mind when Grandma explained the leaves cured colds and bad hearts and ladies who fell pregnant but didn't yet have big bellies.

She called me a witch once and I ran breathless to Grandma

Evadnee asking her to name the thing she was showing me. Her head was bent. The scalp parts of her hair made a hot-cross-bun marking. She carried on patting cow-lick dumplings. *We all call it different, but I've never cursed God*, she said, chopping a groove into the middle of the dumpling with the side of her hand. *It all runs into the same thing*, she said tearing off more dough to begin again.

'Take sawdust, a piece of garlic and alum and grind it all together.' I leave out the bluestone. It's years since I told her this one and I can't remember what I left out the last time. 'Shape it into a body and hold it together by tying string over and over. The person you trying to fix – lay it under her mattress. She will never have peace in her house and nothing with her husband will go right as long as they sleep in that bed.'

Hindy straightens up and looks at me. A short time passes before she says, 'You forgot to say: lay the doll with its head to the east and the feet to the west, like a dead person should be buried, following the sun; against the life of the person it's under.' And then she smiles, and fork-mashed sunshine spreads all over her brow. She thinks she's caught me out, but I skin teeth with her because her colour is a throwback to redwood verandas and early morning mint tea, and because I'm shocked at the correctness of her memory, and because I was right to follow my mind and leave out the bluestone.

'Indyanarriet,' Fardder calls. I widen my eyes at Hindy. She walks further out, water passing her knees. I don't tell her nothing again.

'Coming,' she says, dragging the heavy sea between her ankles. Six strides and she is beside me. She smoothes her dress with the flats of her hands. The flared skirt Mrs McCalla made us, that looked fine on the pattern picture, suits her, not me, and it is not, as Fardder keeps saying, because I am different; it is because I am not the same. I hand Hindy a towel. She dries between her toes and rubs saltwater from the front of her legs and behind her knocked-knees. Up to last year I made fun of her knees them, but there's no point since I find out Monroe has the same problem. It makes them put too much hip into their walking, Marilyn and Hindy. They wear misfortune well; high, like a carnival queen wears a tiara.

The stones on the beach force the whole of my legs to work, calves and toes pulling in tight then gone again. I link arms with Hindy for balance. We pass a family sitting on a brown blanket eating bendy sandwiches with mean fillings. The fardder's legs sprawl out from under the pages of the *Sunday People* like dashed Coca Cola bottles. The daughter smiles and I know she's exactly seven from the size of her teeth. Grandma Evadnee taught me to tell age from teeth, and a woman born with cauls over her eyes who dreamt lucky numbers and kept horses taught her. I walk around seaweed. Shells crunch. Hindy's elbow jabs against my ribs as we walk; our four legs as smooth as two legs reminding me why we are unbeaten in the three-legged race, reminding me of what it means to *be in step* with another person because this is the joined-up way we walked into school on our first day.

Hindy waves at our parents the way Princess Margaret did when she married the pictures man she didn't love, in a small circle as if air cost money. We are bent over laughing, stumbling towards Fardder. Mooma looks tired and cold. She has looked that way since she stepped off the platform at Liverpool Street Station. Fardder warned her. He had the call-up telegram to pick peas and chop celery in Florida where a frost spoilt the crop, so he knows about cold from going to America. But Mooma insisted on summer shoes and would-n't be told. *Those who feels it knows it.* She bore up well all three weeks on the boat, losing colour only when we stepped off to board the train in Genoa. By the time we reached England she looked like she look-ing now and she can feel *one of my heads coming on* all the while. It's the cold, the scrapings-from-the-bottom-of-the-pot sunshine and hard water. England can pickpocket your looks if you're not careful.

'You pickney can't stop the skylarking?' Mooma says, gripping the temples of her forehead. Our laughing when she can't share the joke annoys her, annoys everyone we have ever known.

We are not allowed to be too noisy in England; we must play music low, talk calm, and not be bursting out with laughter all over the place. Fardder looks vex, is angry for Mooma because she is too tired to do it properly herself. Used to be getting up at four and the amount of work it takes to keep cocoa and oranges and coffee, a few pigs and ground provisions was the cause of his troubles. *No time for improving the race*. Now he is angry because he works in scrap metal and has to take two bus to get 'cross town. He wakes the same time as if he worked the land and has to take orders and isn't the boss of his ownself any more.

It's not just her anger he takes on 'imself. He takes on the anger of strangers. Like the Aborigine people. He is angry for them because whites are stealing land (although land don't go nowhere, so can always be given or taken back). Worse still, white people stealing their pickney and raising them in their image, and language and culture, that's another thing again, because when those things are gone, might as well call that the end. Every time Fardder comes into focus his face is bigger and angrier. We laugh harder till I am so full of laughter I can't breathe.

It is easier to be happy *outside*, when all four of us are not doing our cooking and sleeping and eating in a room divided by a curtain, with two windows sized like the suitcase on top of Mooma's wardrobe. Mooma talks of 'going out', but it's really 'going in' to walled-in cinema or food stores or other people's front rooms. And Grandma Evadnee thinks I joke when I write tell her we go swimming at our school, and when I lie on my back and look up there is a roof were the sky supposed to be.

Tears are rolling and all the while I'm thinking of Hindy's royal wave and Fardder's second-hand-mad-as-hell face. I tilt my face to the sky and gulp giant breaths to quiet myself.

White, big-bellied birds with boomerang wings are flying over my head, crying like somebody took something precious from them. Hindy stops laughing and we are acting backwards because I know she has the answer to a question I am holding on to. She has no patience, doubts it is a virtue so don't want none neither. I wait her out with ease. She huffs.

'You don't know that?' she says. 'Seagulls. Them is seagulls.'

Scattered showers: April 1963

Our friend Dolores and her daughter are the first coloureds to move into her flats, and brand new homes in this country are cause for song and dance. The mayor cut a ribbon and all the residents of Cornish House had a glass of champagne.

Back home we built new all the while, on a plot of land shouting distance from family and so close to the sea that our breathing ended up matching the in-and-out of the waves. Here they love old houses, are not afraid of other people's smells and spirits, acting as though the dead stay dead in all cases, so have no worries over how many strangers lived and died in rooms they paper over and call their own.

This is the first time the council have built homes one on top of the other with lifts and chutes to put rubbish in instead of bins. Dolores pays £3 9s a week. Fifteen shillings of that money lets her run deep baths and stay there topping up hot water until her skin wrinkles. She can leave on heating day and night no matter. She has a rent book and there is no knock on her door on a Friday night after last orders because her new landlord is the London county council and all they want from her is money.

'You can see St Paul's from that window,' says Dolores, coming up behind me. The window has one big glass, no dirt-trapping wood of the smaller panes, and according to Dolores it can turn inside out so you can clean both sides. 'Hindy needn't have worried. She could've just bring herself. We have plenty food. It's her company I'm look-ing,' she says, down-growing me, because I remember she was my friend first. I started out as the main course and ended up as the appetizer.

'You want some firewater Honey?' Dolores looks up through a set of false eyelashes and swings her glass of rum.

'Not for now thanks,' I say, refusing to be hypnotized, because even if sixteen and a half isn't too early in life to start with hard drinks, four-thirty is too early in the day.

'What did you girls tell your mother *this* week?'

'We been invited to worship at a friend's church.' I look down at my court shoes. 'Too churchy?' Dolores starts one big gummy laugh-ter. And I see why Mooma thinks Dolores is *full of sin*, but I think I might be too, which would be no surprise to Mooma because *birds of a feather flock together*.

In the street below umbrella tops scuttle like cockroaches. I knew plenty rain was coming since yesterday. I woke up sniffing damp clouds, a bag of 'forget to peg out' 2-day-old washing smell. Before a storm my head feels stuffed up, but it was Grandma Evadnee who showed me that was a sign, had me watching the shape of clouds, measuring light, feeling the weight of water in the air. Before I was ten I could call rainfall before the rainbirds flew.

The English don't love rainwater. I never seen a people so affected by weather, getting more miserable the wetter it gets. It's like Grandma Evadnee used to say, nodding her head in Grandpa's direction, *When something is with you all the time, with no plans to leave, might as well you learn to love it.*

Dolores turns the radio off against some of the Aldermaston pro-testers being interviewed. Seems they are against nuclear weapons. Seventy thousand of them are marching into London tomorrow. Last month thousands of jobless people walked outside the Houses of Parliament. Everywhere people are marching – and not just England. *You know about walking when you have this*, Father said, tapping the skin on the front of his hand. *That boy James Meredith, seven hundred and fifty Federal Marshals, and him just going school to study his books. The first black student to walk into a white school – you think white people doing that kind of walking?*

'You warm enough? I can turn up the heat you know,' says Dolores, and before I can answer she shimmies over to the brown tiled mantelpiece where there are six upside-down glasses, and Wray and Nephews overproof rum, and where the pink-and-gold-framed pictures of the family Dolores is saving to send for are propped up. English money is plenty but it don't stretch far, so up to now she don't send for even one of them. She uses both her hands to point to a dial on the wall like a television model showing off a selection of leather-cased fashion jewellery a contestant can win. She turns the dial clockwise.

'No paraffin, no coal. Magic!'

Dolores lifts the lid on the stereogram and drops the stylus on the record. She clicks her fingers and bends her waist to the opening chords of 'Foolish Little Girl', and then she takes on the role of the 'foolish little girl', singing over the record's scrubbed voice and organ music. 'But I love him,' she is yelling. The other Shirelles scold her – **It's-too-late-to-have-a-change-of-heart.** 'I still love him' (even louder). Because Hindy is tired and excused from church after another boutique job that didn't work out, I take it on myself to act as the backing singers, keep my own time because there is no lead to follow. I snap back, '**Tomorrow-is-his-wedding-day-and-you'll keep quiet if-you're smart.**' I manage fine without Hindy, coming in on the nail, but not liking the empty sound.

Dolores plays The Shirelles like only they can make music. She even backcombs her hair and wears a band over a centre part like

Shirley Owens, the lead singer – imagining they look alike, worse still, she even thinks they *sound* alike. It's how we met her – in Woolworths.

Hindy took a pair of weak-tea-coloured nylons off the shelf in Woolworths and held them at the side of her face. 'Natural?' She scrunched her face. 'In America—'

'They might have *Gay Whisper* Crème Puff,' I told her quick, because she sounded just like Father starting sentences that way.

'Too ashy,' she wrinkled her nose.

Sometimes Hindy don't take the responsibility of beauty on, and that's like a rich person dropping money and not bothering to bend to pick it up. There's a price to pay always; Elizabeth Taylor and Ava Gardner wax and pluck and paint and wear diamonds and scorn jam roly-poly and spotted dick in favour of hand-span waists.

'What about that nail enamel from the advert – Coty, Pink-with-a-wink?' And she went off grumbling, to the make-up aisle and I queued up with a tin of Andrews Liver Salts, a bottle of Milk of Magnesia and lavender wax polish in my basket.

The head-back in front of me belonged to a coloured woman. She was wearing a wig that flicked out at her jaw line, high fashion, like a magazine model. She was holding a little girl's hand and rocking her shoulders and tapping her foot in a coloured way best kept for church. I looked around. In the wide alleys no shoppers knocked strangers as they passed by. They didn't ask *How much for this* and tell tall tales for lower prices because how much for it was stuck on the product clear as day, take it or leave it. I breathed out my longing for green grapefruits and long-foot cabbages, and scallions and bundles of fresh thyme, spread on a cloth on the ground, near to handmade basketware, breadfruit and chickens. The coloured woman was clutching a record to her chest, blocking out the writing on the record cover with her forearms and rocking side to side. When she rocked left the fifth time she noticed me and stopped still to bare deep purple gums. There weren't many of us coloureds in the area so I was curious about how long she'd been here and who she knew and what island she came from. I smiled back. Words gushed like sudden rain. 'They're back in the top five again and them being coloured' and she singing too, 'I sit alone at home and cry. Over you. What can I do? *I can't help myself* 'cause baby it's you. Shala lala-la.' Chewing on the words, giving the song too much up and down. 'Shala lala-la'. People staring into their baskets, or studying labels on their shopping, scared to turn around in case she crazy. Like she care. She just swing her hand (no wedding band) until the little girl (the dead-stamp of Dolores) she holding hands with pulls away. 'I don't want nobody. *No-body.* 'Cause baby it's you.' Then she says, 'Music is good for man trouble', as if an explanation was due. So I tell her, 'If you want to keep in love with a man turn your right shoe upside down under the bed, he'll stick with you, won't be able to do it with anyone else.' She looked at me full eyed so I thought I'd made a mistake and she didn't want the man no more. 'If you don't want him back, get some of his hair and put it in a bottle and go to a river and throw it in. The man will go whichever way the bottle goes.'

I hadn't meant to say all that. I put it down to work where the other typists were so careful not to point out I was coloured that if not for 'natural' tights and 'translucent' powder I might have forgotten myself. Dolores made me realize I hadn't seen my nature, hadn't seen myself, not for a long time, not on the television or in posters or at the cinema or in the pages of *Woman*. Dolores put me in mind of old men with watered-down eyes dancing on the balls of their feet at weddings, of oiled and starched children rushing the chicken seller at lunchtime, or jerking their soft-bones at bus stops to street music.

Laugh? Dolores showed all of her purple gums and whooped till even I thought she might be a bit touched. A woman with eight bars of Knight's Castile soap in her basket turned to look. It was Dolores' turn to be served but she was still bent with laughing. I wondered if the till girl was going to call security because we were going on coloured. I looked around the store. Workmen leant against the wooden bar at the back carried on drinking tea, a record went right on spinning on the turntable, a till from another queue clanged. Dolores handed her record to the shop assistant. I looked at the bell inches from the shop assistant's hand. She only had to press her palm on to it and call for the supervisor. She raised her cheeks and showed a few teeth – a white person's smile.

'Would you like a bag for those?' she said, and that was all.

Dolores wiped mascara away from under her eyes and yanked on the child's hand.

'Say hello to my new friend Dusty.'

I crouched down. 'Hello Dusky. I'm Harriet.'

'Dusty.' Dolores corrected me before the child said a word, and I looked on Dolores again because no sane woman would name her pickney after a type of dirt.

'Like the white girl who sings with The Springfields. I know a drummer says she will go solo any time now and if you couldn't see her you'd swear she was coloured. Listen, I have a stereogram. Every Sunday I have a cook-up and people bring food or drink and we play music. The council is my landlord so you can stay long and act free. You must come. Baby, my friends gon love you.'

I stood outside the store holding Dolores' address. Hindy pushed through the doors empty-handed. I squeezed a fist around Dolores' address and readied myself to tell her about my invitation. It wasn't going to be like the squashed chocolate stuck to the heel of my hand that neither of us wanted in the end, or the small bird I fed with an eyedropper and by the time I was ready to share, to show Hindy my find, she opened the box to a dead sparrow. Billie Holiday sings *God bless the child who's got his own* but maybe the only people holding secrets are the sad somebodies with nobody to share them with.

'White Flame,' Hindy said, pushing her wrist against my nostrils.

I didn't smell it good. My mind was on Grandma Evadnee. I was turning over the day I was born, unexpected. I was wondering whether Grandma could have known we would end up in England where pretty and a passport would get Hindy through but I would need something more to make up for Gay Whisper Crème Puff being the darkest shade Max Factor made, and there being no important somebodies, like government minister or bank manager, in the whole of England looking like me.

'What's that you're hiding?'

'Nothing.'

'There. In your hand.'

The clouds were sharp-edged, and white white, the cauliflower clouds that adults still point to as a sign of rain when children know better, painting them in pictures next to a big sun.

'How long will you need?' asks Dolores coming out of the kitchen, carrying a glass bowl of coleslaw stained pink with red cabbage, which she places in the middle of the table next to the other early arrivals – roasted sweet potatoes, a jug of pineapple punch, salt and a bottle of Encona hot pepper sauce.

'Five minutes.'

Dolores nods and when she goes back into the kitchen she lets the glass-beaded curtain fall closed. I take the salt from the table and pour a palmful into my hand. Dolores is quiet – no singing, not even the scraping of a pot. I talk under my breath, 'I will lift up mine eyes unto the hills, from whence cometh my help . . .' I pull up the carpet in the corner furthest from the window and trickle salt on the floor from the bottom of my fist, loosening my hand. 'The sun shall not smite thee by day, nor the moon by night.' I salt the corner by the window then I turn the carpet back down.

In Dusty's bedroom 180 degrees from the living-room window corner I pull up the carpet. 'The Lord shall preserve thee from evil: He shall preserve thy soul.' In the hallway, in the right-hand corner parallel to the front door, I use up the last of the salt. 'The Lord shall preserve thy going out and thy coming in from this time forth, and even for evermore.' I clap the salt remnants off my hands and stand up.

In the hall I see the back of a stranger blocking the living-room doorway, forearms the size of Christmas breakfast spiced hams holding the top of the frame and hanging like he doesn't trust the ground. I fold my arms in front of my chest, stop from stroking his back, from stretching up to hold his arms. *Do not touch the exhibits*, it says in English museums and there are guards with cringed-up faces and no care for how smooth and shiny the beautiful things are and whether there are curved places crying out for fingers.

'Excuse me.' He doesn't turn round, just swerves his body to one side to let me past. 'Thank you *very* much,' I say, hoping he has been in England long enough to understand that saying a word hard can make it mean the opposite. I sit at the dining table and angle my chair to take him in. I'm reading his face to see if he heard what I'd been talking. He gives nothing away. He's drinking me in from my shoes upwards. Hairs from my hot-combed French pleat are breaking loose. He rocks his hips backwards and forwards, forwards and back, gobbling up space without apology. I try not to hold it against him, telling myself he can't help his height and the swinging might be a habit, a smaller man might have been drumming his fingers on a tabletop.

I have him down as being raised without siblings like Father. The only son, only grandson – too much 'only' left no room to shake off the idea that what he said, or thought, or did, changed the worlds of all around him. I see a barefoot child, running up and down, chasing chickens and goats, believing there is no place he can't go, his mind filling up with ideas big as the sky around him.

Mooma was fond of saying Father's mooma had him on her change and that explains a lot. She says and *that woman* could have saved us all plenty heartache if she had broken Father's spirit at the earliest opportunity; after his first birthday when it was safe to cut off his baby hair without affecting his speech, or else when he first started walking, when spirits, like mumps and measles, are more easily dealt with. But my heart swell up big for Father's ways. Like when he opens his hand for change, and if it's placed on the counter instead, he tips his hat and thanks the shopkeeper for the goods, and leaves the coins right there. And Mooma warms a little for a short time when Father outclasses white people, I seen the blood in her cheeks, so she can chat him all she likes, and I don't care if we walk everywhere when the money done, because I love Father's open-neck-shirt way of walking through life, even if England doesn't.

'Sonny move outta the way man.'

Dolores holds a macaroni pie with both hands and stops singing to bounce against Sonny, flicking him with her childbearing hips. Sonny jumps to one side, pretending the force of her flick has flung him halfway across the room. Dolores walks quickly, her feet flashing purple toenails. She stretches her arms down, exaggerating the weight of the macaroni pie, clattering the deep oval dish on to the table. That's her way of asking for help; making everything look harder than it is until someone takes pity.

'No sugar dumplings? Flying fish?' says Sonny. Dolores sucks her teeth.

'Harriet come for the knives and forks for the table.' She starts singing, 'I met a little boy named Billy Joe and then almost lost my mind. Mama said there'll be days like this, there'll be days like this my mama said . . .'

'I was just about—' I say to Dolores, but I'm looking at Sonny.

'Have we met?' He takes a step towards me bending his long body over my head. The light underneath the curve of his body is brighter than in the rest of the room, like the sky directly beneath a rainbow. He takes my hand in his, I pump my arm, but instead of shaking, he squeezes. When he lets go his touch still buzzes in the centre of my palm. I open my folded fingers full of suspicion, expecting an object, peeping just below my lifeline for an explanation.

'Harriet,' I say and smile, wishing Hindy hadn't got all the calcium and I had the teeth like Mint Imperials.

'Knives and forks,' says Dolores, standing in the doorway with fistfuls of cutlery. I take them from her hands. Sonny is picking at cheese from the macaroni pie, his wet fingers flash in and out of his mouth. *Oooh, oooh. My eyes were wide open, but all that I could see . . .* It's not many hands I want involvement with. I can be spring mouthwater for fish and chips but I'll change my mind before the fish even fry if I see dirty fingernails holding the tail of my battered cod. But he has raised veins, blue and green, under his hand-skin like important wires that could power the switch in my belly, jump start my heart and shock my knee-backs until my toes flicker. He walks to the mantelpiece and unscrews the top off the rum bottle, knocking a photo of Dolores' little brother bottom-down – a position sure to disturb the poor child's mind. He pours a few inches of white rum into a red and gold glass shorter than his thumb, then he holds the bottle in the air. I turn the picture face up.

'No, not for me.'

'Good girl.' He takes a craven mouthful and breathes out noisily. 'Rum is a funny thing. I taste Appleton and swear it is the best rum in the world. And it is. But look here, white rum from St Vincent, and guess what? *This* is the best rum in the world.' I slide the glass on the drinks cabinet and bring out the box of Welcome to London placemats. I start the table settings, placing Buckingham Palace at the head of the table, moving round to position the Houses of Parliament to the right. 'Who else is coming for dinner?'

'My sister Hindy, and Alford and another Johnny-Just-Come Dolores trying to get a job for at the Ford factory.'

'She's a good woman.'

'She does it for the rum they all have when they first arrive. She has rum like stamps collection; a bottle from every Caribbean island, even Aruba makes a showing.'

'You're funny,' he says. I hope he means 'make you laugh' funny. He winks his whole face at me, screwing it up so the bulb at the bottom of his nose heads for the dip in his top lip like a perfect, easy to place jigsaw piece. *Mama said. Mama said. Hey. Hey-hey. Mama said. Mama said. Hey. Hey-hey.*

'You know Dolores from time?'

'Since last Tuesday when he sat his muddy behind next to me on the 56 bus,' says Dolores swishing the glass beads of the kitchen curtain to one side and appearing with a plate of thick overlapping beef-tomato slices pushing into her stomach, dividing her pink and brown kaftan.

'I was coming home from football.'

'What Cassius Clay is to boxing, that's what Sonny—'

'Johnson,' he says. She doesn't know his second name, and I surprise myself by feeling like when my shoulders first dip under the sea on a too hot day.

'Sonny Johnson is going to be for football world. Playing for a big team. Leyton—'

'Leyton Orient. I train with them that's all. Me and a short kid they're holding to see if he stretches out.' He is sucking in all the air on his in-breaths.

'*Somebody* can't think straight,' says Dolores, arching a heavy Joan Crawford eyebrow and making room on the table for a plate of avocado slices with a lemon and cracked black pepper dressing. I look at the table settings and notice the knives and forks are the wrong way round.

'Fork here, knife there,' says Sonny standing over me, taking my hands and crossing my wrists to swap the cutlery over as if I am a child who must learn their left and right. His chest leans over my head. He smells of sin – rum, cigarettes and sweat. Just when I think Mooma is right and I am heading for hell, the clean sweet scent of the soap flakes his shirt was washed in redeem him. Angels hum at London Bridge. I can't take in that this has happened without a piece of lodestone in sight. He is above and below and all around me like a swaddling blanket. *Say you need my lips (come on, come on) come on.* My heart turns over. *Say you need my heart (come on, come on) come on.* I'm pleased for us both, for me and Hindy. I know she will take to him too, because I hear her thoughts following mine like a *shala-la-la-la* chorus.

'Just a sip,' he says. I take the glass thrust under my chin and turn it until the lip smudges are on the side nearest to me, then I press my lips where his were and sip. The skin inside my mouth starts burning at Trafalgar Square. Heat crawls through my body. My heart catches and sparks. We are approaching Big Ben when I realize the world has been lopsided for some time without me noticing because suddenly I shift up on my right side like I let go a heavy shoulder bag and now I am perfectly balanced. When this happens it doesn't matter that we are cusp born and I could be Scorpio all by myself due to my arrival creating a commotion and nobody checking the time, because right now I am sure I am Libra and the other half of my scales is nearby. I look up. *Oh, it may (may, may) just be al-all in my mind (yeah, yeah, all in my mind).*

Hindy stands in the doorway, a drenched pink flamingo; one pointy slingbacked foot wrapped around the opposite ankle. She is dressed from head to toe in newborn girl-child pink. She tucks a strand of wet angel hair behind her ear. Sonny stops moving, but his heart is hammering between my shoulder blades. *You were laughing back then, but now I hear you sighing. (Oh yes I do.) Whoah darling, don't say goodnight and mean goodbye.* His hands cover mine. I grasp a knife and a fork.

'A towel is coming,' Dolores shouts from the bedroom. Hindy holds out a plate tied with a red-and-white gingham tea towel towards Sonny and me. A handbag like a pink, sugared envelope dangles on her wrist.

I couldn't stand for us to part, because I love you much much too much.

'I fried plantain,' she breathes the words out like soft smoke. Mooma says Hindy has weak lungs, but one time past she held her breath under water long enough to find the entrance to a cave no problem. She is softly spoken for people she wants to draw close, those she wants sucking in her words like they nicotine addicts.

Please don't go away pretty baby with that look in your eye.

I won't step forward and take the dish from her the way I took the book she won at school for a poetry recital or the bag with the soft nap. *Take it. It'll match your green skirt.* Not because I wanted it, but to balance the scales, make her feel less weighed down by all she had.

All of a sudden I can't bear these concrete boxes piled upwards, away from grass and back-fence who-and-who-said-what. They are cages fit for chickens (and watch them peck each other, and their own selves, to escape). I hate the smelly toilets *inside* the house, near to where people eat food, can't stand the 260 stairs and the intercom where neighbours are free to buzz strangers into the building, and there's no knowing who's going to appear, it could be the tallyman, but there's no chance to turn out the light and hide behind the sofa.

'Anyone going to pour me some rum?' she asks, and Sonny lets go of my hands. I lose my grip – drop the cutlery. Sonny unwraps himself from me and I remember I didn't answer Dolores about the heat. I shoulda tell her *Yes, turn it high*, because a few months ago the whole country was freeze up and it's not over yet, and all of a sudden I'm feeling the cold, and Jack Frost is no friend of mine.

Let her turn the thermostat all the way. It's not as if it's going to cost her any extra.

Whoah, whoah darling, don't say goodnight and mean goodbye. Don't say goodnight and mean goodbye.

Winds sweeping up from the southeast: October 1965

This isn't the prettiest or grandest town hall in London, but during the Christmas season a pine (a gift from the borough's twin town in Norway) beautifies the forecourt. Hundreds of white lights, invisible in the branches, are switched on by a local celebrity (a footballer, for example), and then you might call the town hall splendid and question its ranking. There is a clock with Roman numerals at the top of the building that locals set their watches by, and clean glass and regularly polished brass in the heavy double doors at the front. The town hall is set at the top of steps in the middle of a square. In the square are wooden benches for office workers to eat their sandwiches and bins for throwing rubbish and flowerbeds planted up with yellow and purple pansies.

We are scattered on the town hall steps, a new and dry-cleaned crowd, under the clock up high like we are on stage, like we something special. Down below horns are honking. Traffic comes out from the road at the left from the back of the town hall and turns right or left on to the high street, but cars are slowing down and people sound their horns. When I take time to study the drivers who are winding their windows down they wave and honk again joining in our celebrations and only then do I relax, because horror and delight wear the same face from a distance.

The English don't do it our way. They *don't like to make a fuss*. If not for their transport, death and life events would be hard to call.

Their cars tell what the clothes do not – a white Mercedes for a wedding, black for a funeral. They are cockney sparrows and we are magpies beady-eyed for the sparkle of sea in a blue sequin, for two-carat stars in paste earrings.

Hindy and Sonny stand like marzipan figures on the hard-iced tiers of the town hall steps.

A tinny tape recorder plays the 'Wedding March'. Dolores sings *here comes the bride* every few minutes, out of nowhere in a breathy Diana Ross voice and then she is silent.

'All thanks to me.' Dolores prods me, and then pulls the tops of her white three-quarter-length gloves (The Supremes wore something similar when they sang 'Baby Love') higher on her upper arms before crossing them across her chest.

It took hours of searching through copies of *Vogue* and in the end Mrs McCalla took different parts from three patterns and joined them together. The gown is ivory white, a fitted bodice with an oblong bow on the front of the waistband, capped sleeves, a boat neck. It is a dress that could have worked for a shorter woman, but it is ideal for a tall bride too, the strips of silk one on top of the other, widening out into a beehive and two extra bands have been added at the bottom to accommodate height without spoiling the style.

Hindy is first to marry, as it should be. I hadn't been born when she was in the world wrapped in Mother's white crochet blanket (the only piece of old clothing Mother dare keep for fear of frightening the unborn child's spirit and causing death at birth).

Although we have had equal practice, I handle loss worse than Hindy who took losing our milk teeth in her stride, explaining the new teeth on their way, and that was all very well but I still thought of the old teeth, all different shapes and sizes like freshwater pearls. Grandma Evadnee died from the loss of us. If she had come here she would have died from the loss of the island, turned insomniac without the sea to hush-hush her to sleep, lost her appetite and turned meagre without the smell of frying garlic and onion all times of day from someone, somewhere, starting a meal. Mother has 'the pressure'. Doctors talk of foods she has been eating all her life being the cause. Her arteries are blocked with coconut oil. A back-home sun would melt the blockage – loss of sunshine is killing Mother. We don't lock ourselves out or leave belongings on buses. We are not a careless family, yet loss is claiming us all.

A string instrument could play out my sorrow, not a harp or an organ with promises of angels and heaven, a violin, only a lonely violin would do. After today, *from this day forward*, my sister will live in a different place. *Indyanarriet*. My name will change. If Daddy wants me he will call out Harriet. When I imagine my name cleaved in half, said in his voice, the sadness deepens until the blues seem too bright and concerned with foolishness – men, when if one has done you wrong there are others, and worry for bills and rent and things you want but can't buy – that isn't worth sitting down and making a song of. A God-fearing church woman, a Mahalia-Jackson type, who can close her eyes, sway, and confident of her place setting in the upper room she can drag through her throat all the passed-down pain of separations – a child who didn't run or hide because he only ran from strangers – diseased cargo thrown overboard separated from brothers and mothers – tongues separated from sense, and girls painting their eyelids blue because eyeshadow can't go *in* the eye, separated from who they are, and separated from the only people who can tell them.

'Come on. I want to offer congratulations,' Dolores says, pulling me clattering up the stairs, past heels and hats, short coats and high hair until we are two rows deep from Hindy and Sonny.

'You don't think it's bad, me not bringing Dusty?' she asks as we wait in line. I shake my head. 'Only it's important her attendance is regular or they won't choose her at auditions. I know she misses real school now and then but as I explained to the school welfare officer she won't need algebra and history when she's a singer.'

Sonny doesn't make me wait any longer. He drops his hand from Hindy's waist and bends over two other people until he is close enough for his stubble to graze my cheek. I peck him where I can reach; the edge of his chin near his ear. Just the once, not over and over like a hungry bird. He kisses my cheek, his lips thick and warm and smelling of Vaseline. When he pulls away I notice the line on the inside of his bottom lip where the pink inside stops and the purple-brown outside begins. I start thinking about anything else – how the streets of London are paved with gold leaves every autumn and the trees act like drunkard whores – swaying and throwing off clothes. Sonny straightens up and gives a second cousin on Daddy's side the same kiss he gave me – the coolness of autumn.

The photographer arranges Sonny's football mates in two white lines on the steps going down. 'Come on. The weather's not looking too clever,' he says. But although winds from the southeast are expected to blow in light rain in the late afternoon I doubt the forecast is correct and even if rain falls, wedding weather is full of double meanings – a shower is bad-luckied, or a blessing, an anointment even. A black bird blocking out the sun and darkening the sky for a few seconds would be more cause for worry. The photographer frowns. He calls in men from the wedding crowd and mixes them black, white, black, white.

'You too, Big Daddy.' He gently punches Daddy on the shoulder, and Daddy acts hard-done-by and gives Mr Anderson a 'duty-calls' look and walks away from his conversation to complete the zebra crossing on the stairs and escapes a one-sided chat and nodding down at Mr Anderson's two-toned shoes the way he does when he is adding up figures in his head or memorizing road directions.

117

The footballers' arms are stretched out with footballs balanced on the tips of their fingers. The photographer stands near the bottom steps looking up. He bends back and smiles with satisfaction, and then he starts snapping, running left and right, forward and back, snapping all the way.

'Nice one fellas.' He turns away from them. 'Now let's have a bit of colour. Ladies, get your confetti. On your marks . . .' Dolores raises peppermint satin away from her ankles and runs as fast as her column dress allows but Mrs Cohen is already halfway up the stairs with her hand inside her handbag. 'Go.'

Hindy and Sonny hold hands on the highest step. Red and green and pink and blue petals gather in paper clouds above their heads.

'Perfect. We'll do one more of the same. When I say go.' Hindy is searching the crowd and when she sees me the outside rays of a weak sun peep out above her eyebrows.

'Go.' Confetti and rice explode around them and flashbulbs go off. Sonny shields his eyes. The lines in the palm of his hand are chiselled out, Braille for those who can't read him any other way. But I see him, even with a long-distance reading: a lengthy unbroken life-line, a forked love-line, a plump mount of Venus.

Hindy takes a pale blue box with a dark blue bow from Mrs Cohen, who is wearing a fur neck-wrap, the animal's pointed face slumped on her bosom. Mother wanted her on the invite list not because Mrs Cohen's only daughter is thirty-one and not even court-ing, but because Mrs Cohen let us stay in her house when others wouldn't, and it's best to forget the high rent and the shilling-fire because after all *the past is the past*. Hindy looks at a tree to her right and points to where she wants me to go to with her chin.

Women line up, knees bent, ankles soft, ready to jump or sprint or stretch.

'You're too young for marriage, step aside.' Teenage girls ignore concerned relatives on the sidelines and take up positions. I move as far away as I can, at the bottom of the steps, almost on the pavement.

Hindy turns her back on me. It is the only back I could correctly call in a line-up. The two shelled walnuts that press through the skin at the top of her backbone when she curves away from me at night. Holding her waist whilst sitting on the tray of the great houses of Grenada Mother gave us because she fell out with the lady who gave it her, sleighing down hills on it, riding with our mouths gaping, our first taste of Epping Forest soft sky-ice. Hiding behind her back when trouble came looking.

Her right arm thrusts up and two dozen roses tied with a pink ribbon from Mother's hair-treats box are looping through the sky. There are squeals and shouts and heels clacking. I don't move. She throws like 'the bouquet' is an Olympic event. The girls a few steps below her gasp at her strength. She hurls the flowers so hard that a few Bird's Eye custard yellow petals fall as the bouquet dashes straight into my stomach and it must be reflexes that make me catch it. There are cheers and whoops.

'Harriet's turn next,' an amateur soothsayer prophesies. I clasp the flowers against me hoping for thorns, but the stalks are smooth.

Cloudy with snow turning to rain: April 1966

The shipping forecast on the wireless, all tune and alien words, soothes like a lullaby. Not that we heard 'Rock A Bye Baby' growing up, but Bible words before bed, sung like a command, *May the Lord bless you and keep you and let his countenance* **shine** *upon you*, with enough surety to have us looking around for a bright light.

The only light comes from a green candle, showing my breath the way it shouldn't when we pay an extra five shillings a week for gas and we're not out of blue paraffin. I wring the rag in the bucket, then wipe the floor smelling vanilla from the vapour, working fast so the water don't cool. I shuffle backwards on my hands and knees, drawing in all good fortune into my home, front to back, not back to front the way I did yesterday when I was too tired to realize I was removing evil intentions instead of creating prosperity. I keep on, topping up the bucket with boiling water until the sky is more blue than black and then I stop.

I grab my husband's heavy overcoat from the back of the door, wear it with the collar flipped up and leave the house carrying the bucket of leftover water down the outside steps, breathing shallow to keep the cold out of my throat and nose. When I reach outside the headlights from the milk van are watching me, and the moon is full and hard-baked like a Jamaican water biscuit. I face east and toss the water out of the bucket into the sky and spin around, turning away, careful not to look back, in case it's mistook for a lack of faith and not a suspicion that water has turned to ice midair.

A last mouthful of molasses and pine tar tea and I wrap my son in a blue blanket, put him in the pram and wheel him outside our room, squeezing past the cooker on the landing. I carry the pram down all eighteen steps. When I open the front door cold slaps me hard enough to start a nosebleed. I tighten my scarf, pull my hat lower. The streetlights show up okra-stew darkness. I pull the blanket up over Anthony's nose. The ground is wet this time of day, this time of year, even when no rain falls.

I push down our road, past dark houses sticking together, pulling damp into their brickwork, past Mrs Stephenson at number nine who keeps her curtains the same at every window so no one will know who she is renting out rooms to, past the light in the corner shop where papers are being sorted for the paperboy to deliver. Make a left on to Bryant Road past the bus stop where I nod to the women waiting for the bus into the City to clean the banks for dreaming office workers. Turn left again, on to Overton Road where Mrs Brown lives. It is here that I slow down my walking. Even with the cold freezing my nostril hair I won't rush to be separated from my son.

I carry Anthony and the pram up fourteen steps. My arms ache so I bump the wheels up the last two. Mrs Brown opens the door before I ring the bell. She watches me.

'You coming in?' she asks. 'Did I tell you I've got a little half-caste coming next week? Father studies law. Mother packs biscuits at Peak Frean's. They call the girl Charity – not something the grandma knows anything about. Still she's a pretty little thing and I won't say no to the extra money.' I don't say nothing, just hand over a carrier bag; inside is the meal I made last night – mashed green bananas, greens and steamed coley to boost his iron. There is a tub of zinc cream to encourage regular changing.

She holds the carrier bag away from her body. 'Like I said before, it's easier if you bring jars of baby food.' She hooks the bag over one of the handles of the pram where a white flannel pouch of lavender leaves and angelica swings.

'I'll be back at seven.' The cold air hurts my teeth.

True, I'm not typing fast. The other girls in the row behind me clack their fingers non-stop. But my mind is being drawn to Anthony who I only seem to spend time with when he is sleeping. I wonder about him getting so little wide-awake love, worry because he sucks cream-of-wheat and Carnation milk off a spoon in his sleep. Hindy says not to fret, that she falls asleep with the radio on sometimes and the talking gets through and changes the direction of her dreams and Anthony will be fine because love is more powerful than the World Service.

'Everything okay Harriet?' The supervisor doesn't like me at all, but I threw a handful of salt over my right shoulder and called her name three times at the end of our first day together and just for good measure I burnt sulphur and salt for three days before opening the door to let trouble out, so now she can't touch me.

'Fine.' But it's not so. The white lady who always has an unwrapped tin loaf in the tray under her pram comes to mind. She stopped me the Saturday before last when I was coming out of the butcher's with some pork belly and a loin chop.

'Anthony is better off with you,' she said and walked off. I didn't know she knew my baby's name and she's never as much as cracked a smile before. White people talk in a way where you have to read between the lines, so it started me thinking but I didn't take the thoughts too far because there is no one else to care for Anthony and Leighton is working all hours, trying to win over the workforce so they don't call a strike when the boss at Trebor promotes him to foreman. In the end I have her down as one of those women who are opposite to women's libbers and don't think mothers should work outside the home.

There is one big hullabaloo. The supervisor is pointing me out and before I know it Mr Perkins is standing in front of my typewriter waving paper, his messy eyebrows pressed down low.

'What's the matter with you girl? A-c-c-o-m-m-o-d-a-t-e – double c, double m.' The supervisor, arms folded in front of her body, foot tapping to the sound of trouble, waiting to witness my comeuppance.

'I'm feeling sick,' I say. It is almost true for my insides are turning over and during Hindy's pregnancies I usually chew ginger in the mornings but I'm cutting back because I ate too many strawberries when she was pregnant with Susie and now her first child lives with a strawberry birthmark on her neck and I don't want this new baby coming out with toes shaped like gingerroot.

'It's not like you to make mistakes,' Mr Perkins says, looking at me good, his eyebrows smoothing down a little. 'Go on home.'

The supervisor looks vex but he is the governor so she don't dare put her razor-mouth on me. I put on my gloves and wrap my scarf around my neck with a solemn face, crushing down my happiness at the thought of the best part of a day with my wide-awake son.

Snow falls, white like basmati rice, but with not enough starch to make it stick. When I walk through the gates of Hindy's flats the bricks look redder against snow collected in white lines on the window sill. In Hindy's block her kitchen curtains are pulled to one side, held in place by a yellow Marigold washing-up glove. She waves and then the nets drop back.

The door is open when I reach it. I kick the edge of the doormat to check; the calendula, alfalfa and the Irish moss I taped to the underside to draw prosperity over the threshold are fresh enough to last a few more days.

Hindy is standing in the hallway wearing two pairs of socks that stretch past her long feet like flippers.

'Didn't I tell you she was coming?' she says to Susie, bouncing her on her hip. I stroke Hindy's belly and then her cheek. I nuzzle my niece, nipping her gently between my teeth. She wriggles with delight. 'No work? Don't tell me you're sick again.' Hindy frowns like a newly appointed Methodist minister confronting a layabout.

'You take everything for me.' I hear her wrong. *You take everything from me*, and then I hear her right again. Susie stretches out to me with lively limbs. I take her off Hindy's hip-ledge.

'I'm just passing. I'm picking up Anthony early.'

'We're in here. Come in the warm,' Hindy says going into the living room. She sits down on the leather sofa Leighton and I gave her when we paid off the balance and collected our new one. I bend down to give back Susie but she digs her heels in and clings. I take her with me to the kitchen, fill the kettle and switch it on.

'It's all right Sonny's not here.' I think of protesting, of 'not being fussed either way', 'not minding', but I won't fool either of us, so I don't bother. 'Blossom – my friend in the other block. She got Sonny to do a job for a member of her congregation and since then word spread. Now he gets bits and pieces – fixing this, mending that. A painting and decorating job came up. Just a few days' work, so he took it. He *wants* to earn money you know. It's not easy for him watching us struggle. When he gets selected for a top team we'll look back on this time and laugh,' she says, and starts laughing but stops suddenly and joins me for a few seconds in replaying the hollow sound.

'You're low on milk,' I say, lifting a cloth over a near empty bottle of milk in a bowl of shallow water and checking the cupboard for a tin of Carnation. On the top shelf are two cans of peaches in syrup, a canister with 'tea' written on the outside, Weetabix and a bag of granulated sugar. On the bottom shelf are dried herbs, a Fray Bentos steak and kidney pie and a third of a bag of American long grain rice. Despite the doormat, poverty is cocking a foot up on her table, making itself at home. I take a cup of dark tea through to the living room and catch the end of what Hindy is saying.

'. . . boxes with torn corners, tins with dents. Last week it was Shredded Wheat. She's good like that Blossom is. She believes we're being tested and we need to hold on. She sounds like Daddy. *Tomorrow belongs to the people who prepare for it today.*'

She stops shuffling her hand through a bowl of rice, picking out bad grains, to laugh for real and Susie, lying on a rug, holding a naked dolly with ink scrawls on its face on to a police car that Anthony left on his last visit, joins her, like she is in on the joke.

'Hindy, you think leaving Anthony with a childminder makes sense?' The somersaulting starts up in my stomach. I pull a blanket off the back of the sofa and wrap it around my shoulders.

'Who else? Daddy still works all hours – paid and "for the people". He makes work enough for Mummy – nothing canned or frozen – everything cooked from scratch.'

Neither of us pretends Mummy is maternal. There are women who favour their children over their men and those who work the other way. We know, but don't discuss our dashed hopes for changing her from one category to another with our offspring. It stays unsaid that Mummy doesn't want to have our children who, just like we did, make jerky movements and mess and noise enough to send her to bed to nurse one of 'her heads'.

'Mummy and Daddy are not young people.'

'Grandma Evadnee—'

'She lived her whole life in the West Indies and one of their years is equal to three-quarters of an English one. Same as dog years are weighted another way. You can't expect them to take on Anthony . . . and after this little madam—'

'Boy,' I tell her, irritated. Her son will repeat Sonny in looks. I've seen photos and his people have arrogant genes on the male side – the same bow lips and square chins coming up generation after generation, refusing to be diluted. 'It's a boy.'

Hindy raises her eyes to the ceiling.

'After the *baby*,' she says, patting her stomach, 'if I can get a job where the boss leaves me the key I'll look about a cleaning position. And good luck if you don't want to leave Anthony with my husband even for a few hours although—'

'Grandma Evadnee would have killed to care our children for us.' We sit in silence smelling Bouquet of Flowers air freshener and pink paraffin, the room filling with hard-handed, warm-hearted imagining.

'Leighton's job suiting him?'

I choose my words, take my time answering.

'Nobody grows up dreaming of factory work but the money puts food in the cupboards and that suits us all.' Hindy turns the rice grains at the bottom of the bowl until they are at the top.

'Uhh, uhh. My pregnancy making you touchy as well as sick?'

Streetlights smoulder and people clip past fast like the weather can kill if you don't get out of it fast. I'm grinning just thinking of how full-eyed he's going to be to see me. I take Mrs Brown's steps two at a time. I ring the bell; it chimes out all eight notes and she still don't reach – now she's coming. I can see her through the glass panel in the middle of the door. She is fixing up herself; checking buttons, shifting hair. She opens the door looking worried, frightened even.

'Harriet,' she says, as if either of us could be in doubt as to who I am. 'You're early. I, we weren't expecting you.' Red ants are marching through my blood. I push past Mrs Brown and enter the house.

In the front room there are two red velvet armchairs. A black cat is stretched out on a rug in front of a coal fire.

'Where's my son?'

I open the door to the back room. It smells like a place frogs and snakes live. The curtains are closed. I turn on the light. And there is my baby asleep in his pram, coat on the same way as when I left him this morning, wrapped in the blue blanket. On one of the pram handles swings the carrier bag, looking just as heavy as it was when I handed it over. The room chills my bones faster than a Frigidaire.

'I've only just put him down. Now don't go disturbing him. Did I mention? Probably not, but I've been meaning to say, what with this new half-caste coming and me getting on, perhaps it would be better if you found someone else.' I back out of the room dragging the pram.

'Don't act prissy with me lady. Who else around here will take in a coloured baby at six in the morning for twenty shillings a week?' she shouts from her open front door as I bang the pram down each step so hard Anthony starts wailing, and I'm thinking how much easier it is to come down than go up and wondering if I can get hold of Angelica roots because without them I'm never going to find the strength for climbing.

Wind easterly fresh to strong: February 1971

Not now, but the first time, it looked like one big, big space; green, green with men like ants running in different directions. But I relaxed my eyes until the chaos turned into football pitches, over a hundred of them as far as I could see, all sides and on each grass oblong the men were connected by movement; running in the same direction, or they all have their hands on their hips and are leaning first to one side and then to the next, or they are a huddle of listeners all ears trained on one talker.

I link one arm through Hindy's and one arm through Leighton's, using them as sideways shields from wind whipping round the flat ground where there are no buildings to protect the body parts sticking out – nose, ears, fingertips. I watch a swell-bellied man pulling his socks up two pitches down.

The bodies here, all shapes and sizes and colours, are not for TV coverage; they belong to The Lions of Judah, Epping Accountants, The Lahore Londoners, Old School Boys, even The Fatboys. Their wives could leave them, their bosses sack them, they could find out the children they been raising are not their blood, no matter, all of them with talent and without will step on to the pitch every Sunday anyway.

Leighton whispers in my ear. 'I'm going to run you a hot bath when we get home. Rub your back.' He drops his voice until I can barely hear him and raises his forehead when he says 'Rub your back.' Leighton is a low talker, not feeling the need to shout. His words are to take or leave and he doesn't seem to mind which. He whispers private thoughts for sharing, not making others move in closer, concentrate harder. The first time I heard his voice he was whispering.

I met Leighton at a shebeen in Tottenham. The walls were covered with egg boxes, stuck floor to ceiling to soak up sound. I was standing next to Dolores when he approached Hindy and whispered in her ear (he had to do that to be heard over the music). She pulled away, *no thanks* and took back her hand (I thought slowly, on purpose, so he could see her wedding band) and carried right on sipping a Cherry B. He moved along the line to me. *Soon as I saw you I knew you would do for me* was what he whispered. I didn't refuse him for asking Hindy first – I was accustomed to coming second, but I objected to his 'would do for me' comment. I knew about 'making do', it was another way of saying 'substitute', which is what I did if the recipe said butter but I only had Stork margarine, and when the cake baked and I tested it the flavour vexed me and left me wishing I'd waited for the real thing.

Later that same year the three of us was at the Cue Club, a double celebration, Dolores' birthday plus The Supremes or The Vandellas were in town, or had a hit in the top ten, or appeared on *Ready Steady Go*. The Cue Club was a snooker hall before Count Suckle gave us a place to relax in and dance to music that made sense. I recognized Leighton from the off and I said yes when he asked me to dance and passed my Babycham to Hindy to hold, because he asked me first this next time. When I stood up the music changed. I remember asking Dolores what the new music was all about. *Rocksteady*, she said, *rude boy music for looking and feeling cool*. She knew all about it from a friend who was 'fraid of fat spiders but was 'fraid of missing out on opportunities for white girls and big money more, so he stowed away in a banana boat and got through on the second try. The music was slower, the strings were being held down and the bass was out front and though I couldn't work out the right way to move at first, the rhythm was telling me to ease off so I did, we both did. I was ready for marriage to a rock-steady man, one I could rely on. I wanted to say 'my husband', and set the table with crockery that did not belong to Mother. I danced with Leighton on the first night in England when ska turned into rock-steady, and to my way of thinking that meant something.

I bang my feet on to the frozen mud to keep life in my toes.

'Lord knows I do my best to get my family to church. Excuses, excuses. But here you all are on a Sunday morning.' It's Mother's first time with us. Since Clyde Best was born in Bermuda and West Ham are playing him, and you can see him running all over the first division on television, a new excitement has seized even those who had begun to wonder if Sonny's talent wasn't like a breadfruit being saved for Christmas breakfast and slowly rotting unnoticed on the tree. Mother has joined the new general accept-ance that fame is on its way *as sure as eggs is eggs* and is waiting for the day his face appears in the newspaper, like Bobby Moore and his Mrs did, before last year, when he was accused of stealing jew-ellery in Mexico. But all the standing is troubling the back complaint she wouldn't have had but for me, and making her mis-erable. It is Daddy who has been behind Sonny, not that he cares for sport but he says with television we can show what we can do (he especially favours live TV) when we are all playing to the same rules. Today he is home caring for the children, to make way for Mother to be with us, changing her normal routine where, out of duty, and fresh from Sunday service with a renewed supply of

Holy Spirit, she keeps our kids after Sunday school, starts off the stewed beans and browns the boiler chicken.

'I can't stand up in one place for ninety minutes at my age.' Hindy and I snort, the steam from our noses staying in the air to accuse us of a lack of caring.

'I'm going to find a seat for your mother,' Leighton says, and walks off in the direction of the groundskeeper's cottage.

'Bless you Son.' We don't look at her. Praising other people is a cuss for us.

The footballers are warming up, running round the outside of the pitch. I count six seconds of safely watching Sonny touching his toes before I turn away still carrying him in my mind's eye. When I look at him again he is balancing on one leg, his grabbed foot pressing into his buttock. Unlike the other players, with arms too thin for heavy lifting, or glasses to help poor eyesight, or a bandage for a weak knee, every part of Sonny seems useful. He is like cho-cho, slice the pear and fry in batter, eat the shoots as you would asparagus, steam the leaves as greens and even the hidden root is a yam.

He is something to watch, not just on my say so. Anything could happen anytime and you don't want to miss out. There's no warning. You can't say he is nowhere near the ball and risk unscrewing the lid from a Thermos. Don't turn away. The ball can go up into the air and he'll spring high and bend far to one side, and a goal is scored from nowhere, from nothing, like a shower of hailstones, in June, when the sun was shining just now. That's what curves the necks of the spectators from other teams' games and in the end has them standing on our touchline. He is *someone* to watch too, for he is going to be famous one day soon and everyone here will talk about seeing him play at Hackney Marshes, because people like to think they've got in on something early, can spot greatness before others, like Dolores who, even though she thinks there is a problem with the distance between John Lennon's eyes, and she isn't a fan of their floppy music, still brags she was in the audience when The Beatles played Lewisham Town Hall in '63.

Leighton comes back with a garden chair for Mother.

'Bless you darling.' Leighton holds her weight under one armpit and lowers her on to the chair. She groans as she goes down. He comes over, stands next to me and rests his hand on my waist.

They are marking Sonny the most. It should be one on one but no less than four men are close by. The players on Sonny's team pass the ball between them scared to give Sonny a touch. Then Sonny breaks away, followed by the man – who stared him out when the referee tossed a coin, who wanted heads and got tails. The man trips him up (hardfaced as you please like a landlord of yesteryear who bags your belongings on the outside step).

'See that? What a way him wicked.' But Mother might as well be shouting at the television screen at Mia Farrow doing wrong in *Peyton Place*. Sonny stays put. Is like he's thinking, or resting. I feel sorry for the opposition. Sonny is the type of man you have to knock down hard enough for him to stay down; otherwise he is best left be. Mother sucks her teeth and then she sits back in her chair. 'Vengeance is mine sayeth the Lord,' she says quietly through Steradent-white National Health dentures, handing her concerns to the Almighty.

'Free kick. You don't know that?' Hindy shouts. She knows football, has passed on words but not their meanings; defender, offside, diamond formation, extra time, corner, midfield. But I saw Sonny before all of these people here and I didn't need *Grandstand* to tell me I was in the presence of greatness.

The referee lets Sonny have the ball from the line despite Hindy's protests. When Sonny gets up he brushes mud from his right side before making vertical patting movements in Hindy's direction to tell her to simmer down. He throws the ball from the sideline on to the toe of Crazy Connor, who isn't crazy, just Irish. Sonny sprints into a clear space, running in the wrong direction, along with the other team, heading towards the wrong goal. I hold my breath, close my eyes, listen to the groans around me. He has a duty to do well, make us proud, make up for our lack of position, respect and sunshine. When I peep Sonny has the ball, has read the game, and is running in the right direction whilst the opposition try to swat him. Sonny rolls the ball under the sole of his boot back and forth before swerving a quarter circle. When he is followed he turns back sharp, and he is off, ball sticking to his toes as he runs and nobody can take it and other people coming over to stand up with us, because boy is he something to watch.

'Score Son score.' But deafness has struck; he is trapped in a calypso. He is lovemaking and can't hold back. He is sucking the stone of the last mango of the season and the sweetness is popping his eardrums. Hindy squeezing me up tight.

'Oh Lawd, oh Lawd.' Mother gives thanks and prays at the same time.

'You can't keep a good man down, eh?' Leighton shakes his head.

'Fuck me, watch that Darkie go.' The ball blasts. The goalkeeper? He is an English sportsman educated on fair play, getting ready to welcome defeat because it's not the winning, it's the taking part. Might as well move paleface. Move outta-de-way! Goalie dives left. The ball lands. No, ball crashes dead centre of the goal, forcing me to rethink the reputation for trickiness predictions have, and wonder if it is simply a matter of being watchful of the present, because with plenty more playing time to go and Sonny's team with a narrow lead, the ball sits at the back of the net like a full stop.

Steam rises from Sonny as he rubs a small white towel over his face and head, then pulls up his shirt and wipes under his arms and across his chest.

'Don't say I never give you anything,' he says, and winks our way, throwing the towel towards us. I catch it before thought, grabbing it like a glass knocked off a sideboard. Hindy doesn't flinch, knowing I will reach out first. I can't stop to worry if knowing I would catch the towel means knowing *why* I would, because I realize what I have in my hands and act to get rid of it fast. I am doubled over the holdall Hindy brought to carry water and quartered oranges. I scrunch up the towel, zip it in, seal it away, but it's too late.

Sonny doesn't wear scent. But that's not to say he doesn't have a smell he knows about, same way Hindy (who favours her hair up and not down) must know about the space at the back of her neck that dips like a baby avocado stone has been taken away. Sonny smells of the caves we explored on the island.

The water there wasn't safe, could tug you away unexpected, so we weren't allowed. *Why? Because it's dangerous and I said so.* 'No' troubles Hindy, affecting her more than 'or' when she thinks it should be 'and'. Say 'no' on its own and you might as well be talking Swahili. Follow it with an explanation and she has still has a problem. She'll rail up against the word, and don't mistake her sitting back down as final acceptance. She's only making herself comfortable whilst she searches round the 'because' in the sentence so she can find a way round, or under, or over.

She worked it out. We could enter the caves by holding our noses and plummeting under water. I should close my eyes, the salt might sting them. She would do the seeing, hold my hand, pull me to the right place, and then we'd come up inside the middle cave and through tunnels leading off there were holes on both sides so we could look into the first and third caves.

Leighton hugs me around my neck, pulling me towards him and away from Hindy. I take her with us. Leighton smells of a rabbit hole if you push your hand in after rain and then sniff your fingers, and there's nothing wrong with that, but I prefer his aftershave, his over-the-top smell. It is the same him with me. When we first courted, when his style was butterfly kisses along the centre length of my body, soft enough to split me like a meat cleaver from my mouth and all the way down past my breastbone and navel, he stopped between my legs. He held his breath. I was opened up like a shelled mussel in coconut milk. *Women smell of fish*, he said, *and I was never a lover of seafood*.

With blindfolds we would not have become lovers.

'Oranges?' says Hindy and I pass her the holdall, catching Leighton out of the corner of my eye drinking water his body hasn't earned. I avoid looking at Hindy, scared she will ask what my mind is on and my answer will either trap me in a lie and grow any suspicion, or I will have to tell the truth, and from the starting point of the cave she will retrace the trail all the way back until she finds the hidden thought. I've watched her with Mother's missing glasses case – *Where did you see them last? – And before that?*

My nose holds on to Sonny's scent. It pulls me like a sea spirit, and even though the current could come and drag me down at any point *I still want to go*. Hindy will walk into the sea before me, drawn by whispering, shaping sound into words with meaning. She will drown first, weighted down by the order of our birth and her fearlessness, because despite being born before midnight Hindy is never visited by bad spirits, who select the haunted carefully and wouldn't waste their time trying to frighten her.

Rain expected: March 1973

Death has a menu – granite, Italian white marble, Nabresina, Portland stone, York stone or dove grey marble. The Carved Memories brochure suggests polite word choices for dead – fell asleep, passed away or departed this life. Your memory can be sacred, treasured, loving, ever loving or affectionate. The dead can rest in our hearts, rest in the Lord, rest where no shadow falls. They can rest after weariness. There are death rhymes to finish. *A tiny flower lent not given, to bud on earth and bloom in heaven* catches my eye.

'For babies,' Hindy says and turns the page on to coffin handles.

'Beef burger,' Geoffhurst says and then Susie and Anthony copy, shouting demands.

'Mashed potato', buoyed up by the hyperactive adults on children's TV. Hindy splits frozen beef burgers apart with a knife, and then stops suddenly, drops the knife on the work surface and leaves the room. When she comes back she gives me a pen and paper. 'Write down the wording you want for the headstone.' I push the kitchen table clear of clutter with my forearm and after five or so minutes I start to write. In the end this is what I choose:

In Loving Memory Of
A dear husband, father and grandfather
BERESFORD RANDOLPH THOMAS
WHO PASSED AWAY ON 14.2.73 AGED 61

Also a beloved wife, mother and grandmother
LOVITA ELEANOR THOMAS
WHO PASSED AWAY ON 27.12.72 AGED 58
REUNITED
For ever in our thoughts

When Hindy shows me her paper this is what she's written down.

In Loving Memory Of
A dear husband, father and grandfather
BERESFORD RANDOLPH THOMAS
WHO PASSED AWAY ON 14.2.73 AGED 61
Also a beloved wife, mother and grandmother
LOVITA ELEANOR THOMAS
WHO PASSED AWAY ON 14.12.72 AGED 58
REUNITED
For ever in our thoughts

Sunny: mid June 1976

Even while I'm frowning with white people at bus stops, shaking my head and wondering where it will all end, I'm secretly happy for my first English summer when the sun has roasted me all the way through, when I haven't been pink and rare inside.

The new prime minister has made up a job and given it to his government man. 'Minister for Drought' is his title and poor Mr Howell is running all over, finding new ways to save the land from cracking up. Everybody watching how their neighbours use water, ready to snitch for the good of the country.

We've set up under an oak tree that sieves strong sun through its leaves. The kids are in the deep shade where the branches are thicker with a cool box packed with cans of Old Jamaican ginger beer, jerk chicken, a jar of chocolate spread and some overripe fruit. The tub of Kwik Save coleslaw, egg and bacon flan and slices of pork luncheon meat are from Blossom and are *best before the 28th*.

Hindy and I have seared ourselves and now we are cooling off in the shadow from the tree's branches. We are close enough to the *Socialist Worker* stall to see white Rastafarians signing petitions and their half-caste kids stealing handfuls of rock against racism badges. Hindy sits next to me, legs crossed – the outside edges of her feet on her denim thighs, her knees lifted away from the ground like a resting frog. I am sun-drunk. I pick a blade of hard yellow grass and stab my other hand. A breeze blows jaundiced oak leaves and carries a mixed-up coconut-rundown of smells and sounds: barbecued beats and glory-be trumpets, vegetable korma and tambourines, bass and fried bananas, spliff and tamarind-sour guitars.

'It's too hot,' whines Geoffhurst. I look at my nephew clawing at the top of his arms under his T-shirt. Next to him Anthony is forcing Action Man to do a headstand in a plastic cup of Coca Cola.

'Just thinking about underwater breathing,' Anthony says.

'Boy, you're too English,' I tell Geoffhurst, because heat makes them sick and the cold kills their old people. They're just not hardy – no direct sun – not too shady, and water every third day or they fold in their leaves and give up.

'Can sun make you sneeze? I think I'm allergic.' Susie tenses up and pulls a tissue from the back pocket of her hot pants. Ugly Jesus sandals are standing on our blanket. I look up at a small boy with his eyes quinge-up against the sun; he looks six, but he has eight-year-old teeth.

'My friend says your dad is a footballer. I say not. Is he?'

'Yeah,' says Geoffhurst, his chest high.

'Is he famous?'

'A bit.'

'Is he on the telly?'

'Not yet,' Geoffhurst says, scratching the back of his neck. The boy shrugs and runs off.

Hindy closes her eyes. Her hair falls behind her neck as she raises her face towards the heat like a greedy sunflower.

'Mum, I saw a programme on TV about this little boy who had to keep the curtains closed for ever. He couldn't play with other children and he lived in a tent with windows – a kind of plastic bubble,' Susie says, and then she sneezes again.

'Germs. Yuck.' Anthony hides a chicken drumstick under his T-shirt. 'Mum can you open the chocolate spread lid? It can't undo.'

'Ask *my* mum, she'll do it,' says Geoffhurst. 'She's superstrong. She was trained to be a warrior on Themyscira, an island far away. She's in exile. That means she can't go back where she came from and live happily. They gave her gifts. See the band in her hair? Well it isn't, not really.' Geoffhurst shakes his head to show just how mistaken we are. 'It's an indestructible boomerang and those bracelets—' Hindy yawns.

'Why don't you all sod off . . . go play . . . find Daddy and Uncle Leighton in the beer tent,' she says, shooing them from around her as if they are yard fowl.

'Can we have ice cream?' The queue for the ice-cream van starts at the swing park in single file and thickens up where the woman with a red velvet dot on her forehead is selling vegetable samosas and miniature flying saucers of meat and spiced pastry.

'Okay, but all stick together. A Cornish Mivvi for your mother and an Orange Maid for me,' I say, giving Susie my purse. '*And don't rush back.*' And off they go fighting over who should hold it. A Dobermann passes, panting and tossing saliva strings from its jaws. It snarls half-heartedly not wanting to disappoint. The heat has changed all of our behaviour, with dogs saving their energies for burglars and other emergencies.

As soon as the children are gone, we lay down side by side on our fronts resting our weight on our elbows. The soles of my feet are toasting. The blue sky has a curling white line left from an aeroplane. My spirit won't settle. It could be 'mother nerves' because my child is out of sight and worry, like relaxing and sleeping, has changed and won't turn back since having Anthony.

I look across at Hindy's swinging feet. My mind is shuffling tragedy pictures. Anthony face down in the paddling pool, his blood turning the ambulance stretcher slow red. My heart beats regular, doesn't jump. I try closer to home.

'You and Sonny . . .' Hindy sighs, as if she is bored with the subject already, turns her face away from me, and rests her cheek flat on the brown and cream wool blanket.

'Do you think you and Leighton will grow old together?' Hindy asks through the back of her head, turning the subject back on me.

'Leighton is old from time.'

'And us?'

'We'll be in our rocking chairs on the veranda slapping mosquitoes and watching the sunset drinking rum sent over from Dolores in Barbados.' Hindy laughs and turns to face me.

'Me and Sonny *us*.' My heart twitches with loneliness.

People say, *It's the Sonny and Hindy Show* when my sister, brother-in-law and I walk into a room, as if I am off screen, or at best a featured guest. Sometimes they start by singing the music that starts the show. Inside I'm shouting *No it's the Hindy and Harriet Show*. I can't believe they don't know that. Daddy knew. I long for his impatient voice to call out, *Indyanarriet*. I recover enough to speak.

'You two are like Ike and Tina,' I say, determined to move away from Sonny and Cher but not liking where I find myself, because there *is* something of Ike and Tina about them – passion wrapping in on itself, snarling at outsiders, capable of providing the turning-inside-out-Saturday-night sex all days of the week. 'Ike and Tina will be together for ever. They've got "fierce love". Not many couples got that,' I say, thinking of Daddy, whose heart would have lasted longer if he hadn't loved his race too tough. 'Fierce love don't let go easy, they love each other too powerful.'

'Together, for ever, and never to part,' she says and pat-a-cakes her hands against an invisible partner. I don't dare ask if it is him or me.

Sonny is walking towards us, pushing back his baseball cap to mop his brow with a white handkerchief that he waves in the air as he talks, as if he's signalling 'peace', although he doesn't look peaceful, flaying his arms, taking up sky space. He's talking and though I can't see anyone else there must be someone. Sonny wouldn't talk to himself. There are no thinking people past going crazy, but he is the careful type and they don't hear voices when they flip. They check the cooker is turned off twenty times and wake up at four o'clock in the morning convinced they forgot to lock the back door. It is Leighton with him, and I can't see him yet because of the crowds and Leighton not being a tall man. (I wouldn't call him *short.*) In the beginning his height put me off. Hindy pushed us together. *You're not exactly tall yourself*, she reminded me. But a man is a chance to get what I didn't get given. Hindy says it isn't so. She quoted the feminists when I was thinking of marrying Leighton to encourage me to accept shorter, accept less. 'You can become the man you want to marry.' She is complete already and if I were Hindy I would've just looked for myself too.

I recognize the feet in the sandals, stretching distance from my face. The second toe longer than the big toe, which signifies wealth or luck, or a bunion on its way. When I look up Leighton is standing next to Sonny in front of us. I kneel up and sit back on my heels. Leighton is holding a bottle of wine by the neck. There is a wet triangle spreading out from Sonny's breastbone, darkening his blue T-shirt. Hindy sits up suddenly, tall and cross-legged as if the headmaster just walked in to morning assembly. Sonny blocks the sun, throwing a shadow over Hindy. She stretches up, grabs a fist of his T-shirt from the middle of his chest and Sonny drops down slowly until he is kneeling between Hindy's splayed knees. Hindy pulls the back of his head towards her and kisses him. They join their tongues, the tip of Sonny's tongue pushing into the root of Hindy's. Round and round they go, twirling like blind majorettes.

'All right mate.' Leighton bangs Sonny on the back. Sonny sucks the length of Hindy's tongue up and down, all the while stroking the back of her hair, pressing it into the in-and-out shape of her head and neck-back. They rock so slowly you could believe breeze was blowing them. The air feels like lemon curd.

The only excuse for their behaviour, at their big age, is they are bound together. Grandma Evadnee warned me about binding together, told me not to do it lightly due to the problems it causes if one of the couple wants to part. Elizabeth Taylor and Richard Burton is the example I give for the reason I won't do binding. Bound-together couples can hate each other but let them try to separate. They can search, but there is no drink, or drug, or food that will dull the agony of apartness (and between them the Taylor-Burtons have tried all three). The Burtons – probably an accidental binding. You don't need to tie a beefsteak between your legs to bind a man. Time past I suspected I might be bound to Sonny too – it could have happened when I was sixteen and he helped me lay the table and I turned the glass and drank St Vincent rum from the side of it wet with his lip print. It can happen without knowledge if a man and a woman swallow each other's private fluids (I've never been able to find out the quantity required) and that can happen all sorts of ways, which makes me wonder if Leighton, who insists I colour code kitchen and bathroom rags and says *I don't business what English men are doing for their wives*, when my turn for pleasure comes, knows more about the old ways than he's letting on.

'Where are my kids?' Sonny asks as soon as they separate. My sister rolls on to her back, sits up and leans back on her arms. The muscles in her neck stand up like strands of uncooked spaghetti. Leighton passes me a plastic cup of wine and Hindy snatches it away before searching her armpits for the missing children.

'They're under my arm in a sweat bubble.' Leighton passes me another cup that I hold firmly. 'Liebfraumilch,' he says. Sonny scratches his head through his cap. Hindy shrugs her shoulders and studies blotches of sunshine coming through the leaves and moving on her knees. My wine tastes sweet and cold.

'Gone for ice creams,' I tell him.

'Thank you Harriet.' *I can't help myself, ooh ooh, 'cause baby it's you. Shala-la-la.*

'Good old Harriet,' Hindy says, cutting the song. 'You had your chance,' she adds in a lower voice. Then she laughs, and her laughter sounds like a dry cough, as if she's choking and can't keep the sentence in her throat. I want to whack her behind her knees with a baseball bat, watch her concertina to the ground. I hear Daddy. *Indyanarriet! In this family there'll be no whippings or beatings. We're not carrying on where they left off.*

Sonny unfastens the buckles on his sandals.

'Always running your mouth,' he says clouding over, slipping his sandals off. 'You keep on.' The inner soles of his sandals have pebble-shaped toe prints.

Leighton is lying on his back, his forearm resting on his face blocks out his eyes. *See no evil, hear no evil, speak no evil.* Hindy crosses her spidery legs at the ankle. She is slurping wine down her long throat too fast to taste it, and when she has drained the glass she stretches her neck, points her chin at the empty sky and pretends not to notice the rumbling at ground level.

'You know something?' Sonny says to the side of Hindy's

upwards-jutting chin, and it feels like lightning could strike at any time. He sucks his teeth. 'Leighton you coming?' And without doing up the buckles he flip-flops away in the direction of the beer tent.

Visibility very good or excellent: late June 1976

Seven, eight, nine. Hindy holds her forehead with a flat palm as I brush long strokes from the V at the start of her hairline. The sides of her face are damp. The space above her top lip bubbles sweat like a salted aubergine. I make sure the bristles scratch close to her scalp; keep going past her neck-back and on to the middle of her shoulders where her hair ends.

It used to be mother's job: wash Hindy's hair, and with a blob of grease balanced on the top of one hand, using the first fingers of her other hand she'd dab and draw oily lines in her scalp, massage her head and brush her first born child's hair 100 times as if Hindy was a Victorian princess and Mother her lady-in-waiting. *Rapunzel, Rapunzel.* Locks long enough to free her and, as Hindy said, free us both if I climbed up her dropped-down hair with the key in my mouth to unlock the door so we could escape together. She didn't leave me out, but still I couldn't help grudging her the fairy-tale hair and grudging Mother for the chance to play in it.

I am eight or so, Grandma Evadnee is turning me pretty with seventy-two plaits, five yellow ribbons, a lick of La India, four short bursts and a cloud of eye-stinging Afro Sheen. She pulls my hair from the comb, rolls it between her palms and hands me a ball of my dead hair to put in the toilet as usual, but after six flushes it won't go nowhere, is still floating on the surface. I can't wait to pop style on Hindy but I'm not allowed out to play until the hair is gone. I am sobbing, waiting for the cistern to fill up again when Grandma Evadnee bursts in. She pulls the chain. We watch the hair whirl and suck away. I'm not surprised it is gone now. *Everything happens in God's time*, Mother says, and again I put Grandma Evadnee in the sentence and take God out without the sense taking leave. Grabbing my wet jaw with a hard greasy hand that presses on to my back teeth she locks me into her gaze. *Do you know how easy it would be to hex somebody with that much hair? They can go in the swamp to some tree or other and bore a hole and put your hair in there and put a plug back in that tree. And you'll go crazy. Or they can throw your hair in running water and your mind will wander on just like the hair is wandering on in the stream. And do you think I could help you then? Think on, because not even a black hen buried alive can save the day.*

Twelve – Hindy is sitting on the floor, a cotton skirt between her legs spread wide, her toes pressing into the base of the smoked glass cabinet Mother left me, full of framed photos of all of we, the crystal glasses and the *for best* rosebud china. I sit behind Hindy on the edge of the sofa, the backs of my legs sticking to the leather, the inside of my thighs relaxed against her shoulders. I push the bristles of the silver-backed brush into her damp hairline and sweep back – fifteen.

'Shut the window. Bugs are flying in.' I catch sweat about to run into my eyes with the back of my hand and blow a ladybird off my shoulder.

'It's too hot to close it.' It is the third week of the heat wave. In the first week the weathermen were happy to be the bearers of good news. Jack Scott was flinging facts like frisbees – hottest summer in

200 years — lowest rainfall since records began. But the heat has burnt away his pleasure. He points at weather charts, dressed in long shirtsleeves and a tie, hopeful of changing weather, waiting for cold fronts and travelling showers. I keep brushing, wondering if Hindy has forgotten real bugs with legs thick as shoelaces. Cher is on the telly. I wouldn't call what she's doing *dancing*. Her singing is nothing to write home about either. This week she's wearing a crocheted purple dress with trumpet sleeves and the tips of her fingers take the place of musical notes.

'She's got style,' Hindy says. 'For a white chick.' Hindy knows about style, can set trends accidentally. At school she started a fashion with nothing but laziness and loose elastic in one sock.

Hindy leans her head back on to my lap and looks at me with her upside-down face.

'Mother used to part my hair in the centre and brush from top to bottom.'

'I never seen her do it that way,' I say, wondering why she is lying. The electric fan whirrs, keeping the net curtains away from the window glass.

'Harriet, you only ever see what you want,' she says. But isn't that true for us all? Eighteen. I jerk her head and press the bristles hard on to her tender scalp until they bend. Her shoulders race to her ears.

'Sorry,' I say. 'I'll get the comb.' I take the ashtray with me to empty. In the kitchen I press the dustbin pedal down to the floor. I empty the ashtray full of bent stubs Sonny and Leighton left before they went off to the pub. They fall into the bin. I take my foot off the pedal and let the lid snap closed. Tiny red ants make a moving pattern over the kitchen sideboard around a saucer of oil that was butter at breakfast.

'Tea?' I call out in friendly singsong whilst shuffling in a drawer past dead batteries, Sellotape, elastic bands, red bills. Under a letter from the school asking for money for a trip to the zoo l find a comb.

'Okay,' she shouts back. I flick through the pages of yesterday's *Daily Mirror* waiting for the kettle to boil. I still can't do the crossword, stuck on nine across and four down, so I flick to the horoscopes, ready to read Scorpio and Libra, check who's about to have the best time before I decide what sign to claim as my own. When Mother died in '72, I stopped reading the zodiacs for a while out of respect, *Jesus didn't do astrology. You shouldn't either.*

I don't set much store by zodiacs for forecasting the future, dreams are better, if only people would make time to think on them for long enough to spot a premonition dream in with the message dreams and desire dreams. But Daddy knew the difference when he planted ground provisions in Taurus, and I've noticed better results if I tie my work to the planetary positives of the person needing the help. Besides, it's like Grandma Evadnee used to say behind Mother's back, *There were ways of knowing and doing before the missionaries and what is it with niggers and Jesus anyhow?*

'Lemon cake,' I say to Hindy's confused eyebrows and place a mug of tea and a cloggy slice of cake with a wet bottom on the smallest of the nest of tables beside her.

'It's the recipe book's fault: one *and a half* lemons and the yolks of two eggs. What am I supposed to do with the egg whites? I blame rationing – a *sprig* of parsley – a *pinch* of sugar – a *slice* of lemon. White people can be so mean – especially to their own selves.'

'Mother always said you had no eye for measurements.'

'It will let you down in the end,' we both say in Mother's voice and titter, the tea in our mugs sloshing from side to side.

When I settle back into the sofa, I clamp Hindy's shoulders between my thighs and line the tip of the comb with the centre of her nose before parting her hair.

'What number now?' I brush down from her crown, past her right ear.

'Nineteen.' On the telly Sonny and Cher are waving goodbye.

'They choose your Sonny for any match yet?' Hindy's neck stiffens. Sonny is no age, but footballers retire at thirty (earlier with injuries), his cheerleaders are too old to star jump more than a few inches, and Dolores' daughter Dusty knows a boy who was spotted playing football in the park near his estate where scouts go searching for the black in the Union Jack. Sonny has just a few more seasons to impress in a game, get snapped up by a first division team, make a fortune and retire.

'Not yet.' Twenty-five.

'I been burning a red candle with his name tucked underneath.' I don't tell her I think I've been burning it on the wrong day, although there's no shame there, even Grandma Evadnee admitted candle use is a specialty that takes a lifetime's work to master. 'You see if that manager doesn't change his mind,' I tell her. Hindy sighs. Thirty. 'You see if a match doesn't come to meet Sonny soon,' I add – not from confidence in candles, or in the manager (who came to dinner and made 'natural talent' sound like 'lazy', and is weak-kneed under pressure from the players and Daz-white supporters) – but because life can throw an opportunity so hard and unexpected if you're not careful it can knock you out clean.

I listen to a mumbling of nonsense words with a complaining rhythm. The children are sleeping with kicked-off covers, their damp bodies sapped by the sun. On the top bunk Anthony and Geoffhurst lie back-to-back, upside down from each other, one head next to the other's feet. On the bottom bunk Susie's fingers trail through a stream of cool dream-water.

Hindy puts down her mug of tea and pulls her knees up until they nearly nudge her chin and holds them in place with clasped arms.

'I had a visit from Jason's mother the other day. Came to my door. Make-up this thick.' Hindy spreads her finger and thumb. 'But her cheek was barefaced enough, telling me to keep *my* son away from *her* son – accused Geoffhurst of bullying. I'm not one of those women who can't call their children's faults.' She presses one index finger on top of the other. 'One, he's a bit handy with his fists and he's touchy sometimes – it's his lazy eye. I told her *Boys play rough, they just* do. *Ask yourself*, I said, *why would Jason want to stay best friends with Geoffhurst if he was bullying him?*'

'You spoken to his teachers?'

'They say he has an overactive imagination. He's a child. But they add his intelligence and so-called aggression and two-twos . . . Daddy told me. They start off stopping the pram to coo and ahhh, and ten years later, especially if he's big for his age . . . He blames his eye.' She looks away. 'But you can hardly notice it. I'm up to here,' she says, chopping her forehead with her hand, 'with, *Are there any problems at home that might be contributing to his recent deterioration in behaviour?*'

Childhood ailments need early attention, something science has cottoned on to, catching up with Grandma Evadnee by putting right a baby's flaws in the womb. But when Hindy was pregnant with Geoffhurst I was distracted with my own troubles and I missed the incubation period. Hindy puts his eye defect down to him rolling off the bed when he was a few months old. She asked for my help but I was scared of getting it wrong so I turned her away. I was beside myself, watching a strange self – a new mother and wife – and I was quietly nursing a lust so bad just thinking on him could make me vomit.

'I know Sonny needs to practise,' I say, 'but he could spend a little more time with that boy, get him away from the television. Geoffhurst would sit inside the box given half a chance. Mary Whitehouse—'

'I put it down to environment – lack of trees,' says Hindy, cutting into my talking. 'People behave better in places with a lot of trees. She never would have felt fit to come bad-mouthing my child if I had two elms either side my front door.' She rubs the lowest part of her back. 'Mary Whitehouse nothing. Children see all sorts of things, but they're not stupid. Even with his bad eye Geoffhurst can see, right from wrong, pretend from real.'

I wait on her; hoping silence will pull out the tissue of words packaging what she really wants to tell me. She drops her forehead on to her knees and is silent.

'I picked up extra at Tesco – a few bits. The bags are in the kitchen,' I tell her.

Hindy strokes my knee as if it aches and both the knee and the ache belong to her. Thirty.

Hindy purrs. Play in her hair long enough and sleep follows. Her head nods, bending lower and lower behind her until the weight is all rested on the top of my thighs. I part her hair once, grease her scalp with sweet yellow oil and then I do it again in another place. I stop when a parting shows a half moon of scalp. I slide my finger into the gap and move her hair aside. When I flatten her hair to the sides of her head I see a circle of scalp the size of a 5p piece. I run through cures for hair loss – rosemary oil, red meat – even though the rest of her hair shines with health.

There was an old woman who swallowed a fly. A nursery rhyme about an old woman who keeps on swallowing insects and animals booms in my head. Is like I swallowed a bird and it's in my throat trying to raise its wings over and over. I start checking Hindy's head, pulling apart hair with my fingers. Searching. I'm full of anger, the way a doctor would be if he diagnosed a common cold, told the patient to wrap up warm and drink plenty fluids, and all the while it was meningitis, and worse, it was his own child he dismissed. We expect more from trained people and they expect more from themselves. I can forecast a hurricane from the temperature of the sea. I can say whether the rain on its way will last for days or minutes, and before I was ten I could predict rain before the rain-birds flew.

I curve her head forward and release my hands either side of it. She stops breathing for a few seconds and then shudders like she is in a dream and stepped down one step and discovered three. She sleeps on, her nose inches from her chest. At the base of her neck are eight red and yellow marks, four on each side nearly opposite each other. I hold back laughter and admiration, because the bruises aren't chaos, aren't ugly. Like all of we, damage is charmed by Hindy, turning orderly and rainbow beautiful on meeting her. The bird presses in its wings and darts to the centre of my chest.

We have no parents. A dead father can't threaten to slice Sonny like a Christmas ham, snap his neck like a wishbone. There are no elders to put their mouths on him. Shaming isn't effective in England where it is more closely related to embarrassment than honour. Back-home-shame can lead to death whilst English-shame colours fast, raises the temperature for a while, but does not change behaviour, won't train hands to their sides. *Don't dance abroad if you can't dance at home.* Sonny is in London gyrating. His thighs are limbo-level with the floor, the palms of his hands waving in the air carnival high.

My femaleness hits in a high, wash-up-me-up-on-the-shore wave, fresh and shocking as 12-year-old blood appearing with no cuts, as terrible as coming to England and driving in a car twenty times the speed of a truck, as finding out I was coloured and realizing it meant something lesser, something Kelco-Cochrane-dangerous. We have been more than enough sibling for each other, but now we need brothers, other men, because men need bigger, stronger men than themselves around to hold their dark side down. Leighton is too small and I have grown accustomed to his ways and I'd rather give away hair from the mould of my head than change his nature. I won't wear his hair in the toes of my shoes.

This is not the Sonny and Cher Show. This Sonny won't argue with his wife in front of viewers. He is no jester putting himself down. He is careful, pays attention to detail, like the policeman with a mattress in the back of his van, beating his prisoners without marking their skin.

Loving Hindy is like being a worker in a grand house; dusting the chandeliers, polishing the mahogany floors, giving more strength to that house than to my own, until I could argue the house is more mine than theirs. Lock me out without warning and watch me shatter the windows, collapse the house, crumble it low down where ferns and croakers thrive. If I can't live there who but me has the right to douse the petrol, light the match?

Get nine across wrong and four down can't work.

I know the answer. The bird in my chest spreads its wings full span.

I sit pulling long angel hairs until the brush is picked clean. On my way to the toilet I roll weightless hair between my palms the way I've seen my mother and both grandmas do all my life. The ball gets smaller and tighter, starting out the colour of potato pudding, finishing up dark as the muddy sand crabs favour. I hear Grandma Evadnee. *Flush it away, all kinds of hexing start with the hair from your head.* But for the first time ever I disobey her. The bird is bashing against my heart, trying to escape. A few loose feathers stick in my throat when I think of going against Grandma Evadnee who always had a long reach and could, no doubt it, even from the other side, scrape me up and grab my neck-back.

I tuck the hair into my bra. In the kitchen I look for an empty jar to seal the hair away from the air when I remember the ashtray. I press the pedal on the dustbin and mess up my hand searching for a cigarette stub, picking out a long dog-end tipped with black cherry lipstick. With my clean hand I search through the food cupboard. Behind Jacob's Cream Crackers and sardines in oil there is a jar of thick-peel marmalade with a few spoonfuls left which I could wash out and use, but Tupperware is best, could have been made for this use alone. I wrap the fag end in foil and drop the hair strands in a freezer bag and knot the top. I lock them in the plastic container, forcing my hand palm down to dip the lid, squeezing the air out. A recent picture might prove useful, but it's difficult to think of any with just her. Beautiful people don't get much alone time, what with the everyday people always wanting to be close to them. As I seal the edges closed I hear Grandma Evadnee. *Keep the ingredients fresh. Remember how newly picked feverfew has more flavour, more strength, more power?*

Apart from lodestone – for pulling towards (good quality, too, because skimping on a drawing force is a false economy) – most of what is called for is here. And being prepared brings peace, like looking at your dried fruits plumping up fat and boozy in a tall glass jar of rum in October, and knowing poverty or supermarket shortages can't catch you. All the ingredients for your Christmas cake are in sight and when the time is right it will be baked.

The bird stops flapping. Wings tucked in. Feathers smoothed down. Its body is quiet and tight. I could convince myself of heartburn, imagine undigested meat stuck in my gullet. If I hold my breath and listen I can hear a soft heartbeat quieter than a human life starting out. I listen to the tick-tock-tick-tock and know it isn't dead, just resting.

Fine and sunny: early July 1976

The record 'shop' is a shack, a garden shed without a door. There's a wall-to-wall counter at the back, full of records labelled A–Z, and any record you name Curtis can put his fingers on and pluck it from the wall first time. He shuffles records, then spins them with his forefinger on the centre like a Harlem Globe Trotter, playing tune after tune until someone in the crowd can't stand it any longer and reaches for their wallet, because worries start when the music stops, and for less than the cost of a prescription they can 'rewind and come again' as many times as their neighbours can bear. There are less than a dozen of us crowded into a shop that smells of peach pomade and frying hair from Mavis' salon next door.

The stinging sun and the jump-up music are reminders that carnival is coming: a time for noise without petitions, when purple can sit next to orange, and blue next to green without sideways looks, and our men can gather in groups without others looking fearful, and we can thrash our arms and kick our feet and sing loud calypso and call up the ghosts of the past without psychiatrists queuing up to stick schizophrenia on us, and just for a few untouchable days we are free.

We all making small movements, bouncing a finger, tapping a toe, shaking a shoulder; trying not to push up in anyone else's space. Lord Creator is singing *Kingston Town the place I long to be*, and I let him carry me along, and what with the heat oiling my joints I soon forget the other people and I'm rocking, remembering the warm black air stroking my shoulders and the white stars gathered in a group like a gang of young girls on a night out giving me a downtown rude-gal stare-out.

'Dolores, I'm going to leave you here and meet you back. If I leave it any later all the best—'

'Yes darling, you g'long,' says Dolores winding her waist and sorting through the records that have been put by especially for her. 'Play this one for me nuh?' She slips a 45 from its cover, holds the record by the edges with her palms and passes it to Curtis.

Next door to the chicken stall where the upside-down fowl hang, are deep-pink pig noses and curled tails dangling on hooks across the top front of the stall. On wooden trays slanting towards me are dusty pieces of salt fish, some as thick as T-bone steaks. The smell of salted cod passes through my nostrils and raises the top of my head, and I imagine the sea under my back, keeping me afloat and seeping into the corners of my mouth. So I stop and buy a flat salt-crusted fish, even though they are stacked like cardboard, one on top of the other, in my food cupboard.

'Three pounds for a pound. Threepounds forapound. Threepoundsforapoundthree poundsforapound.'

Bare-armed people jostle me skin to skin as they push through the crowds on the pavement, giving up the wide-open road and the chance for bargains from the stalls on either side of the street for the pavement where stripy canopies offer a little shade.

The honey scent from hundreds of egg-sized yellow mangos slows me down. The pregnant stall owner is stretching up to a plastic bag hung from a hook high on the wooden frame.

'Put the bags lower down,' I tell her as I pass, because an expectant mother raising her hands too high can tie the baby's cord around its neck. And then I add, because the high round bump must be a boy, so there's heartache ahead, 'Place scissors underneath your back when the baby is born, it will help cut the after-pain.' I don't stop to see her reaction, not all people like advice, especially when it comes to their children.

'Hot enough for yer darlin'?' He twirls a paper bag full of purple grapes at the corners until they seal with twists at each end. He is naked from the waist up. His pink chest sprouts golden hairs. He winks at me, cheeks shining like the American Red apples behind the *Do not handle* sign.

When I reach the West Indian stall there is a queue. I stand behind a frowsy-smelling woman who is taking the water shortage and using it as an excuse. And like Mr Ling from Daddy's dominoes club says, his teeth spread out like fork prongs, *Joke is joke, but damn joke is no joke at all.* I look past her at the crates of vegetables – dark green calaloo leaves flop in between tiger-print plantains and skinny red seasoning peppers.

Mrs Williams is chopping a grey-skinned yam with a machete. Her wide-brimmed hat is bigger than the sun. She holds up a buttery circle of yam like it's a winning medal. The customer she is serving nods his head and Mrs Williams wraps the yam in newspaper and longs her hand for payment. She acknowledges me with a quick glance. I pull my T-shirt away from my back and flap it in and out.

'I'm not asking 70p. I'm not even asking 50p. I'm giving them away at 30p. Come on ladies, quick before I realize I was robbed.'

I pick up four green oranges and a bunch of swollen-headed scallions.

'Harriet.' Mrs Williams takes a slatted box covered with a cloth out from under the stall. 'Come,' she says and I follow her to the side of the stall where she hands the box to me. 'If there's anything that takes your fancy I'll give you a special price.' I remove the cloth and finger the top of glass bottles reading the names. Go Away Powder. Follow Me Girls – Follow Me Boys Powder. I feign interest. Every now and then I buy a box or two to nice her up; because it's not everyone can get red dogwood or fresh blacksnake root at short notice. Passion Oil. Good Luck Perfume. Never Part Oil. Easy Life Oil. I lift Spanish Love Drops, take the square-necked bottle out of the box then put it back. Get Together Powder. I pull out Love Powder. *Ideal for attracting or holding the one you love. Smooth lightly over face. Spread on your body at night.* Get Together Powder – *Does the one you seek to hold say no? Then this is the powder for you. Sprinkle it in the palm of your sweetheart's hand.*

'The pocket is short,' I say patting the top of my thigh. 'Just the regular order.' I hand back the box before accepting a bulging Sainsbury's carrier bag. I can't resist checking inside: prickly ash, black dogwood, ginseng and burdock. I dig to the bottom of the bag looking for blacksnake and angelica roots. The few jars of powder at the bottom include rattlesnake. I prefer to grind my own but I don't complain. I am more than pleased with what I have, I could dress the inside band of Sonny's hat and in this heat the sweat would act as a carrier to run the powder into his eyes to blind him. I could tighten his bowels until they locked, or rinse his clothes in a poisonous root that won't start working until his pores open and I could be in another country when he died and not even Columbo scratching his head and asking *Just one more thing* on his way back into the room could catch me.

Mrs Williams won't let me pay. She shakes her head and pushes my purse-holding hand to my side. Then she drags my left arm until we are as far away from the waiting customers as possible, pulling us into the Babygros and frilly shawls from the stall behind. We are under the shade of her hat when she whispers, 'I could only find you four devil's shoestring.' The friend of Mother's who moved out of London to a house with a garden front and back, whose neighbours say she makes too much noise and are collecting signatures to chase her away, if she is to stay, she'll need nine strings – all the same size. I'm about to tell her not to worry they'll do fine, when she says, 'My son Alby him gone. His girlfriend didn't want him again. She spit him out like a plum seed and he just take off. See a picture here.' Alby is sitting on a sofa covered in plastic wrap. On the floor on the left of the sofa is a vase filled with peacock feathers. I stifle a sigh. It is hard to be sympathetic when people bring problems on themselves. Feathers will have bad luck flying and that is as basic as shoes off the table, don't eat from strangers and don't leave an unplucked chicken in the house. 'His toothbrush and my phone number in the bag.' She wraps my fingers around the carrier bag and pats the top of my hand. 'Do your best.' There is no time to cut her short, to tell her if you want a particular person to come to your house just get a snapshot of them and lay it face downward on your dresser under the cloth, and they will come inside of three days, or to tell her how fast anvil dust works for bringing parties back together, because Mrs Williams is putting two sun-blackened plantains on the scales for the next customer.

'If you want everlasting life see Jesus and get it.'

If my head wasn't full up with Hindy, helping Mrs Williams would be no botheration. Binding together, love getting, nature tying, straying – all Grandma Evadnee's favourites (although she turned her hand to restoring lost nature if she could lay her hands on John the conqueror root and a man was foolish enough to offer over the odds). There are all kinds of ways of bringing people back who are running around or have run away and ways to help those left behind – persimmon root and alum to close an open vagina so a lover won't have suspicions – a ginger root remedy for women who catch pregnant for one man but want to return to another. Ways to bring on miscarriage or delay birth – *hot green coffee, whisky, turpentine. Everything hot, hot, hot. A brand new lead pencil, sharp, never used. A bucketful of boiling water*. I'm no braggart but I cut my teeth on straying spells – lots of body fluids and calling out for the missing person. They come to me as easily as my four times tables. I've been able 'to tie a man's nature' from when I was a girl too young to realize it was a way to fix a man's cock so it only works for one woman.

'Wimbledon strawberries – sweet and juicy – four boxes for 50p.'

There are pulling-apart plans to consider – mixing their head hairs with black pepper and wrapping them in greaseproof paper (it works as well as parchment paper). I could push the paper under the airbrick at their front step – where they have to walk over. Wait, and watch them pull apart. Nothing would save them (except red peppers in brown paper stuffed into the toes of their shoes). Or I could bury

one of Sonny's shoes, have him walking the earth until he found it.
Not seeing him ever again? No. The best-suited spell for Hindy and
Sonny (that will have him where he belongs, under her foot) calls for
the dead skin from my sister's heels and there's no sensible way of
getting that, which is a shame because dead-skin powder mixes well
with drinks and Sonny is thirsty for rum like a bottle been under his
porch for three weeks and then poured into a fire.

'If you can't see this is a bargain Mummy you shouldn't be allowed
out on yer own without a white stick or a guide dog.'

Love powders can't be beaten – but they are not without problems.
I wouldn't use them for very young couples. They fear separation,
get het up and are prone to suicide pacts after deciding eternity is
their only option.

'Repent! Repent! For God so loved the world that he gave . . .'

By the time I get to the record shop the shack is moving. The walls are
jumping and the floor dips with the weight and movement of the two
dozen or so bodies jammed inside. A calypso leaps into the street. It is a
song made for carnival, telling people how to move and when to jump,
and when the singer calls there is an answer to fling back, and then John
Holt starts singing, cooling everyone off like a lemon ice after a goat
curry. People limp outside. Dolores looks surprised to see me.

  'You been out here long time?' Her hair has lost its curl and has
started to frizz. Her cherry-red lips have been eaten away.

'Just come.'

'Get what you wanted?'

'Ah ha.'

'What sweet you?' a bug-eyed Rasta with pencil-thin locks tied in a high ponytail asks me. I can't help skinning my teeth. It's the dead skin heel spell making me laugh, the under-the-foot part – imagining all six foot six of Sonny with Hindy's high-arched high-yella chicken-foot holding him in place.

Mainly moderate: mid July 1976

I hold the pestle at the bottom of my fist crushing bark and pods, breaking down roots and dried leaves. All the while Grandma Evadnee is pushing herself into my head. She says nothing, just sits quietly in my thoughts. But I can tell by the look on her face (not smiley-smiley but her eyes are soft) that she thinks I've done well.

Today is the hottest day of the year. The duration and intensity of the sunshine has not been equalled since the eighteenth century, the radio weatherman says, and then he switches to a 'for your own benefit', mixed in with a 'we're all in this together' tone I notice people old enough to remember the Second World War are partial to. *Those with asthma should stay away from traffic and remember their inhalers. Between twelve and two unless absolutely necessary avoid going outside. Old people should drink plenty of fluids. Dogs shouldn't be left in cars with the windows wound up and bowls of water must be put down for cats.*

Grandma Evadnee is not one for praise. Her silence sounds better than applause. It is something I have taken on as my own. I don't allow myself excitement at Anthony's mathematics grades. I don't swell up when they praise his upbringing, his manners. They expect one thing. I expect another.

I have chosen today to send out a clear message of my confidence. It is the reason people marry on Valentine's Day. In future years Anthony's birthday will bring layered pleasure like lovemaking on sheets fresh off the clothesline, or eating *mille feuille.*

I checked my original weighing twice over, taking no chances, the way Grandma Evadnee reweighed oranges from the grocer, checking she had the full two pounds she paid for. I don't expect problems. There are no distances to work out, no lines to get straight. And Mother, who mistrusted my ability to measure sugar, flour, feet and inches, good and evil – she is where Grandma Evadnee being in the right always put her.

A thin line of sweat runs round the outside of my face and drips off my chin. Not enough food. I didn't underestimate. It's not that I measured wrong. If not for the heat I would have singed the hairs off chicken thighs and drumsticks and wings, seasoned them with jerk, all except the wings, they're not worth the work without a sticky-sweet barbecue sauce to dip them in.

Just as I'm pulling the length of a cocktail stick loaded with a cheese cube, a sticky cherry, a pineapple chunk and a silver-skinned onion into my mouth the floor starts to tilt, just a little, like I am a picture that looked lined up and fine until someone took the spirit level out and, of course, I wasn't balanced right, because now I have shifted and I am dead straight once more.

'Someone get the door for my sister,' I call out, washing my hands, scratching at the black minced cake-mix under my nails, waiting for the half of my zodiac sign to come. The water runs warm from the cold tap like back-home water where the pipes are exposed to the sun. The bell rings and Susie, Lady of the Manor, here a few weeks and acting like she owns the place, pirouettes past the kitchen on her way to open the door.

'It's Mum and Dad.'

'The Sonny and Hindy Show,' Leighton calls out from the garden.

'And Geoffhurst,' Geoffhurst says, poking his head around the kitchen door. His right eye is looking elsewhere when he gives me a worried half smile.

'Come on in trouble.'

Susie bounces past him. My special occasion scent trails behind her.

'He stole sweets from school and Mum and Dad will have to pay money they don't have. He's been asked to leave early.' When I don't react she adds, 'He's been *expelled*.'

'Suspended,' Geoffhurst says.

'He is in trouble at school all the time for being cheeky, telling stories, lies. He has an overactive imagination,' she says, as if that at least is indisputable. Geoffhurst picks four cocktail sticks from the grapefruit and strips two down to the wood before taking a drink from the fridge and following Susie through to the garden.

Hindy and Sonny are projected in the kitchen doorway in glorious Technicolor. Sidney Poitier took a rock-stone to the handcuffs binding him to Tony Curtis, left *The Defiant Ones*, ran clear to *Bhowani Junction* and stole Ava Gardner from under the ski-sloped nose of Stewart Granger. Her bronze shoulders shine against her pink halter-neck like newly minted pennies. They are holding hands behind their backs, entwined so each one's highest arm links with the other's lowest.

'I knew you were coming,' I tell her without putting down my glass. 'Sonny,' I say by way of greeting.

'Harriet.' He says my name through a smile.

'Leighton's out the back,' I tell him but he doesn't drop Hindy's hands. He rocks his hips looking at me. 'With a cold beer.' He catches Hindy in a hard stare before he leaves.

'One minute,' Hindy says, disappearing into the hallway and reappearing with three stacked Tupperware dishes.

'What's that?'

'Chicken. Just in case you didn't cook enough.'

'What's in the small one on top?'

'Barbecue sauce.'

I carry a platter of fish into the garden. I catch Leighton giving Hindy the sort of look I use for prawn roti or raspberry Pavlova. It can't be helped. Her beauty surprises him every time he sees her. He is the only person I know who can be predictably surprised.

'Son, a cold beer for your uncle.' Leighton pushes Anthony off his lap. 'Hindy, beautiful as ever,' he says. She doesn't blush, or argue, or even say thank you.

'Happy now?' Leighton asks me from under the rim of his straw hat. I slam the tray of fish – jack and sprats and snapper and red fish – on to the little wooden table at the side of the barbecue. Silver sprats jump up then settle.

'Not as happy as you.' I have never met a more typical Capricorn. He can be relied on to say the same thing in the same situation in the same way. It makes him popular for pickney's bedtime stories.

'The sausages.' I cut my eyes at Leighton and flick the charred sausages to the cooler edges of the grill with a fork.

Hindy shifts to stand up. I wave her back down and grab a handful of thyme from a pot and toss it on to the coal. A paper napkin Hindy was holding flutters to the ground and Leighton jumps up to pick up after her. I strap three snappers in between two metal grids shaped like a fish and rest them on the smoking barbecue. The fish are turning slow golden pink in no time. I watch Anthony stretched out in Leighton's lap, collapsed back on his father's chest. Their top halves are naked. They are the same colour, a perfect seam-free match. From a distance I can't tell who owns which arm, and that might prove useful if Anthony is caught in a fire and survives, but needs a skin graft. I turn the fish over and go inside for the hard-dough bread.

When I come back out Hindy is sitting next to Leighton on the higher kitchen doorstep, her feet crossed at the ankles trapping Sonny between her denim thighs on the step below, where he and a bottle of Johnny Walker whisky sit side by side. I wave away a drowsy wasp from in front of my face and watch it land on Hindy's arm. She brushes it off her shoulders on to the ground, where it lies there wriggling. She gets up and stamps over and over on its life-less body until she catches herself and then she stops and sits back down.

'They sting at this time of year just because they can,' I say by way of explanation.

Sonny's watching Leighton. 'You're looking on my wife like she wearing something that belongs to you.' Hindy pushes the back of Sonny's head and stands up.

'Listen to yourself,' she says.

'Bollocks,' Leighton says, taking off his sunglasses and balancing them on his head. 'You're talking bollocks.'

'What about my cake?' Anthony asks.

'What cake?' I tell him, enjoying holding him back because I couldn't stop him crawling or walking or pulling my hands away when he wanted to button his shirt, and because he loves numbers more than people he'll end up with a job that makes people say *that's nice* when he explains it and women will take advantage of him and today he is one year nearer to his future and there is nothing I can do about any of it.

'Photos.' Leighton gets up. 'We'll take them in the living room. C'mon.' Susie turns the page of one of the comics spread out around her. Anthony watches Geoffhurst flick a marble with his forefinger.

'Inside.' Sonny jerks his thumb at the house. Like the *Sound of Music* pickney when the whistle is blown, they stop all play and walk silently into the house.

'Why not outside?' I say, rubbing my lips against each other spreading the waxy colour and trying to grab Anthony's face.

'Get off,' Anthony says, flicking his head out of my reach so I miss half the crumbs on his cheeks.

'The sun would be behind us.'

'And the new wallpaper will be behind us in here eh?'

'You made enough fuss to make me put it up.' Leighton takes the basket of silk flowers from the dining table and places it on the floor in front of our feet.

Sonny takes his baseball cap off and throws it on a chair. He smoothes the front of his hairline before snatching Leighton's sunglasses off the top of his head and putting them on.

'Anthony and Susie, move closer together. I can't get you in. There. Nice. Hold it.' Leighton snaps a blinding photograph.

'And again,' he says, but I break up the picture by walking off into the kitchen. The others head outside into the still-hot sun.

By the time I come out again wasps and flies have flown off, excused themselves and gone home early like polite English dinner guests. I hand Hindy a paper plate with two triangles of bread and a fish. She cuts the fish lengthways and then flips the flesh to one side leaving an oil stain on the plate. She thumbs flakes of fish and pinches onion and pimento and red pepper between before leaning back to drop fish and relish into her mouth. Snappers are her favourite. I've seen her chew the heads. *They're the best bit*, she'll say, triangular fish teeth showing between her pearly whites.

'Pepper.' Hindy fans her mouth and pokes her tongue out. I hand her a long glass, stir the jug full of punch with the tall spoon, hoping I have mixed this drink right. Love powders are like Victoria sponges – exactness is called for. Use too little and nothing much changes in the relationship except sex is more frequent, a plus for some couples, but not others. Use too much and the real trouble begins. Grandma Evadnee knew of it only once (and the girl mixing the powder was hard-headed and had no proper training), but love powders can lead to extreme violence, or death. (Love and hate being separated by a hair's width, nudging into the other side is easily done.)

Hindy drinks fast, not stopping for breath. There is movement behind my navel, fluttering. *Miss Molly had a dolly who was sick, sick, sick.* I sing inside my head, blocking my thoughts from being read. Ice knocks the side of the glass. It's not surprising that people under-estimate the dangers of love, mistake it for romance, tie it in ribbons and roses. No wonder people get confused when hearts are symbols of love, but blood, arteries and veins are nowhere to be seen. *She called for the doctor to come quick, quick, quick.* It makes people care-less, and heavy-handedness has severe side effects.

Sonny stops eating. Up to now he don't feel the heat, then he does.

The crescent moon sits upright, full of water it can't hold, a wet moon sharing sky space with the sun. I have waited through the shaved-off-coming-down moon (good for taking away a spell, but useless for gaining control over others), now it is coming up (an ideal time to butcher meat that won't shrink in cooking). It is perfect for my purposes, full of gathering power, and not yet a quarter old.

'Your sister's killing me,' Sonny says, coughing and grabbing his throat. He is sweating under the bulb of his nose. Hindy passes her empty glass to me and I fill it for Sonny. *He came right away with his bag and his hat.*

It's unusual this way, carrying out work for someone who hasn't asked, doing it on someone else's behalf (although don't take me as typical, because Hindy's almost myself). It is the person wanting the work who takes the consequences. There will be a pay-off some-where along the line. Nothing is free.

And he knocked on the door with a rat-a-tat-tat.

Hindy helps herself to another glass of punch. 'Tastes funny,' she says, pulling a sprig of mint out of the glass, showing it to Sonny and making a face as if it is the culprit. *He looked at the dolly and he shook his head.*

'Cake,' I say, heading for the kitchen. It will take away the taste. If I don't measure up now it will mean more than sunken cherries, pastry that won't hold together, but if I get it right the credits will roll on the Sonny and Hindy Show.

I'll be back in the morning with a pill, pill, pill. I'll be back in the morning with a bill, bill, bill.

There are two cakes shaped like two number ones, white with silver balls. I light six candles in one cake and five in the other and then I carry the square silver tray with the cake outside. I am pleased for an opportunity to sing, shout out, to hear my voice instead of my thoughts.

'Happy birthday to An-ton-eeeeeeeeee. Hip-hip.' Geoffhurst claps his hand over his mouth making Red Indian noises.

'Hooray.'

A changing front with storms expected: late August 1976

On the last bus before the night bus, with powdery moths flying around the light in the panels inside, and nothing to write home about outside, I still choose the front seats with a view of the ink-spill sky and the Friday night walk of men with their wage packets pulsing in their pockets. But I am suspicious of free will when I remember Hindy likes the same seat too, and then I hear Daddy. *Rosa Parks. Montgomery, Alabama. December 1955. Go sit upfront girls!*

The bus accelerates and a rush of welcome air bends my afro, and then we slow down, crawling along to a standstill outside Wimpy. It is the third time we've stopped at a place that isn't a stop. In cooler weather people might be using the opportunity to hop on or off the bus, but nobody leaves or joins. I lift the cotton sleeves away from my shoulders and drop them back down in damp patches. The words of an article in the *West Indian World* swim until I stop reading and look out at the sky frowning like an eyebrow. I listen out for thirsty tree roots, clambering over each other, pushing aside soil in anticipation of a soaking.

'He's on a go-slow. The one in front was early,' the clippie explains. She takes my fare and winds her ticket machine before pushing her damp fringe away from her face.

'The bus is too early so all of we have to suffer? Is who the service is for?' asks the West Indian woman wearing stewed-tea tights who got on the same stop as me. She kisses her teeth and the vicar sitting in front of her turns round and nods in support. The clippie sighs. Her face is the shape of an upside-down heart.

'Seventy-seven degrees today,' she says, handing me a soft ticket. I don't doubt her for we are at the end of Dog Days when the Dog Star is ascending and they are the hottest days of any year. When I look up to take my ticket the edges of her face bleed out of focus.

'Thanks,' I say through a cat yawn, emptying as much breath out of my body as possible. The air inside the bus is fattening up. I stand up and hold the top part of the wound-down window for balance.

'Are you going to be all right, love?' the clippie asks.

'Yes, just, need . . .' I gulp air without turning around. Eyes screwed shut I put my arm out of the window with a half-cupped hand palm up and tightly locked fingers, so nothing escapes and I don't get a false reading, and I measure the weight of air. When I have a reading I sit back down. A meagre man is hammering my head to win a soft toy at the funfair. He swings blows to my left temple. If he gains strength he will shoot my stomach up through my mouth.

Someone pulls the cord twice. The bus buzzes.

A throbbing at my left temple before a shower – a queasiness, even sinus trouble before rain clouds gather, I'm used to that. This is different. A storm. A hurry-build-your-ark downpour is on its way. There is a trembling in my stomach which is maybe what Mother felt when the blood clot that gave her the second stroke (before the stroke that killed her) was starting out, making its journey to her brain. *The war finish so long and they still rationing milk? You can't see the tea too dark? Pass the . . . Pass the . . . cow from the fridge*, she'd say, her tongue weighted with surety and sarcasm. I pull myself together. There is bound to be a build up of pressure when it hasn't rained for forty-five days in a country where everyone owns an umbrella or a raincoat. I feel as if someone is wrapping three strands of my hair in parchment paper and nailing it to a tree at sunrise – or worse, driving a rusty nail into the left-hand side of a tree when the sap is rising. It isn't likely. But that doesn't help when I've known so many unlikelies, like Mr Wells (the church organist who played at Grandma Evadnee's funeral) who until Grandma sent him to the crossroads and he received a visitation on the third night couldn't play a note.

I am heaving; scared to actually vomit in case I can't stop. The sky turns London-pigeon-grey. It is hard to be accurate at night time. Shadows of buildings block my view. I can't spot the vertical band of mist where rain begins and ends. But rain feels close. The evening holds water like a sponge. A small squeeze, a little pressure and it will pour. We jerk to a halt outside the shop that sells tea strainers and Jeyes Fluid and kosher crackers for Passover. I close my eyes and start to breathe deeply. The bus moves on.

'Look Mummy it's raining,' a kid says.

'Don't be daft.'

'*It is.*' A hush echoes through the bus. A small clear bead pings on the front window of the bus.

The pings speed up.

'See.' They hit the front from different angles, carried by the wind. The teenagers smoking at the back of the bus start cheering and stamping their feet and then someone starts clapping and suddenly the whole bus is applauding as if rain is famous. A branch scrapes the side of the bus, waving and joining the fan club.

'About frigging time.' The clippie blows out and up. Her fringe jumps away from her forehead.

The vicar bends his head and rests his forehead against the metal bar at the back of the chair in front.

Now water is rolling down the glass at the side windows and my sickness is ebbing away. The big-footed birds weighing down my head and shoulders take flight.

The rain turns carnival noisy – drummers pounding fast, fast, fast, forcing the bus to slow down, turn on front beams that spotlight the rain's showering needles. The kids at the back of the bus run downstairs, two, three stairs at a time, trailing smoke-fog they jump off the platform in front of cars that beep, stall and flash their headlights, spotlighting the 'now you see me now you don't' downpour. They spin and skip through the rain, their clothes turning see-through and clinging to their thin bodies, hard and bendy like green bamboo. I wipe the steam from inside the window with my newspaper to see them better. A girl's heavy-metal eyes run on to her cheeks.

Everybody caught short, a lifetime's warnings about the dangers of rainwater, the colds and chills and ruined shoes, are wasted, there are no umbrellas, or hats or coats or plastic bags to hold above their heads, and they look glad for the excuse to get soaking wet in unexpected rain, look like they been waiting for years for the chance to get soaked. They are wet under their arms and in their ears, on the soft spots in the middle of their scalps. They are being watered, baptized, and even grey-headed people look slimy and newborn.

Gallons of rain whoosh wasted down drains and puddles by the sides of roads. It is rain impossible to stand straight in – knock-you-down-and-bend-you-out-of-shape rain. There is enough water for dozens of protective baths. Not that they have worked well in all my time in England (even when there is no water shortage, and a bath nine days in a row is no botheration). I don't doubt people when they say they wash downwards and dispose of the water in the right way. I put it down to plumbing, because there's no substitution for free-flowing rain, spring or ocean water.

I am English for true because I start to understand streakers at rainy day cricket matches. I feel to pull my dress up over my head and run outside too, even dance maybe, rain-dance. I see why children beg to go out in wellington boots to splash in puddles and feel water pour between their fingers, and I remember why back home we hear rain and are glad someone else has taken charge and changed the pattern of our day. Schoolchildren hang back up their steam-pressed cotton shirts and stay home because the pathway has flooded and earth has shifted somewhere inconvenient. Lovers make love, or take a walk, and old people and those used to time on their hands drift off to sleep to the soft, soon finish, tap tap tapping of sky water on a tin roof – a sound the steel pan drummers make when they are playing for themselves because they are in love, or heartbroken, or tired of excitability.

I am stopped in a shaking bus listening to rain hissing like streaky bacon in a hot pan. I remember the nudists on the news last week. Since the heat wave they've been fighting for their own beaches. Dolores says *They've left their clothes where they left their senses*, but I'm not so sure. If rainwater hid nakedness like the sea we would all rush from our front doors to skinny-dip in the rain. Water and bare skin are meant to be together. Naked on the red roof of the 73 bus with Leighton's feet planted either side of me and my legs wrapped tight on his back so we don't roll away and raindrops can lick the inside of my ear. My bare back against the living dirt under a big-leafed breadfruit tree. My rain-washed toes stretching ballet-straight, lifting my bottom in the air to touch the underside of wet coffee beans shining like emeralds on low-slung branches. But the fantasies are spoilt when I remember that Leighton won't even lie next to the patio doors on a rainy day with the curtain open, even though we're not overlooked and sex cures my rain-headaches.

Rain batters the roof of the bus, cuffs the front window, pummels the side panels. The temperature won't pull down. It is hotter than the first breath of Caribbean air when the door of the Boeing 727 slides open, thicker than corn-meal porridge. I swallow – choke.

Fear grows fat on my nerves. Rain from the open window stings my arms. A woman smelling of 4711 cologne and mothballs slaps my back between my shoulder blades with heel of her hand. I suck in mouthfuls of air – in, in, in. My heart acts like a beginner knitter – rushing, dropping odd stitches. My throat tightens. My windpipe crushes – in, in. I close my eyes.

Rain blows towards me in grooves like a downtown zinc fence in a hurricane. It is so grey I tremble. Not long ago the world was bright – a loadful of green and blue, yellow and orange and purple washing, and I have opened the machine door to grey. The colour of the world has drained away and I won't be able to slice a cucumber and see the dark-green skin and white-green seeds side by side.

Pain crumples me down but when I try to straighten up, breathe slow through the gaps in the hurting, I can't. I am lopsided as a hunch-backed troll. I have fallen into a smooth-sided pit of darkness, and up up up at the edge I don't see Hindy anywhere. *Rapunzel, Rapunzel*. There is no time to find my missing balance because the pain returns, delivered as a message stuck on a burning arrowhead and fired through the centre of my breasts, and now I understand the truth – thunder hid the sound of the trumpet. She has been torn from my side. The first earth has passed away. The world I knew is no longer, and every one of my hundreds of eyelashes, every skin pore and every fingernail knows for sure that the hot pink-orange of a nearly dead jerk pit and the blazing up orange-pink of orgasms and day burning out and smashing against the rocks of Breakneck Point has gone from the world for ever.

Sonny

Mrs Wong's

'How's your back Mrs Wong?' I ask, cupping my hands together and blowing in the gap between my thumbs, hinting for the two-bar electric heater she keeps under the counter.

'All fine now,' she snaps, keeping her face closed. She is carving a carrot into a palm tree. She does this on Wednesdays. Wednesdays are quiet, giros are spent, and workers, even if they are paid monthly direct into their bank accounts, still act like they've been handed a Friday brown envelope.

I pick up a plastic menu from the counter and scan the menu, lingering on the appetizers I don't usually look at, expensive morsels that won't fill you up but cost the same as dishes that do – crispy seaweed, chicken satay, butterfly prawns spread out like whores. It tickles me to think of buying a hundred pounds' worth of starters and the Saab 900 I'd need to carry all the foil cartons home.

A hundred pounds' worth of starters and I'm not talking soup. I wouldn't care if I got grease on the cream leather upholstery of my new wheels if Mrs Wong stammered and forgot to speak English and got the numbers mixed up, and her mum stopped spooning noodles from the plastic container into the giant frying pan with high edges out the back to check she heard right. I look up at the strip lighting then down at Mrs Wong and sigh.

'Number 36 for you?'

It can be comforting, people remembering things about me, like I don't eat hot and cold food together (it ruins your teeth), and it's best not to pick arguments with me on rainy days, but it's also a way for others to tell me about myself. And that can be restrictive, as if I'm not allowed to change. Those who've known me longest do it most and are least likely to update their information. They enquire after The Silver Surfer when you'd think they'd know I lost interest in superheroes in my early teens, once I woke up to the idea that the Caped Crusader only ever staged rescues in Gotham City. And when Bruce Banner gave his gamma-irradiated blood to his cousin who turned into She-Hulk I couldn't enter into the spirit.

'*Actually* I want number 22.'

She snatches the menu and runs her finger down past sticky pictures of Peking duck and spare ribs and egg and chips.

'*Special fried rice?*' she asks, and frowns as if one of us has made a mistake. Mrs Wong's mum, in the kitchen at the back, is already on her way to the fridge for the plastic container with number 36 written on the side.

'*Yeah.* Twice,' I say, nodding my head. And just to make sure she understands that I *can* be spontaneous I add, 'And give me a curry sauce while you're at it.'

♠

Me and Jason sit in the window seat waiting for my order. J is listing his day's spending in the financial section of his Filofax. He has included 'four second-class stamps' and a 'prawn and avocado sandwich'. The stamps bug me. Why miss an opportunity for first-class anything? Flights, trains – they cost. But postage? From their invention to their use there is something white and mean about second-class stamps. Who the fuck would bother when for a few pence more a letter can go first class and arrive the next day?

I stand up and look out of the shop front at the blue neon light from the burger bar across the road. *tarburger*, it says because the 'S' is missing. It's not even six but it's dark enough for my reflection to come back at me. I stretch to my full height and try to go beyond, to another inch and a half to see what six feet six feels like. I stroke my chin with a sideways glance at Jason. There's nothing wrong in noticing my good looks. It might piss Jason off, but then he can afford to be ugly. Muhammad Ali understood. He was beautiful. Simple as. (Don't get the wrong impression; believe I'm headed for an early death from a gay disease.) All the boasting and bragging about how pretty he was? For balance – to regain his equilibrium. Forget Smoking Joe Frazier and the Thriller in Manila. The most powerful nation on earth was forming a queue to call him a thick-lipped coon. And perhaps when Rusty Lee stops rolling her eyes like a Black and White Minstrel, and running around the *Good Morning* kitchen in bare feet and fucks off breakfast TV for good, taking her pineapples with her, maybe then I can stop admiring myself quite so frequently. I'm not blaming J, nobody could accuse him of insensitivity, but he wouldn't get it. He doesn't have to. If I wasn't a player then the rules of his world wouldn't be something I studied too tough. With me and J it's like Auntie Harriet says about her marriage – *What's his is mine, what's mine is my own*.

Above the railway arch the sun isn't going down without a fight. It's bleeding all over the sky.

'How much d'you spend on Chinese a week?' Jason sucks the end of his pen again waiting for an answer. The back of his tongue and the gums around his bottom teeth are blackening with ink.

'Don't worry about it,' I tell him. I'm rarely skint. Not a lot of people on the dole can say that, but I watched Mum; a jam jar for every day of the week, and say you don't use Monday's money up? Well you can empty that into Tuesday. My sister said to add a jar for savings. I did. But I labelled it 'emergency fund' because Susie has a spare key and if I die my sister's the type to feel pleased because I took her advice. I don't smoke either – that's a mug's game. They should introduce a government health warning with sound effects: a gun on the front and *bang bang* each time you pull out a cancer stick. I used to smoke, nine years ago, Embassy Gold – ten, fifteen a day for two months solid. It was after Mum died, before me and Susie went to live with Auntie Harriet, when we were left alone a lot because of certificates, registers, plots, engravers, hymns and wreaths, chapels of rest, funeral directors and hearses. There were three cigarettes Mum didn't get around to smoking, and one day when we were still dumb but no longer numb, when we'd had all that time with her smell still in the flat but we'd been too fucking dozy to use it, and it was gone, it wasn't in her pillow or her headscarves, it was gone, on that day I picked up her cigarettes and smoked them, and there she was, blowing all over the flat. I know Susie appreciated it because she gave me 18p and offered to go halves on the cost of my new habit. One day Auntie Harriet smelt my breath and sat me down for a talk. I couldn't have been at it long enough to become addicted because after the bit about passive smoking I stopped.

It's one thing mashing yourself up, but killing your loved ones, there's no excuse for that.

Mrs Wong waves to a buzzing fly.

'Coohee,' she says and smiles as it darts at right angles, drawing triangles in the air. Last summer she was chasing flies round the shop with shoes and other weapons, breaking glass and knocking stuff over shouting, *Not paying rent. Not welcome here.* It's a lot calmer all round since her son installed the fly electrocution machine.

'It can't be good for you. All that junk.' I am about to put my finger over my lips and nod my head in Mrs Wong's direction, but when I look at her she is already staring at me. She drops a rose that used to be a radish into a bowl of water and doesn't look best pleased. I feel the need to explain that J eats grapes when he isn't sick.

'There are loads of vegetables in Chinese food, ones you haven't even heard of because they're difficult to pronounce so they don't sell them in the supermarket,' I say, and smile a sorry on Jason's behalf.

'And fat and sugar and monosodium glutamate,' he says, raising a finger for each evil ingredient.

'They have a very healthy diet and live on for ages. Quite a few of them have telegrams from the Queen I expect.' I look at Mrs Wong for confirmation. She raises her eyes and says something in Chinese to her mother in the back. They both cackle. I turn my back on them all and look out of the shop front. Eddie and the guys from the leisure centre are approaching on the other side of the street on their way to the floodlit courts. I turn my back against the shop window, but not before I have a glimpse of the future: Eddie and his posse, their middle-aged legs, ill-fitting stilts, struggling to finish a basket-ball game started twenty years earlier.

'Peter Walters. They let him out,' says J. 'Looking crisp too. It's the weight training. That's all there is to do in there. The boredom nearly killed him. He's calling this stretch the last. Have you noticed? Peter never plays the big man.'

I clench my fists and my biceps jump. Five-a-side builds your thighs but don't do shit for the upper body, and bench presses and curls don't work overnight. I tense my stomach muscles, and then relax, aware of the damage a hard punch to my gut could do right now. Because it doesn't matter how strong you are if you're not pre-pared.

I watch Jason in the glass and then I look through his reflection at leaves squashed on the pavement like wet cornflakes.

'Did I tell you about my dad?' My words mist the glass and

evaporate leaving no trace. A picture of my mum's foot, liver-red nail polish and long toes, on lino with green diamonds and yellow circles jerks then fades out. I can think of him and bad memories about *her* come too, as if I've used the same folder for two separate memories. I told Auntie Harriet about the fucked-up filing system. *Don't think about him then*, she said. And ages later, when she was washing up the Sunday dinner dishes and you could've thought she was talking about something else, *That'd be right*, *stuck to him like jam on bread*.

Jason pulls his little finger until it cracks.

'I knew he was due out . . . I heard.' He pulls the knuckle on his forefinger. I regret bringing up the subject at all. J isn't one for pushing up in my private business without an invite – but give him an opening and he's like a bailiff with his foot in the door. If you're not careful he's busting into your front room and even though the TV and video will cover the debt he's eyeing up all your personal stuff and nothing's safe.

'From?'

'An ex of Mum's got out. Knew your dad in Dartmoor.' Jason weaves his fingers in a sharp-knuckled clasp and lowers his head. His dopey hair falls forward.

'I'm not interested,' I say.

'I knew it.' J stands up and shifts his weight in a swaying motion. 'I told her so. All these years, not even a birthday card. Not as if he didn't have time. Like Mum says, let sleeping dogs lie.'

I flatten the image of him sitting down with his redneck mother discussing my family over a cup of tea and a custard cream.

'When I want your opinion . . . Forget it. Cancel the conversation.' His mouth opens, closes back, and then his lips part again. I stoop until my head is level with his and get ready to bite the head off his next sentence.

'I—'

'What part of "shut the fuck up" are you having difficulty in understanding?'

He sits back down. A red blotch spreads from the centre of his left cheek. He opens his Filofax, selects the 'financial' dividing tab, flips a clump of pages over with his finger and writes 'travel costs' in shaky writing.

Next door to Starburger, the Halal butcher stops chopping a slab of traffic-light-red meat into cubes with a machete to wipe blood from his hands on to his apron. Jason closes his Filofax. He takes a *Daily Star* newspaper from the window seat. Keeping his gaze low so he doesn't catch my eye, or have to look at me, he starts reading last Saturday's *Daily Star* – staring at the centre of sports pages when it'd be fair to say he's not the sporty type.

♠

We stand under studio lights, our legs hidden behind a curved booze-free bar. On the punters' side our name is brandished, THE JOHNSONS, although Les calls us 'the lovely Johnsons' at every opportunity. Fair comment – we scrub up well. We explain ourselves in relation to our father.

Sister-in-law, Les.

Son.

Daughter.

Dad (fake exasperation – to be translated as pride – and cock of the head towards Susie and me) *for those two, Les.*

We watch our family representative on the podium. Les wishes him *all the luck in the world mate* and then he reaches up to pat Dad on the shoulder.

We asked one hundred people to name the most effective way of destroying a family without using a machine gun.

I can't think why he hasn't buzzed in. It's an easy enough question. Susie and Auntie Harriet are itching to press the red buzzer, but it's all on him. Only he knows the top answer.

♠

'Jace.' He doesn't move his eyes from the page. I nudge him.

'What?' he snaps back, pulling the paper taut.

Instead of taking J on, I think about the girl on the second floor, whose door I nearly knocked on a few months back when I didn't want to be by myself cause instead of an earthquake there was a skyquake, with lightning dividing the sky into two parts and the stars were gone – fallen into the abyss.

I'm hoping to sex her one day soon. She hangs underwear in the bathroom – lace knickers and bras with pieces of foam in them and tights so sheer they'd be useless if you did a burglary. I don't mind that she pads out her tits because she's the sort I could talk personal with. I wouldn't tell about Mum. I'd just say, *Mum isn't around* and if she asked why I'd say *reasons* and leave it at that. I wouldn't want to confuse any future sexing with a sympathy fuck, but I could talk and she'd listen because she's a girl, and generally they're good at listening. They don't interrupt or use words that hurry you along, or bring you back to the point, and they know when to touch your arm or let you put your head in their lap.

Jason is still blanking me so I watch Mrs Wong wrapping matchsticks of carrot and spring onions in an oblong of the thin white paper you can eat.

If my father died I would be an orphan, and so would Susie. 'Orphan' is a terrible word, a new scary label that will turn our clothes to rags and trigger other people's hidden stammers. Before '76 being an orphan would have excited my sister. She was into adult death back then. She snuggled against a live parent and settled into loss and sadness with a box of Maltesers and a toilet roll. There was *The Little Princess* where a rich girl was turned into a servant, beaten, starved and forced to sleep in the freezing attic with rats because they thought her dad was dead. *Oliver Twist* and *Annie Hall*, and I must've watched *Who Will Love My Children* a zillion times. It's about a woman who has cancer. Her other problem is she hasn't heard of contraception and won't stop breeding, but the film doesn't address that. Instead it deals with her 'race against time' to find a new mother for all twelve of her children before she dies.

Mrs Wong places a white plastic bag on the counter.

'Number 22,' she says, and makes a show of adding a grease-stained brown paper bag of free prawn crackers.

'Split a portion of banana fritters with me J?' I nudge him in his ribs. The side of his body is stiff with stubbornness. Mrs Wong's fritters are one of the few foods we agree on. They come in balls. The outside is hot thin toffee that you crack with your teeth and the inside is squishy, and sweeter than you'd expect for fruit.

'Nah,' he says without looking up. And yeah, I *was* a bit harsh, but as God's my witness, if he gets any more fucking sensitive he'll need Tampax.

'Go on, you know I can't eat all four,' I say, approaching the counter. 'Banana fritters Mrs Wong.' When I look through the back her mum has already stripped two sides off a banana.

There is a crackling then a sizzle. A fly vibrates on the pencil of blue-white light in the box on the wall before dropping on to the corpses of other dead flies and innocent moths.

That's the thing with aiming for one target – there will be other casualties, and it doesn't help that you didn't mean it for them.

Billingsgate Fish Market

Ruby snapper, blue fin trevally, goatfish, jackfish. Foot-long strips of overhead lighting shine on aquarium-bright fish. Their perfect bodies are laid out on a white background, their overpretty colours intensified with water, touched up for final viewing. Plastic markers stand up in front of each tray of wet fish. Black mouth cut shark, black sea bream, blue lined snapper.

'What you fretting about?'

I shrug at Auntie Harriet in reply and turn to watch a man with squid-white hair brushing a big-headed fish with a rotary grater. He holds the fish at the tail end and brushes cataract scales into an old cardboard box. 'Are you hearing me? *Keep your eyes open for yellow croaker?*' Auntie Harriet walks off dragging Uncle Leighton's boots on her child-sized feet. I look down at the ground wet with hosed water and follow her green wellingtons, pushing my hands deeper into my pockets.

'Yellow croaker. Got it.'

I'm trying not to worry, I don't hold with it. I'm no fan of guilt either, but at least it serves a purpose. Shouting *scab* at a miner might keep him on the right side of the picket line, and if it doesn't, feeling guilty convinces him he's an all right bloke. But worry? It's the fake of the future; a possible, a probable, teaming up with chance and creating chaos. Maybe. Perhaps. It fills up your head with imaginings. Then, out of nowhere, some *unworried about* disaster smacks you upside your head, and when you take the elastic band off the brick and unwrap the note it reads *Now you have something to worry about.* Chance, Worry and Chaos have all signed their names and you can hear the titter of their held-in laughter.

Auntie Harriet turns her head and drops her voice slightly, low enough to be mistaken for whispering, loud enough to be heard by the fish men in whitish coats.

'That coley's seen better days,' she says. 'If we don't find cheaper salmon we'll be back.' Fishman shrugs and takes the money for a box of kingfish steaks from an African woman with a tall blue and green headwrap.

'You won't find better.' He lifts a grey flap of skin. Inside is the red that rims your inner eye if you pull the bottom skin down. He gives the salmon an intimate slap with barnacled hands.

♠

The yellow croakers are a foot long and have watered-down golden stripes. Auntie Harriet wants twenty-four. The first scaled fish with innards cut out is coiled in a bucket, and a slit has been made in the white belly of the next.

'They're letting him out,' I say, turning my concentration away from slabs of decapitated flesh with dead-red centres and on to a whiskered catfish with a lemon clamped lengthways in its jaws. Auntie Harriet makes no sign of having heard.

'When you've finished do me a couple pounds of prawns. Prawns are sizeable,' she warns the fish man. 'If you plan on giving me small ones charge me the shrimps price.'

'Good behaviour,' I say, and chew on my bottom lip and on the ridiculousness of the word being applied to him. 'I'm not saying I'm going to tell the journalist—' I stop because 'journalist' has a stench, a stronger presence than the buckets of fish-heads, livers, tails, scales and tiny hearts and piccalilli-yellow guts. 'It's just they got it wrong last time. They wrote a whole heap of rubbish. Remember?' Auntie Harriet watches prawns being shovelled out of a box on to the weighing machine. 'You said so yourself,' I remind her. She doesn't answer, so I look over to the right at seafood. Not jellied eels or cockles for soaking in vinegar and selling from clapboard stands outside pubs where old men in corners sip from pint glasses in daylight hours. No, this is posh seafood – oysters and scallops and crabs – spider crab, stone crab, soft-shell crab, and crab claws detached from their bodies, looking nonsensical, like a porn shot of a fanny without its owner.

Auntie Harriet watches the last few prawns being sprinkled on and carries on staring at the scales even though the black line has stopped a few ounces over two pounds.

'And you think you'll do better?' she asks. 'What do you know? It wasn't about them for starters.' Her shoulders and neck move closer together, hunching her shorter, reminding me that she and my mother were twins, and as Mum was six-two, height was one of the things she took from Auntie Harriet *that she had no right taking*. 'It was about us. Your mother and me. Indyanarriet.'

Crabs and lobsters stumble drunkenly up the edges of the tray before dropping back down. 'Can we have sprats?' I ask, pointing to a helter-skelter pile of silver. My stomach turns against the raw smell of sea flesh.

'You can stop being a husband or a wife, but you can't untwin yourself,' she replies.

♠

We drive home in silence. My eyes have been closed for five minutes. I listen to my sound-asleep breathing.

'So, are you going to see him?' The question pushes me onwards like Santa stockings and mince pies in supermarkets forcing me to think about Christmas before October is done. Time doesn't care if you're ready. You go to the funeral on the day they dig the hole in the ground, and even if you're burping Brussels sprouts and can't breathe for turkey, you eat Christmas pudding on Christmas day.

'I'm talking to you,' she says and pushes the side of my head with her fist. I give up pretence, open my eyes.

'Probably,' I say before realizing that our meeting needn't be an accidental bucking-up. I can go and meet him – have the upper hand – be the seeker. I don't have to wait to hear him call out *Ready or not I'm coming* . . . I can change the ending. There have been technological advances; new paint colours bright enough to remove all traces of blood without an undercoat, hi-tech all-around sound loud enough to drown hissing and swallowed screams.

'It'll end in tears.' I add her words to *It might never happen. It'll all come out in the wash. Worse things have happened at sea.*

'It already did.'

'There's something belonging to you in the glove compartment.' She is gripping the steering wheel like a teenager with a provisional. Her chipolata fingers join together in a lump of sausage meat. 'Go on, open it.' I press a button on the dashboard and the flap falls open.

'What's this?' I unfold a green Marks and Spencer carrier bag, inside is a pile of white envelopes tied with a skinny ribbon. I wouldn't call my right eye lazy right now. It's working hard on looking away. I read my name and then Auntie Harriet's address below. I flip to the letters underneath. They are all addressed to me. Words lean to the left. Loops are closed on the circular letters with nothing allowed to escape. I have seen this writing on school permission slips for after-school clubs or trips to the seaside, the name of a horse written in the margins of a newspaper, on lists *milk, beans*. Each envelope has a second-class postage stamp in the corner. I flick the top right-hand corner of the stack. December 1977? February 1982? I breathe in and start counting to ten. Five. *See what I mean about second class.*

'What were you doing with them?' I listen to my words travel on wobbly waves. I'm asking a fair question. It sounds reasonable, but pointless because I can't think of an answer that would be of any use.

'I was keeping them until you were ready. I didn't want him messing you up again.' My throat is dry and sore as if I have a clear lead in a cracker-eating competition.

'You know you had no right.' Buildings whip past. I look down at her right foot pressing harder on the accelerator; the veins on her feet push on the thin skin as if they want out. She stamps on the brake. My head and shoulders roll forwards. My teeth bang against each other. 'What the—' The car behind is sounding the horn in angry punches. She leans over me and clicks the inside door handle. The door swings open.

'Out.' I don't move. She starts shoving me, so I know she means business. 'Move. Out of my car. Get out!'

'All right. All right.' I get out. 'Uncle Leighton's car,' I say and slam the door behind me. The window shakes. She bends over and picks up the bag of letters off the car floor and throws it out of the window. She shrieks off with no regard for Uncle Leighton's advice about slow changing through the gears if you want to save on fuel costs.

I sit down on the kerb holding the bag of letters against my chest with my knees, pressing my fingers against the sides of my neck where my pulse rushes. The traffic in my head is speeding up; thoughts overtake on bends, race each other, swerving in and out of their lanes. The smell of antiseptic. *One more time?* Dad took the ticket out of his wallet. Nineteenth June 1976. Stalls. £3.00. Block 19.

Seat 32. Bob Marley and the Wailers. *Pull the trigger shoot the nigger*. They threw banana skins on to the pitch. He held my hand for seventeen minutes, dragging me through Hammersmith Odeon newly painted in red, gold and green. They all lived happily ever after. Gurgling. Whistling rain. He sat on the reserve bench at Crystal Palace. If we'd waited until 1977 when Bob played The Rainbow it would have been too late. When he transferred it was to the sugar machine at the Trebor factory. Rain. Beating. Rain. Beating rain. A spaghetti junction of thoughts that don't give jack for road markings. I am heading for a pile-up. I obey my body and stand up, stiffen, tip on to my toes before vomiting on a single yellow line, over and over and even when there is nothing left to come up the dry heaving goes on. As soon as the shuddering stops the traffic slows down and there's not as much lane jumping. I rub my face into my T-shirt. The lining of my mouth tastes sour and I feel roughed-up but I walk on anyway enjoying the emptiness that follows vomiting, the scooped-out hollowness of body and mind. I've been walking for ten minutes or so when a car slows down beside me.

'Geoffhurst wait,' she says through the open passenger door. 'I'm sorry.' Her face is broken up under the skin like a television face when the aerial is knocked out of place.

I turn a corner and the wind that was at my back blows into my face stinging my eyes.

'I didn't read them.' Her words sound strangled with snot. 'Come on little G,' she pleads; her voice smoothes me down. Now I am capable of freezing my hand mid-slap, finding a way to put the money back in her purse, apologising, circling her hips with both arms and grabbing my wrist to hang on. 'Get in.' But I can't risk being softened up, so I keep my head down and keep walking. She knows I prefer the low buzz of goodness to a bad-boy high.

'I should have used lodestone,' she says and drives away.

I walk on. By the time I get to the end of the road I have lost the image of the poorly glued cracked pieces of her face. I remind myself she stole from me, lied for years. The wind makes my eyes run. I finally figure out what her last sentence was. *Your heart's made of stone*, is what she said. But I don't care. In fact, I'm really pleased. Actually. Like Uncle Leighton says opening his toolbox, showing me screwdrivers with different widths and handles and heads, *the right tools for the right job*.

The Cutting Edge and Sergio's

If Jason's house hadn't backed on to the synagogue, and I hadn't seen hundreds of black velvet top hats and kiss-curl sideburns bobbing up and down as Jews prayed in a noisy, joyful way I hadn't known their God allowed, and if laughter from Susie's squealing friends hadn't cut out every time I opened her bedroom door, I might never have realized that some religions have it sussed, because there are times when separate spaces for men and women are a good idea.

The Cutting Edge
Curly Perm (Wet Look and Wave Nouveau), Relaxing, Hot
Comb, Tonging, Singeing, Weave, Bonding (yak, synthetic,
straight, wet and wavy, super wavy, kinky), Plait (extensions),
Colour, Steam and Treatments, including electric stimulation of
the hair root useful for breakage, hard-to-grow hair, itching,
dropping off, bald patches and general hair loss. Cut, Style and Set.
Barber on premises. Beauty treatments upstairs. Human hair for
Sale. Ask at reception downstairs. Open Sundays.

A buzzer sounds and two feet away a woman with a vibrating clock in the palm of her hand dips out with freshly baked hair from underneath one of five giant crash helmets. An operating surgeon shifts her fat backside to block my view and I bend my neck to see what she's doing out of spite. A comb. A thick needle. A four-foot stretch of dead hair with a high sheen. I watch hair being sewn on to a cornrowed head, unable to look away even though my innocence is being stolen by an operation as intimate as any gynaecological procedure.

I'm on nodding terms with a few of the bredren leaning against the walls, shifting their feet, looking at the floor or studying the photographs of possibilities: a high top fade, the shag, the cameo, the box, wavy lines carved in the back of the head, a map of Africa, D&G, a Nike symbol. Hairspray catches in my throat. When I cough a few other coughs join mine. I count eleven bredren including me. They are waiting for Antoine who studies photography and wears shells on his belt. If they had got out of their pits earlier they coulda gone to Winston's where it smells of the talcum powder brushed on the backs of necks and the lemon cologne he slaps on your chin after a wet shave and warm towel treatment.

Winston grades hair, never people. For the short time you sit in his chair, wrapped in a purple gown, it doesn't matter what you've done or who you are. Sooner or later even the countryside lawyer will park his BMW outside some Winston's or other. He will wait his turn behind a boy from the local estate on his way to big school, holding his ears down flat and flinching from the buzz of the clippers. In the queue he can order fried chicken, ooh and ah over a football game on TV, listen to the latest tunes, purchase knocked-off goods from an entrepreneur, pick up a flyer for a rave, contribute to a fundraiser, advise a brother who ran his mouth to the Old Bill when told to produce his driving documents for the fourth time in a week. He can forget the taste of rice and peas. Maybe. His friends at the country club might never mention his colour. He can take a blonde, lose the lingo and buy his suits in Savile Row, but it has to stop somewhere. Hair is where it stops. He has no fringe for his wife to trim. He cannot put a basin on his head and cut round the edges. There is no Wash and Go for us.

I've been sat in Winston's chair when a hernia was diagnosed and, once, an old-timer married for thirty years shared his sex secrets. I learnt how to deal with an air pocket in a valve and a finicky Yardie, who turned weak at the sight of other people's blood, showed me the cleanest cut to kill a man. All that, and a Curtis Mayfield track too. Instead we are trapped in a his and hers salon, both sexes embarrassed into silence.

'Did Susie say how long she'll be?' I ask the hairdresser nearest to me, who is wrapping three inches of hair around a hot silver tube. A clip traps the hair in place as it sizzles.

'She's with a client.' She looks away from me. 'Joanne,' she shouts to the ceiling, 'how long does a half-leg and bikini take?'

'Fifteen minutes,' a voice booms through a curtained section where smoke and ankles of varying thickness are visible at the bottom.

'Fifteen minutes,' she tells me, as if Joanne had whispered the reply in her ear. She hands a tub of TCB Straight as a Bone to another girl, who is scratching her head through her beret. I imagine my dentist with false teeth, or a manicurist in gloves. A half-caste girl is gripping the armrests of her leather-and-chrome swing chair. Flat white gunk is being pasted on to one side of her hair, within seconds it foams and fizzes. The smell of ammonia drop kicks my nostrils.

'Mum. It's stinging.' The surviving hair is bunched into two afro puffs about to be blown away. She screws up her face. 'Now it's burning. Don't tell me it's supposed to burn.'

'The hairdresser said if it doesn't tingle it isn't working.' She flicks muddy blonde hair over one shoulder. 'It'll be nice when it's finished. More manageable.'

I hide from 'manageable' in the pages of a creased copy of *Black Hair and Beauty*. Teachers, police, politicians, hairdressers: everyone is so keen on 'manageable'. I first noticed this with Ken. He lived in the flats I grew up in. He walked at night and one day he went too far and they found him walking through Blackwall Tunnel. The police put him in the nuthouse. The drugs to make him 'more manageable' stiffened his muscles and he was tired all the time. It worked in a roundabout way because he stopped walking after that.

When I look up Susie is standing in front of me dressed in white – dress, tights, even shoes. (They're not actually shoes. They slide on. Old ladies with no ankles and feet problems wear them.) I stand up and kiss her cheek. She kisses me back, then holds me by the shoulders at arm's length and eyes me silently.

'I thought you might want to treat me to breakfast,' I say, knowing she thinks breakfast is the most important meal of the day and terrible things can happen by leaving the house without a hot drink and a few rounds of toast. She is twenty-one. My smile hides the pity I feel for her years of unrewarded efforts, for the gallons of tea brewed, tower-blocks of toasted Mothers Pride.

'It's four thirty-seven. Why haven't you eaten already?'

'It takes me a while to build up an appetite,' I say, wondering why she is so exact, so digital about everything. If she doesn't change her ways she'll end up with small cans of vegetable soup in the cupboard and a stinking ginger cat that leaves hair on her black clothes that everyone sees but no one tells her about.

'I've got clients booked. I can't just—'

'See what you can do.'

♠

I haven't eaten since yesterday lunchtime, because I'm saving for the fare to Dartmoor and even if I take the coach it doesn't come cheap. Susie's paying so I order Sergio's special: bacon, fried egg, sausage, beans, grilled tomato, black sausage, mushrooms and a slice of fried bread. Tea and coffee is all in with the special, including refills. I stay away from blood where I can, so Sergio gives me an extra rasher in place of the black sausage.

'How's work?'

'You know,' she says and shrugs, dipping her bread into my egg, bursting it all over the beans.

'What?'

'You upset Auntie Harriet big time. Even Uncle Leighton thinks you're out of order.'

I study the tablecloth. It is wipeable plastic with pictures of vegetables. The courgette has dew on it. I take a triangle slice of fried bread off the side plate, cut a corner off, use it to absorb the liquid from my breakfast and put the soggy bread on the side of the plate.

'She kept the letters he sent me.' I'm not sure how much Auntie Harriet has told her, but I figure Susie can't know this or I wouldn't have to work to get her on my side. She puts her knife and fork down and looks at me. I watch her nostrils waiting for them to flare with indignation on my behalf. Her eyes search my face. My right eye spins slightly with the strain of holding eye contact. 'They date all the way back to when he went down,' I say, edging her along, impatient for understanding. Susie's face is blank with shock, but her lack of expression annoys me all the same. I glance around, giving her time to process the information; an old couple are taking advantage of the 10 per cent off for pensioners' dinners on Tuesdays. Sergio exchanges their empty dinner plates for bowls of pineapple upside-down cake and custard.

'She thought it was for the best,' Susie says. I sit back not convinced she has come to her senses.

'Come again.' Susie cuts into halves a singed tomato, puts one in her mouth.

'She thought it was for the best,' she says, and touches a forkful of fried egg and bacon against a blob of tomato sauce on my plate – a friendly action designed to remind me she is my sister, a person so close she can eat the food off my plate without me growling.

'She *thought* wrong then,' is all I can think to say.

'Yeah,' she says into her plate. My anger for Auntie Harriet still needs company so I am willing to reconcile treachery and disloyalty being family traits carried by the female genes.

'She might have letters belonging to you.' Her face goes quiet. Her pain is a bonus. 'Ask her.' She is separating the fat and rind from her bacon carefully. I don't care that he might not have written to her at all. I load bacon and a mushroom on to the side of my fork with my knife, then I squash beans on the back of my fork.

'I had my letters.' Daddy's little princess picks up her coffee cup. 'We write now and then.' The palm of her hand touches his through reinforced glass. I stab two mushrooms. 'I didn't tell you. Didn't think you'd understand.' I catch the side of the next mushroom and it jumps off the plate. I throw the fork after it.

'Am I missing something? Am I?' My hands are either side of her plate and I am inches from her face but she won't look up. She places her cutlery slowly and soundlessly at the edges of her plate. The old couple stop talking and look over. Susie blows out gently. I sit back down. The old folk start talking again. Bean juice is splattered on her white dress.

'Who'll put up my bookshelves?'

'Uncle Leighton will do it. *I'll* do it.' She doesn't have books. She thinks they smell of geography teachers' jumpers and expectations. They are dead and dusty. Mini tombstones. The information on the back cover about the author reads like an obituary.

'There'll be a gap in my wedding pictures.' She has swapped places with me without me noticing and now she is the victim and I have the job of propping her up.

'You don't have a groom so, of course, there'll be a gap you dozy bitch.'

'Why is everything about you Geoffhurst?'

'I was there remember?'

'Fat lot of good it did. What were her last words? Maybe you *should* sell the story so I can read it. What happened that night?'

She's right. I did jack. That's when I start laughing. Laughing so hard my eyes flood and I shake like a spaz. It sticks me under my navel and eases upwards slicing all the way, hurting so bad it could have been written by Richard Pryor, that bug-eyed brother raised in a brothel with a whore for a mother. It is sick, perfectly timed, painful and so serious, laughter is the only possible response.

'Fuck me. You're jealous? *You're jealous* because she's dead and I was there? See these beans?' I shove them towards her with my knife. 'I eat them first. I move the egg to the edge of my plate for pro-tection, because if the yolk breaks and the yellow runs into bean juice on Sergio's green plates it reminds me of their blood on the lino when he killed her. Don't you get it?' I ask, jabbing my finger in her forehead. 'It affects everything. I spend every minute of my life trying to get away from that last day. *And you want that?*' I push my chair out, scraping it away from her. I lean back, close my eyes and count the disappearing family members: Mum, Auntie Harriet, Uncle Leighton, Susie. At this rate I'll never be able to apply for *Family Fortunes*.

The baked beans are developing an orange skin. I get up to go. 'Your breakfast's getting cold,' I tell her, standing in the open door-way of Sergio's. Darby and Joan are muttering about the draught in that sneaky, letter-to-the-council, anonymous-call-to-the-police way, so I leave without closing the door. That's people all over, negative vibes, focusing on trivia. I witnessed the murder of our mother, but she's on about photographs and shelving. And these old people have a 10 per cent discount and have just enjoyed Sergio's smooth custard, but they're moaning about a little fresh air.

Victoria Coach Station

The real McCoy. I haven't seen this much poor white trash in one place since I took the wrong bus from Stepney Green and ended up on the Isle of Dogs. These are confusing times. Poor people play rich, and rich people play poor – dressed from the clothes' rails in Oxfam, denying themselves meat and taking up spaces on buses for no good reason. In the end it comes down to teeth and shoes. If it wasn't for teeth and shoes I could make mistakes, forget who's who.

I hike my scarf higher over my nose and mouth. I hadn't expected early mornings to be so much colder than later in the day. They're unexpected all round – nearly worth getting up for. On the tube suits read *The Times*, clean copies, folded like origami so they didn't take up too much space. People smelt unused and their faces looked ironed. Not one teenager with a cardboard sign begging for food and no tramps picking up cigarette butts, which is a shame when you consider how much longer six a.m. butts are. But for all that, early mornings are like new shoes and I prefer the day scuffed, a bit worn in.

I taste other people's cigarette smoke and the exhaust fumes from a packed coach revving, eager to get to Birmingham. When the coach pulls out I look round and notice a sweetshop booth. Folded newspapers cover the length of the right-hand shop front. On the counter are plastic teaspoons, sugar grains in a neat cocaine line and a cup of tea in a white polystyrene cup next to a round sugar bowl with a silver spout. I walk over for something to do and stand at the counter out of the way of the 'fireworks sold here' board propped up near my left foot. I buy a cup of tea, grey as papier-mâché water. The sugar bowl is the type you have to turn upside down and when you do it releases just one spoonful of sugar through the spout. I last saw one when I was eight and Susie was ten when Mum and Auntie Harriet took us to a fish restaurant near Leigh-on-Sea. (Anthony stayed home with his dad because the trip coincided with his bus obsession and he wanted to memorize a new timetable he'd got from the depot.) On the table was a sauce bottle shaped like a tomato that did fart noises when you squeezed it, and the same clever sugar bowl that understood when enough was enough, which was more than the grown-ups did. I upend it another four times for old time's sake.

The payphone on the landing rang at five this morning. In movies the suckers answering five o'clock calls have to identify dead bodies or walk lame friends around the room fifty times until an ambulance arrives to rush the self-centred victim to hospital to have their stomach pumped. I nearly didn't answer it. I walked on cold cracked lino with the outside edges of the soles of my feet. It was Anthony.

Sorry to wake you. I just want to say, keep your head. Don't mind Mum. She's the same with me, shooting off her mouth. She balled me out for telling my age to a woman in the West Indian bakery, because, get this, now that woman can hex me by numbers. We both know she's a bit crazy, but you know what? She loves you. Like fried chicken loves coleslaw, like ackee loves saltfish, like . . .

Mackerel loves dumpling. I get it.

Stay safe blood.

♠

I sip tea that tastes of the polystyrene cup and watch a kid poking out of a blue Puffa jacket, alone at ten past seven in the morning. He is asking passers-by for a *penny for the guy*. I look round and then I suss the situation and laugh. There is no guy. The kid's got more bottle than Unigate. If the world were straight he'd end up on a documentary about young achievers. He'd be tipped as a Richard Branson of the future. But the world's fucked, so one day his mum will be on the telly, wearing all her jewellery at the same time, holding up a school picture and making a tearful plea for the paedophile ring that snatched him off the street to return him. Unharmed.

The Plymouth coach opens its door and a woman with corned-beef legs hands fake Burberry luggage to the driver to load into the space under the coach. I try to pick out the people with friends or relatives in prison. A girl with black eyeliner and the fat from Asda's frozen dinners showing in her hair could have a visiting order between the pages of *Hollywood Wives*. I am travelling light, just a rucksack. In it I have the packed lunch I found outside my room door: sandwiches, cucumber, a wedge of fruitcake and an apple. There was no note but it was from my sister. She must have let herself in. The raw vegetable has *Susie* written through the centre like Southend rock. There's the letter and a knife to core my apple, and a personal stereo in case I get stuck next to some bore who wants to talk shit for the whole six hours. When I booked the ticket I asked the clerk *How long?* When he told me I asked him again. He said they stop for an hour on the way, but even so. There's a conspiracy to waste the time of skint people – the DSS, the doctors, they're all at it. *Take ticket two hundred and sixty-three and have a seat over there. Thank you sir. Number seven . . .*

I climb on board and sit near the back, seat 12a, away from the smell of Air Wick and pine disinfectant from the toilet cubicle. I press the recline lever and lie back with the hood of my sweatshirt over my head because the seat in front has a long hair on the headrest and the window is smeared. I switch my headphones on without

a tape and close my eyes. I imagine all the things that can go wrong –
they let him out through a secret exit – he got into a fight and they set
back his release date – he has been tipped off and *he* is waiting for
me. My stomach starts grumbling. It isn't hunger. It does that when
the thing scaring or exciting me is about to happen, and then, the best
thing to do is screw the girl, or look at the porn, or open the present,
or shape up to the man with a telephone cut.

The coach must have twenty passengers, mostly old women
smelling of face powder and decay. We pull away slowly. A bookie's,
a snack bar, a kebab shop, a pub with benches outside. In a few minutes London brightens up. Rows of four-storey houses with naked
white walls, a barge called *Veronica* painted with daisies, a man in
sweat pants with an obese paper under his arm, walking a Dulux
dog. The five o'clock start presses me back against the chair. A silent
movie plays on to the blank screen of my closed eyelids.

He is pulling my mother out from under the bed by her legs. She
holds on to the wire springs under the mattress and he drags and
shakes her ankles and the bed screeches and slides around the room
bashing against the walls until her fingers are too torn to hold on and
when she comes out it is slowly, like a seaside winkle pinned out of
its shell waiting to be eaten.

I unzip my bag and pull out the letters quickly the way Mum
taught me to pull off a plaster so it wouldn't hurt, even if there was
an open wound yellow and pus-filled underneath. Once they're in
my lap I ignore them, slow down my breathing and try to get my
balance back.

I could use a cup of tea.

Tea makes me feel better. The betterness isn't in the tips of the tea,
or in foil-wrapped freshness, or in the shape of the bag, or in the tiny
perforations. It isn't in the continent. It isn't in the thing itself.
Typhoo. PG Tips. Brown Label. Tetley's. Red Label. Quick Brew.

I'm-sorry tea. *Good-morning* tea. *There-there-don't-fret* tea. *I-forgive-you* tea. *Don't-go-yet* tea. *Your-mum-is-dead* tea. When there's fuck all else to hold on to, a cup will do. And drinking starts you swallowing and swallowing starts you breathing. *Tea is filling a vacuum in this country. Tea-drinking up. Church attendance down. A God incidence,* Auntie Blossom says, because she doesn't believe in accidental happenings. She and God are close and he doesn't like tea-drinking, not coffee either, they're stimulants, although I'm not sure 'stimulant' is a Bible word. Ask her if she wants a cuppa, *I only need the Lord to get high,* she'll say.

I untie the ribbon from around the letters, not sure why Auntie Harriet didn't use one of the elastic bands she hoards in different sizes and colours, why she didn't use string. I throw the ribbon under the seat in front along with a flash of Mum ironing, her eyes stuck on a Saturday afternoon film where a woman with rolled-up hair ties ribbons around perfumed letters. I wrap my fingers around my fist and grip them to stop the shaking. *Sticks and stones may break your bones but words can never hurt you.*

♠

The postmark has faded on the first envelope I open. Inside a card is folded lengthways. I bend it back against the crease but it is set and refuses to lie flat. It must have been sent a while back – when I was sixteen and Auntie Harriet gave me the option of staying on at school or leaving her house – when I was seventeen and I got the key to my own front door, and one knife, fork, plate and spoon that Susie had sneaked out of Auntie Harriet's. Perhaps I was twelve. 'Dear Son'. There's a picture of a fishing rod and a boat with a blue sail. Inside it says, 'A son like you is a dream come true, I wish you success in all that you do. Many happy returns. From your father.'

I am stuck in the groove of the first two words, 'Dear Son'.

A few years after they banged him up, when I was thirteen, a man on a market stall with dirt circling his fingernails and overblue eyes called me *boy*, not in a Ku Klux Klan way, but in a he-had-a-son-and-maybe-his-son-had-a-son-and-in-different-circumstances-I-coulda-been-either-of-them way. He even called me *Son*, tossing the word away like the outside leaves of a cabbage, or a pear with a dent in it, as if it was going to waste and anyone could make use of it. I spent my pocket money hoping he would lob it my way again. He was forever trying to educate his customers, introducing new potato varieties that they rejected – Charlotte, Pink Fir Apple, British Queen, Edzell Blue. He pitied them their overreliance on Maris Piper. He was one of those old geezers who whistled complicated tunes through clenched teeth, and he called every man twenty or more years younger than him 'Son'. I knew that, but sad sap that I was I kept going back for Granny Smiths and pounds of King Edwards' that stayed in the vegetable rack and sprouted before they were chucked.

I tear his card along the crease and tear it in half and half again, and keep doing that until the pieces are really small. I don't remember any card from him, ever. There is a Christmas card from them both but written by her. I kept it by accident. I hadn't gotten round to cleaning my room. It was mixed in with hardening underwear and *Hulk* and *Silver Surfer* comics and Cabana wrappers. It was just rubbish, but death can turn rubbish to gold, although mostly it works the other way round. I fingered it too much in the early years and the red glitter on the robin's chest has worn away. *Dear Son*, she wrote in blue pen – tall upright letters, and I scratched out *and Dad* at the bottom, sacrificing three of her kisses to make it look like it was just from her.

I am the son of Sonny Johnson. It is not a line from a Western, it is the truth, the whole truth and nothing but the truth. So help me

God. It is also a lie. Not even Uncle Leighton would dare call me *Son*. Good old Uncle Leighton – shed owner, Sunday morning car-washer, nine-to-fiver, bedtime-story-reader, shoeshiner extraordinaire, chauffeur, dispenser of back-hand pocket money, teller of told-me-a-hundred-times-already stories, who paid for my school trips and bought me shoes every autumn and spoon fed me ice cream in hospital when they took my tonsils out and explained in minute detail how to use a condom long after Mates Natural were my favourite brand. He is toast – reliable and comforting, when everything else has run out. Old   Mother   Hubbard. But there is always toast.

Dear Son.

And they can break my arm at any point they choose, but I think I can kill him, with justification, for those two words alone.

The Plymouth Belle

I search out my sandwiches. It's a trip and everyone eats on journeys into unknown territories where food may be scarce, or maybe we haven't evolved to understand fast moving transport, and our bodies assume that after this many miles it must be time to eat.

I had a few outpatient appointments after Mum, for a lump in my throat that throbbed with pain when I ate. It started out the size of a nut. If I overchewed it still hurt but food passed round the edges so it seemed worth the effort. The lump kept growing. In the end I couldn't take the pain so I gave up on eating for a while. I hardly spoke either because the words were stuck on the wrong side of the lump.

At the hospital I met girls with sticking-out bones, eyes as big as their vowels and the fluffy hair (that grew on my face before the real stuff came through) on their arms where their bodies were trying to keep warm. The doctors tried all sorts: food charts, emotional blackmail, force-feeding. What they didn't try was putting us all in a train carriage, closing the doors and driving off. Rail companies selling clammy sandwiches at steep prices understand this, and now I come to think of it I've known it since I was a 6-year-old on a school trip to Chessington when eight out of twenty of us had eaten our packed lunch before we got to Stamford Hill.

I'm about to bite into my sandwich when I stop and look up. A girl is peering over the top of the seat in front of me. I'm not sure how I know she's a girl. She has no earrings and her hair is hidden by a red and white bandana. She is older than nine but younger than twelve. Her skin reminds me that white people are pink or grey or beige but hardly ever white, but this girl is, and it gives a raw, unfinished impression.

'Nose ointment,' I say tapping my nose, but she doesn't take the hint. Only the top third of her head is tied so I can't work out why her hair doesn't show.

'What's the problem?' I ask, my mouth full of cheese and pickle sandwich. She is about to speak and then she changes her mind and shrugs but doesn't look away. I notice she doesn't have any eyebrows and then I realize she has no eyelashes. *What's the problem* not *What's your problem* is what I said. I want to make that clear but she isn't looking at me. I follow her gaze to the top of my rucksack. 'Cheese and pickle,' I say. I wipe both sides of my knife clean on the paper the sandwiches were wrapped in and then I put it back in the leather pouch. 'For cutting my sandwiches.' I shove it into the bag wondering why I'm doing all this explaining to some kid I don't know. 'It's not feeding time at the zoo.' She shrugs as if to say 'who said it was', but she doesn't move.

'Your hands are shaking,' she says. I put my sandwich on my lap and thread my fingers together.

'What of it? Listen, can I eat in peace?'

'Yes,' she says as if she was keeping me company and if I wanted to be alone all I had to do was ask. Her head disappears. Her grown-up travelling companion lolls her dead-weight head into the walkway.

In replying to this letter, please write on the envelope:

Number ...... K47P9602 ...... Name ...... Johnson ......

Wing ...... C ......

```
HMP DARTMOOR
PRINCETOWN
YELVERTON
DEVON
PL20 6RR
```

14 March 1977

Dear Geoffhurst

Give my regards to your Aunt Harriet and thank her for looking after you and your sister at such short notice. I hope she
does not poison you against me. I do not intend for you to be
there long only until this sorry mess sorts out. I am here a few
weeks already. They let me out of a windowless van after
many hours and even before my legs straightened I see a
blinding mist reminding me of when we first come to this
country for it is similar to fog made from people burning coal
for warmth. When the mist pushed back was sheep and more
sheep dashed on green fields and rocks. Then my eyes accustomed and I see bushes and low stonewall cutting fields into
squares and running along one side was silver water. The mist
pull back again uncovering a wide flat building spread out
with chimneys blustering smoke and though it looked like a
factory a place for things not people I knew that was where
they would put me. Tell Blossom there are no burning fires for
sinners. Hell is squat and grey with screaming winds and
rock-stoned earth without fruit or flowers and the sky presses

down on your chest like a forty-pound barbell. They watch us all the while until I start to check my teeth for food and check on my trousers front. Because of the way I feel they put me in a giant birdcage where they watch me through the bars a parrot beating my wings but cant fly nowhere. I would ask that you to check LOYALTY and RESPECT in your dictionary and when you finish ask Blossom about honouring your father. Without your help I will stay here until after my appeal. The English believe in the innocence of children. I have no business here but my voice is hoarse from protesting. Small spaces crush me on all sides. I left my island because of the smallness but now I remember I never heard throat clearing or metal doors slamming or keys turning or men crying through the walls when I slept back home and I could sit waist deep in the rock-pool with only Jack-knife fish for company and when my eyes ran out of sea there was the never-ending sky.

I am your father Sonny Johnson

In replying to this letter, please write on the envelope:

Number .... K47P9602 .... Name ... Johnson ....

Wing .... C ....

HMP DARTMOOR
PRINCETOWN
YELVERTON
DEVON
PL20 6RR

12 October 1977

Dear Geoffhurst

Your grandfather on your mothers side used to say there is no place on this earth that is the same for a black man as a white man. Foolishness. The sky is the sky. The sun is the sun. Of course your mother saw it his way. She said English churches were the worst places in England for us black people what with their cold stone and joyless singing. She stopped attending service when the Christian committee at Christchurch Methodist who collected bread and milk from their front doorstep decided after two centuries to have separate glasses of wine for communion. I hope you never find out that the worst place for us is prison and the worst prison in England is Dartmoor. Not just on my say so. The screws who argue amongst themselves agree on two things alone. Dartmoor and prisoners. They hate us both. The language I ran from on the football fields is all around me. Violence spreads like the common cold in here. They all come in infected and pass it on. They sneeze brutality. There is one prison guard who is not too bad. He knows plenty general knowledge. He is one of those people with facts stick up in his head. There is nothing about the history of this place that he cannot tell you. The prison farm has 1600 acres. The Dartmoor pony has been running wild on the moors since Henry the first was on the throne. That sort of thing. None of the other prisoners like him. They call him a know-all. In here everything is topsy-turvy. Know-nothings come higher than know-alls and do-gooders come lower than do-badders. I am not . . .

The sound of air-conditioning joins together with my heart knocking at my chest. We are moving fast, tearing up the motorway, blurring together scores of trees into a giant trunk with enough rings to be a billion years old.

♠

At least he could feel, eh? If there was a loud noise he'd have jumped, and if he came up on the football pools he'd have felt happy. I was brainstem dead. If I'd been plugged into a machine in intensive care it would have been silent, no beeps and no zigzags on the screen. There'd have been a dead quiet line for me in 1977 – jubilee year. I remember there was a party in Hyde Park for all the kids in London. I don't know who paid. It might have been the Queen. Invites came through the post. It was like *Willie Wonka and the Chocolate Factory* except we all had a golden ticket. I slid down a giant slide, all the way down was nothingness. On the big wheel I stopped at the top and heard other kids squealing when we plunged, but I may as well have been sat in Uncle Leighton's armchair. I sucked sherbet – might as well have sucked sand.

♠

I didn't trust my body to keep me safe. I pressed a glass on my arm to study the pattern of spots dismissed as pimples, as heat rash. I checked daily for swollen glands, cancerous lumps, for signs of the illness or disease that would lead to my premature death. When Auntie Harriet cut her finger slicing onions and called out for a plaster, I insisted Uncle Leighton drive her to casualty for a tetanus injection. We waited five hours with the down-and-out drunks and fretful new mums and all the others who were non-priority.

I went on about fish bones in cod until Susie switched to pie and chips on Friday nights.

Jason was a brother to me and I couldn't watch him die. There was no hope for him and he was beyond my powers of protection. Truth be told he'd been dying since infant school – dizzy spells, wheezing. He was a goner in a hundred different ways. There were lampposts and broken paving stones and bollards only visible if you were looking down, and objects that could be knocked out of windows only visible if you were looking up, and those were just the *walking* dangers. I told him his mother was an ugly whore, a pig-ignorant racist. Twice I said this, emphasizing mother the second time. When he showed no signs of wanting to fight I told him he was a liability and probably a poofter too. I wasn't crying when I told him I'd been carrying him since he was seven years old, and I was tired. I didn't cry. I just told him to fuck off out of my face. He said he hadn't meant to be a burden, and left.

I rescued a bag of nuts carelessly left on the dining table. I lay in wait for Auntie Harriet to return from shopping. By the time she came home it was as if I had been stung by a bee or a wasp and I was one of the 3 per cent in the country who didn't know they were allergic and I didn't have an antihistamine to hand and it was no point phoning for an ambulance because my throat was closing and even if speech was possible I didn't want to waste my dying words on the emergency services operator. I pointed to the packet, urging her to read the warning the food industry and the government thought important enough to print on the back of every bag of peanuts in the country. *Small children can choke on nuts*. She raised her hand as if to slap me, and then she changed her mind and left the room returning with a glass of water that she made me drink down in one go. Anthony was *eleven*, she said. I couldn't talk, couldn't explain that her only son took after her in the height department. It was a size, not an age, thing.

The protective nature of our bodies was above ants (we couldn't easily be killed by stamping on us) but below worms (we couldn't join our bodies back together without the help of professionals). With our eggshell defences you'd have thought they'd have taken more care. They went outside with wet hair, didn't wear warm clothes, started the day without a hot drink, didn't look both ways, ignored speed restrictions, ate old food courtesy of Auntie Blossom, Mum's friend from the flats who was so sure of eternal life in Jesus she didn't mind cutting our earthly existence short by poisoning us with food teeming with bacteria, teetering on its sell-by dates. They cut their toenails so low, so rounded at the edges, they were begging for ingrowing toenails, followed by a localized infection, then gangrene and almost certain death.

I stayed in my room most times to escape witnessing their kamikaze approach to life and to think of ways to get us all to pensionable age in one piece. I came up with new inventions all the time. I had a few sketches and had begun to list the materials required for a polo neck with a built-in neck brace for Auntie Harriet.

Sedgemoor service station

Eating a Kelly's vanilla ice cream in a service station canteen in November sounds strange but isn't. It's a local specialty so they sell it all year round, plus I nodded off with my mouth open and the air vent blowing in my face, and when the coach stopped my throat was dried out.

The combined age of the people around me, drinking tea, reading papers and eating hundreds of eggs and billions of beans, is 56,000, and oldies fart more than youngsters, so although the air conditioning is up too high it might not be a bad thing. Pensioners sit at tables arranged round the edges of the room, on patterned carpet broken up by a curved path of plain lino in the centre where you queue and collect trays. The path is the sort designed by gardeners who don't want you walking on the grass. You are only allowed on to the carpet when you've collected your tray and paid. I just had an ice cream so I didn't take a tray. *You need a tray to get to the tables*, the cashier told me. *It's okay the exercise will do me good*, I said. She looked nervous, so I smiled. She didn't smile back. *Hang on to your receipt*, she advised.

The afternoon sun slow-roasts my right arm through a glass wall where I watch people exiting cars and lorries perform elaborate stretches. A guy with chart-topping hair, wearing a checked apron, is collecting a tray at the next table where a group of Brylcreamed old geezers with beetle-black shoes sit. They laugh a lot for pensioners and nobody says 'Blitz' or 'penny farthing' or 'air-raid shelters'. The tray collector sprays and then wipes their table. I'm not saying his job doesn't have its good points. He can talk the most shit about himself and listen to the tallest stories and everyone goes home happy and unexposed. But it's no job for a man.

Like I told the careers adviser I'm not doing women's work. I wanted to ask the best way to get into TV advertising or production but the question, asked in my head, sounded like a new tune set to the music of an old tune and I kept hearing 'tell me how to be a movie star', in the background, so I kept quiet, although when you check it I've spent most of my life watching TV. I understand the viewing public, what they watch, how they think, what makes them laugh. I could sink a bad programme so low it gets talked about and everyone tunes in. I have a good imagination. Everyone says so. The careers adviser clasped his fingers together behind the back of his head and rocked his chair until the two back legs alone supported it, and then he came up with a half-hearted list of deadbeat ideas. *My people have done slavery already, so I've no intention of doing a youth apprentice scheme for 50p and a packet of chips* is all I said, and we left it at that.

A siren goes off. Behind me, red lights flash on the one-armed bandits. Three cherries in a row, and coins clink-clink-clink on top of each other. I pull the bundle of letters out of my rucksack. There are thousands of his words in my hands. You'd think they'd weigh more. I take another bite of ice cream; this time my teeth sink deep. There is a biting-down jolt and freezing anaesthetic spreads out from the centre of my head.

In replying to this letter, please write on the envelope:

Number ....K47P9602...........   Name ....Johnson............

Wing ....C...............

> HMP DARTMOOR
> PRINCETOWN
> YELVERTON
> DEVON
> PL20 6RR

20 October 1980

Dear Son

If your mother was alive we would have made fifteen years married. When we were married five years your mother called the type of anniversary I think it was wood. Tin is for ten years. She came to England as a youngster and got used to the way things are labelled in this country. I keep thinking on the first time I see her. I know your mother tells that we met at one of Dolores' Sunday dinners. I listened to her story many times never interrupting. She came late with fried plantain. She wore a pink dress with buttons like marshmallows. Her legs were tangled and wet from the rain. She wore shoes with no back and no front just a middle and her toenails were polished clamshells. I worried she would catch a chill. If I followed my mind I would have gone for a towel and dried between her toes. There was not the first time I see her.

I will tell you a story now.

It was autumn. I hadn't seen that many seasons pass and the sick trees still shocked me I had to keep reminding myself they would come back to life in the spring. I passed the bus shelter across from the Co-op. Used to be you could catch the 36 from there. It might not still be so. She was leaning against the bus stand hiding the timetable with her long back. Her legs reached all the way past the night bus schedule. They were thin and they touched at the knees putting me in mind of a child who had put its shoes on the wrong foot for her left leg looked made for the right side and the right for the left. She was eating. People didn't eat much on the street those days. Kids ate the odd bag of chips or packet of crisps but she was a woman eating big square crackers from an orange wrapper and the crumbs that weren't stuck to her lips blew in the air. Her eyes were brighter than custard-apple seeds and her spirit was amber. The Highway Code tells you to be prepared to stop when you see that colour. I never was. Plenty men were slamming on the brakes. Emergency stops all along the high street. There are no people in my blood family who can read dreams or tell the future in the leaves of an upturned teacup so I didn't know how things would turn out. Three weeks before I see your mother I danced with a girl with a green spirit at a shebeen in West London. We were doing all right. We could have kept going.

Love and blessings

Your Father

Sonny

In replying to this letter, please write on the envelope:

Number ....K47P9602...... Name ....Johnson....

Wing ......C...........

HMP DARTMOOR
PRINCETOWN
YELVERTON
DEVON
PL20 6RR

7 July 1980

Dear Geoffhurst

I hope this letter finds you and your sister in good health. It goes without saying that I miss you both but I miss the strangest things. Last week it was shoes. I missed a pair of tan bendy shoes that understood my corns and held the shape of my foot whether I was wearing them or not and I missed the shoelaces pulling tight the slack leather sides. Do you know I have Jan Ernest Matzeliger to thank for those shoes? He was a Dutch West Indian Negro who died in 1889 but not before he spent eleven years making the first machine for sewing the soles of shoes to their uppers. This week it is your mother's cooking haunting me. Not the fancy dishes she could do when she put her mind to it no. Just a plate of plain white rice well washed of starch so the grains are by themselves and swelled just so until they are soft but still you need teeth. I would like two green bananas and a spoonful of buttered cabbage to go with it and a piece of oily fish probably mackerel but there would be no complaints if it was a little red goatfish. I miss garlic. I try not to think on it. It may sound strange but I didn't used to think. It seemed a foolish way to pass time when there was so much to do. Now I hardly do anything because there is so much to think about. I think about big things and end up deep in Dartmoor mist and suddenly things I am not thinking of at all become clear. Today is a good example. I was making a list of the early black footballers that got through. I went all the way back to Arthur Wharton from the Gold Coast who was goalkeeper for Preston in the mid 1800s and Walter Tull who played for Tottenham Hotspurs in the 1910s. Everyone has their time. Mine has gone. Be watchful and recognize yours. There is nothing sadder than someone trying to reclaim their time. If I had my time again I would have studied how the black footballers that went before me convinced their managers to play them and got the fans behind them. I could have come through with football if I had played the right game off the pitch. I would have given you all a house near Epping Forest with an old old oak upfront and a Jaguar parked on the gravel drive. And then she would have looked at me with a coconut rundown of love and respect. I should have chosen a short woman if I wanted someone to look up to me. Ha Ha. I was thinking all that and out of nowhere I suddenly remembered garlic and I understood why the Israelites wanted it so bad they were willing to turn their back on Moses and freedom.

I send you my love and best wishes

Your father Sonny

Your father Sonny. I wonder if he isn't pushing that message home too strong, but then the hand on my chin slips and catches my jaw. Clint Eastwood. Him . . . And the split-second elation vanishes.

I throw back my head and as I straighten up I scan the room. I doubt any of the oldies are more than eighty-five, and that seems like a fair innings. I don't see myself drooling on past ninety and I won't be freezing my body for defrosting when technology catches up. It will be a sad day when all those who knew my mum are dead except me. As long as there are people who remember her she exists. The perv who used to watch us play in Charley Park stopped me a few months back and told me what a beautiful woman Mum was. I was really pleased, him being more attuned to adolescent boys and what not.

In the end Auntie Harriet is the only one holding my mum's life all the way through, and even if she didn't use the same words as Mum a lot of the time, and they didn't smell similar, and she hadn't fronted the authorities on my behalf, I'd have to get back with her because swapping memories of Mum leaves me feeling like a kid who has traded a grubby copy of *The Metal Master* for a extremely-rare-and-in-beautiful-condition copy of *The Hordes of General Fang*.

I tap my pocket for coins and head for the counter. The assistants are both busy serving, but I don't blend well and, besides, I'm breaking the 'where to stand rule', so one of them stops entering the cost of breakfast items into the till and looks up warily. I mime phone. She points to a wall, next to where I came in, with a call box hanging on it.

I walk over slowly, thinking all the while.

A black man, Garrett Morgan, invented traffic lights in 1923. They told me that, Mum and Auntie Harriet (either or both of them). I think Granddad told them. The first traffic light system had amber and green – stop and go. Kids' stuff. Stop isn't a word that's open to interpretation. It won't have hundreds of dictionary entries. They teach you 'stop' before speech to save you from being scalded – burnt – electrocuted – killed. The first lesson for life on the street. Rule one of the Green Cross Code, because deaths occur from ignoring stop signs.

If he had understood 'stop' I wouldn't be getting an ice-cream headache in a service station somewhere off the M4. He wouldn't be visiting the Queen. And I'd have a mother.

I shove my coin in.

'Jace, it's me.   Yes I'm fine – no nothing too stupid.   Let's call it a day trip.   Dartmoor.   A man about a dog.   Listen, that trainee-advertising thing – if I get through today.   I figure it's my time now is all.   Maybe you were right all along.   About me being afraid.   Well, after today it will seem like small fry. I doubt I'll be scared of anything much again.   A big accountancy firm doesn't have its own creative services department? When you get the time do a bit of research. Now's as good a time as any.   Yes, 100 per cent sure.   If they can't, at least they'll be able to tell me what to do next.   Could be.   If you can.   I don't see why not.   The pips, yeah.   You're the Don.   Ah ha yeah. Laters J. Laters.'

Not far from Bovey Tracey

Taunton. Taunton Deane. GOOD FOOD. 1/2m to a petrol pump, a knife and fork, a cup, and a bed. Slow down. Speed kills. Yeovil. Tiverton. 40km to Barnstaple→Tip Top. Pour-over topping with a light creamy taste.

In replying to this letter, please write on the envelope:

Number .... K47P9602 .... Name .... Johnson ....

Wing .... C ....

HMP DARTMOOR
PRINCETOWN
YELVERTON
DEVON
PL20 6RR

21 December 1983

Dear Geoffhurst

Seasons Greetings.

It is as if I have been writing to you for ever. Years of letters and visiting orders. Hoping you will turn up one Sunday hoping you wont. Watching the post for word from you and full of relief and sadness both when nothing comes. Writing to you is like prayer. I wonder if I have been given a wrong contact number or wonder if God is engaged or he has put the answer machine on because he is dealing with an earthquake or giving instructions to angels or else he doesn't pick up because he knows it is me and knows what I have done. Most of all I wonder if there's anybody there at all. I was thinking of telling you a story about your mother for no other reason than I like to tell it. But I am going to end up telling you a story about your aunt because it is hard to pull those two apart. The way your Aunt Harriet feels about me now has doubled in size fed on grief and by sucking the marrow of your mothers energy and dreams but she set against me long before your mother died.

I'll tell you a story now.

I met Harriet first. Your mother second. There was a tight feeling between Harriet and I that could have pushed us together or just as easily pulled us to opposite sides of the room. Given a choice I would have taken her for my own for I took to her but when your mother came along I stopped having choices. The reason she is against me goes back to 1964. It was spring. I was young and getting accustomed to England. My body was changing. Where back home in the hot sun my nature was always high over here it lay low until spring and then took charge telling me where to go and how to spend my money and what to do with my time. Whenever I could be with Hindy I was. Around that time Malcolm X went to Mecca and when he came back he made a speech calling himself a true Muslim and if he was true what did that make them? They must have heard that speech as a cussing. It was a dangerous time in their relationship. Your granddaddy was making a hullabaloo. Martin Luther King was organizing people to sit down when they needed to be standing up. He was of the mind that now Malcolm had stopped saying white people were blue-eyed devils he had the potential to be a world leader. There was to be a meeting to start fundraising for Malcolm's new group in the basement of a man who sold incense sticks and carvings and books about Africa outside Finsbury Park tube station. We called him the Professor and your granddaddy was forever boosting him up to Hindy. The Professor talked self-reliance and education and love of his people but when it came to lying down with women he chose white. He wasn't unusual. The black men raising the tightest fists in salute with the loudest cries of black is beautiful were often the light-skinned brothers or the black brothers who preferred pork to beef. I can't talk with two heads. Without them we might not have had Malcolm or Bob or even Martin for that matter. I didn't blame the Professor we were taught to hate ourselves for hundreds of years and it leaks out in the oddest places but some people backbited him. I could see how Hindy might suit him. Hindy couldn't quite pass but if he imagined she'd caught a slight tan? Plus she was the daughter of a respected race man and it was a time when black people looked up to other black people. Hindy said her daddy needed help at the meeting. I disbelieved the old man but looking back it could have been true. They were all for the liberation and equality but they wouldn't fry a dumpling or pour their own drinks. I thought there was a fix-up going on and said she should stay away. She followed her own mind. It was the first time she disobeyed me to my face and I couldn't settle. Felt haunted. I was living in a bedsit them times. Harriet came round looking for Hindy. When I told her where Hindy was her face crumpled down. I didn't like visitors. Only Hindy and the postman knocked my door. There was nothing in the room except a mattress on the floor a television a radio a fridge and a milk bottle with daffodils. I invited her in. She sat on the mattress and I gave her a Heineken without a glass. We both looked at the flowers and I knew that she knew who put them there. She drank from the can. I sat next to her. She had a big brave afro that the family fought over her daddy wanting her to keep it Hindy wanting it for herself and her mother not appreciating it at all. She had the same rice sticking to the bottom of the pot smell as your mother. Seems her daddy never asked her to go places with him. Hindy Hindy Hindy. Harriet saw a thing first and touched it and smelt it and held it in her hands and then along came Hindy and snatched it away. Finders keepers losers weepers. The finder wasn't supposed to shed tears. We had intimate relations. It only happened once. Harriet said we could have been together if not for Hindy. I knew we were lying down only because of her. None of us were married then and anyway it was '64 and the rules were different but not so different that I didn't know I had done a wrong thing. Harriet been angry with me ever since. In the end she married Leighton when was me she wanted. Leighton married Harriet when he wanted Hindy. Your mother and I were the only two who got what we wanted. The Sonny and Hindy Show. For a while.

With best wishes for a happy Christmas and a prosperous New Year

Your ever loving father Sonny

The little girl's companion in the seat in front reaches over to pull the cord on the blind at her window, moving slowly, smoothly so as not to disturb the girl using her cushiony bosom to sleep on. A purple firework fountains into the air just as she touches the cord. I am tempted to put my hand on hers, stop her closing it because the girl will miss the free fireworks if she wakes up with the shade down, and it is suddenly important for her to see the impact of energy lighting up the skies even when, especially when, it won't last long. We exchange glances through the glass before the blind is pulled closed. She looks away first. I open my mouth to speak but nothing comes out. By the time her seat reclines into the space in front of me I realize what I really wanted to say. *I am for real*, I wanted to tell her, *an honest person – straight as the Mile End Road. My truth is so big I can trip over it accidentally – it stretches all the way back to before I existed.*

I pick at a strip of Velcro at the opening of my memories and when I close it back there are fibres that need picking out. *Intimate relations. It only happened once.* I remember all the times he called her *crazy, a Cadbury's fruit and nut case, away with the fairies* and (tapping his temples) *touched*, but there's no crime there. It's not as if she killed someone.

♠

A billboard zips past of a man chasing a woman. He's carrying a giant bunch of flowers. Her face says 'for me?' in a fake way, because she's that happy you know she's selecting the right vase in her head. She is one of those women with lots of the same thing for no good reason, like Auntie Harriet has more than one type of glass – tulip for white wine, a flute for champagne. At first I think I have hiccups. When I start to tremble I cotton-on to the fact that I'm laughing. My shoulders shake from trying to hold it back, and just below my ribs on my left side I have a sharp pain. There is nobody to slap my face and shock me out of hysteria so I talk to myself in my head asking *What's so fucking funny?* I have no answer, but searching for one calms me a little.

I guess I'm slightly tickled imagining Auntie Harriet once drank from a beer can.

♠

Wiland. Honiton. Impulse. Men just can't help acting on it. Chudley.

Past two scarecrows

The sky pokes through geometric gaps from two electrical pylons. Lower down Worzel Gummidge and friend wear bucket hats and squashed jackets, wave straw hands. I strain my neck twisting it as far as it will go, following the scarecrows until they disappear and all that remains to be seen are miles of Argos-gold crops topped with blue. If I joined all the pieces of sky I've seen in the past five years it would add up to less than I've seen today. You have to make a big effort for nature in London; take buses for groups of trees, set your alarm clock for a sunrise. Seeing the sea is a day trip. This low-down sky is flushed with white light. There is no need to stretch my neck or remember to look up. It is all around. Love's the same. You take it for granted until you wake up naked and alone in a field at three a.m. in the dead of a starless night.

In replying to this letter, please write on the envelope:

Number ...K47P9602........... Name ...Johnson.................

Wing ...C..................

HMP DARTMOOR
PRINCETOWN
YELVERTON
DEVON
PL20 6RR

8 June 1982

Dear Son

I hope this letter makes sense to you. It is hard for me to write and if I go back and change it to read better I know I will never send it. There is a talking group here for men who sex children. They call them nonces. Before I came here I imagined they lusted after force-ripened girls with colt's legs and cow eyes but these people sex baby girls and boys some not out of diapers. The nonces are exercised at a different time from us and have their own wing for safety. We do not have any contact with them so praise God I know nothing more. Group two have done bad things to women. One of the men shaved a woman's head with an electric hedge cutter then used her shorn hair to tie sweet peas to bamboo sticks so their shoots wouldn't get damaged. Then he raped her with garden instruments. He left her body on a compost heap. If you saw him reading *Gardener's Weekly* you wouldn't guess the stench of evil sweats from his pores like the odour of fat garlic. I need to tell you I am part of his group. At first I didn't know why they put me to join. Four weeks passed before I said a word and then I was just answering for politeness sake. It was a fight that got out of hand. I kept to the right-hand side of a bed barely three foot wide and hit my arm against a brick wall when I reached left for her. She had taken her body from me and left me without a woman for the first time since I was fourteen. It was self-defence. Now I know why they put me to join. It was me caused what happened to happen and if not that day it would have been another for I had been UNKNOWINGLY training my thoughts and actions towards that event like an Olympian for years. When I realized what I had done pain spurted and kept gurgling until I was convinced I would drown and I would have been glad but instead I have stayed in the first five minutes of my head being held under water. Only now I can talk underwater though the words echo. I eat underwater though the food tastes salt. I sleep underwater dreaming of wrapping seaweed tightly round my neck or ripping my underbelly against jagged coral and I swim with my mouth wide open searching for squid with poisonous ink.

The summer she died you couldn't just say the weather was misbehaving or acting out of character. You would have to say it had gone stark raving mad and when the natural order is upset all manner of creatures are unsettled. Blossom and the God squad were attending to their souls convinced we were living in the last days spouting passages about the sea drying up and though I didn't take that on I couldnt help wondering. The sun all topsy-turvy with the rays meant for Australia or

Africa turned on us. She was my wife. Little England with her bus queues and zebra crossings was spinning out of control. Whether I played football and if I got paid and how much and whether the rain would ever come back. Honour and obey? My marriage. My business. She did not look dead. Before rigor mortis a sleeping dog on a hot pavement lies much like a dead dog. But I thought I could recognize the emptiness of a departed soul. The prosecution said she was dead when you were sitting on the kitchen floor cradling her in your lap. Perhaps her soul was late in leaving. I AM NOT LIKE THE OTHERS. Do you remember she kept coming at me? You must remember that. In this group they like to put words on to you. INSECURE. Insecurity is based on fear they say. I thought of the time when I was twelve and my father was gone walkabouts and I sat down at a gambling table with Cowboy and a man who never stood a round of drinks because he claimed never to have enough money whose name was Jimmy but who we called Small Change. I took my mother's rent money knowing that win or lose she would tear a strip off my hind. I won. I took a pig home. Stabbed it in the throat and drained the blood into a vessel. We roasted and grilled and fried for weeks. Side belly. Leg loin. Shoulder blade. Pig's trotters. Neck bones. Ears. Jowls. Liver. Kidney. Tongue. And there were reminders of my courage in the months to come when we took jars of salted pork off the shelf. So when they first called me a coward I laughed out loud. I have never been scared of another man it is true. But I have always been scared of myself. Scared of what I would do the day her orange light shone so bright I ended up lost in the shadow. Her daddy fill up her head with ~~what I considered~~ race-pride ~~nonsense~~. Had her walking around with a longed-out neck. He was of the belief that knowing George Washington Carver got the Roosevelt medal in 1939 for extracting 285 products from the peanut and 118 from the sweet potato and knowing he was offered big money by the light bulb man Edison to work for him but he wanted to go his own way this was the type of knowledge needed to keep his girls healthy. Vaccinations against racialists he called those facts. To my mind he was controlling my family heading them for trouble and I could not pull them back. Descending from kings and queens and an ancient civilization was all well and good but I couldn't see a use without having inherited a share of their gold and jewels too. At least then we could have pawned them or sold them for a down payment on a little house. The one your aunt and uncle have would have set us up at the start but the way she talked down to the housing people they were in no rush to give us a nice place. Before we married our plan was for her to put everything behind me until I came through with the football but even before you and Susie came along it did not work that way. I wouldn't talk against your mother to anyone least of all you but ~~just to say a different wife would have worked to support her husbands dream~~. you ~~know~~ may recall she didn't take to telling so the jobs she took were where they gave her keys to come and go but she and the employer never got on for long and soon met on a happenstance that would be enough for her to ask for final payment.

I had been sitting on the factory bench for 136 hours. The factory noises played tricks with me. The electric mixer used to blend the rhubarb and custard flavours together sounded like an aggressive tackle. A four foot needle for injecting chocolate into eclairs sounded like aiming a wet ball a short distance with the inside of the right foot. I stopped walking home through the park because of the excited voices of men calling out to their friends for a pass. I wanted to knock over and steal the balls from wobbly toddlers. I envied the lifetime of goal scoring and keep-ups and dribbling in front of them. I walked home fast. When I didn't play football all the energy battened down inside my muscles I could feel it there looking to be set loose. In case of stray balls from a street game I looked down at the pavement. The sun played my neck-back like a xylophone.

When I came home the house was empty. Susie was staying with her auntie and some kids from the flats had knocked for you to play out. I could hear laughing from the stairwell. Inside the flat was a glow coming out from under the living-room door. It puzzled me. My guess would have been fire but there was no additional heat in that direction. Nobody was acting in an emergency way and I couldn't smell smoke. I went in a little. We had a sofa and two chairs so they could have sat in different places but they chose to sit close with their thighs touching and Leighton's arm draped across the back of the sofa. Leighton was at my house playing messenger boy. Your Auntie Harriet was always sending herbal powders and health-giving teas for your mother. She was wearing a wrapover housecoat. You remember silky green with red dragons. It covered her up all except her out-of-doors legs knocking against Leighton's. But the worst part was her spirit. I'd been carving pieces away for years trying to keep her ~~from harm safe safe~~ from leaving me and of late I had been working hard at it and believed I was getting somewhere until I saw her spirit blazing like a driftwood beach-fire. I knew she had the grow-back kind but to see it so intact and strong. I shut the door back fast. I bathed. I could not eat my corned beef and rice because my emotions stopped up my throat. You came in around five. The heat knocked us all into sleep early. They say the gods feed a sleeping man but I woke up late late hungry and fretful. I went into the kitchen to make a corned-beef and pickle sandwich out of leftover dinner. She followed. I couldn't accuse her of a naked spirit and of growing it and polishing it in secret so I made something of her and Leighton. That made her plate-smashing mad. She said there was nothing doing but even if there was what about Harriet. Why did I follow her into the house at Anthony's birthday. It was all so crazy I laughed and laughed. I asked what lies Harriet had told her. She said no lies. Harriet hadn't said a word. I took bread out of the breadbin. I dropped the loaf. She mentioned the intimacy between Harriet and I over ten year earlier and by the time I'd counted the five slices spread on the floor I real-

ized she had known all along but ~~and~~ had not minded ~~much~~
at all. That was what she thought of me.

'Want one of these?' The bald girl is kneeling on her seat; her chin is
on the headrest of her chair. She looks settled, as if she has been
watching me for some time. She is waving a tube of sweets.

'Thanks, but I'm okay.' I feel myself vibrating, emitting low-level
sound waves that only animals can hear. I have a strong urge to curl
into a ball and hold myself tight enough to stop the movement.

~~I can't remember. Maybe~~ I said something about the time I
was intimate with Harriet that I should not have. When I bent
to pick the bread up she jumped on my back and pummelled
my head. I threw her off. It cut me that I would never make
her need me for survival like air or water and there I was half
stifled because she could choke off my air supply any time she
was ready. I unscrewed the lid on a jar of pickles. I didn't take
my eyes off her. She came back at me. I held my fist out in
front of my body and she didn't break her speed just ran right
on to it. I took the chance while she was stunned to box the
side of her crazy head. Calm yourself and keep quiet woman
the punch said but she had turned deaf. I lost my senses. Sorry.
Forgive me. Was as if a magician threw a red blanket over my
head and when he grabbed the corner and pulled it off the
world was different. I was spent. Heat had been washed away
by a storm that cracked low in the sky. My wife was twisted in
a corner and the colour surrounding her sorrel red or pink like
the fat veins on a sea grape leaf and thick like forest or misted

like the moon at certain times I could not see it. If the writing
is messy and hard to understand again I beg forgiveness.

I am your loving father Sonny

'Sure you don't want one?' Chewing, she stretches the sweets
towards me. I shake my head. She draws the sweets back but stays
kneeling on the chair watching me. I give up on making her sit back
down. There are clusters of thin veins beneath the transparent skin
of her temples; blue, and writhing like a bucket of East End eels. She
is in transition. Her hair, her skin, her body – she is shedding her
earthly self. I ache for us both. There is nothing I can do for her
except pray for fine weather, hope it stays dry. The angel of death
loves bad weather. When speed is essential – for sudden death – he
holds on to lightning, but he prefers to be leisurely, breezing in on
cushions of rat-coloured clouds, with wet raven's wings and breath
like an old lady's mildewed winter coat.

It's as if I watched a private showing of a one-night-only movie
years ago that wasn't worth talking about because it was horrible and
quite frankly a bit far-fetched, and it's pointless discussing a film
with people who haven't seen it. And years later when you would
swear to anyone who asked that you recalled every detail, but you
aren't *exactly* convinced you remember it right, the leading man is
stepping out of the screen, breaking the rules and talking about his
actions, witnessing, giving testimony, like he was in the *audience*
that night.

I lie down; pull my tracksuit hood up over my head and rock
gently from side to side thinking about the pig he bought with the
gambling money, the screech it must have made when the person
it trusted, who had been feeding and petting it, plunged the knife
in to pierce its throat. I remember Auntie Harriet telling me how

much she looked forward to the sound pigs made as they were slaughtered during the festive season because it marked the beginning of Christmas, and from then on in the celebrations began.

Dartmoor

'Princetown,' I say, pronouncing all the letters, so I sound untraceable, as if me and the BBC newsreaders were born in the same hospital.

'*Where* in Princetown?'

'The town centre,' I say, a bit annoyed because my plan was to use single words only, close down conversations. I couldn't find a map but I assume it will be a short walk to the prison and this way the taxi driver can't eggs-up in my business. He nods and I jump into the back seat of a blue Granada and slam the door closed. There is a sticker below the handle, *thank you for not smoking* it says inside a red circle. We drive along traffic-free roads at 25 m.p.h. There is an air freshener disguised as a set of miniature traffic lights hanging from the rear-view mirror. The car smells like a hearse full of the hundreds of bigheaded blooms it takes to spell out a relative's family title.

'I only ever take a fare to the prison once. I had a prisoner's fiancée in the back this time last year. She couldn't stop talking about how much she loved him. She was going to visit every Sunday, write every day and keep her knickers on until he came home. I never saw her again. They don't make the journey twice. The moors are too bleak and the journey's too far. Especially if you're from London. That's right isn't it? You're from London?'

'Uhmmm.' Bangers go off outside, one after another like machine-gun fire. Blue. Green. Blue-green. Purple.

'Yes, course you are.' I wind down the top of the window hoping to smell gunpowder and sausages and baked potatoes, searching for kids waving sparklers, or a dad in a back garden lighting rockets. Cold air whooshes in. I close it again quickly, leaving a gap at the top to counter the air-freshener effect. 'I wouldn't live in London for all the tea in China. All the . . .' He is searching for a right word. 'Community,' he says, pleased with his choice. 'Yes, all the *community* has gone out of it. People used to look out for each other, now they can't pronounce their neighbour's name. Not to mention the crowds,' he says, mentioning them. 'Londoners brag about the museums and theatres, but when you ask them the last time they went they uhhhmm and ahhh. I read the reviews to keep up. I've eaten in a Berni steakhouse more times than I can name. Madame Tussauds. Seen *The Mousetrap* three times. The changing of the guards. St Paul's Cathedral. Regent's Park. I know the capital. But no, they can keep the big smog.'

Trees are turning black. A witch's chin I recognize from child-hood shadows protrudes from the bushes blurring past. 'You weren't involved in the Brixton riots were you?'

'No.'

I don't take black taxis in London, or to be more accurate, they won't take me. I'm all for boycotting South African apples if it'll help to end apartheid but sometimes I look at the *Free Nelson Mandela* T-shirts and I think, if he was freed and he came to London, and was on the corner of Piccadilly Circus hailing a taxi after a night out with Desmond Tutu, he'd have some wait because the cabbies would switch on their yellow light and drive past empty, and that ought to have us staging sit-ins and marching, although personality-wise minicabs suit me better. I like to know costs and consequences upfront so I can make informed decisions. But right now, I'd sit in traffic with the meter spinning numbers beyond my wallet just for the convenience of slamming closed the smoked glass between driver and passenger.

'Toxteth? Did you see the Toxteth riots?' he asks, as if he wants a review of the latest blockbuster.

'Nope. Never been there.'

'Broadwater Farm?' He continues his roll call of recent riots.

'No,' I say quietly, rubbing my forehead, wondering if I can conjure enough civility to redirect the conversation to other rant-worthy topics. Does he think Maggie will succeed in starving the miners back to work? The Brighton bombing? And then he could ramble and I wouldn't be getting wound up because I've never met a miner and I don't know any Tories, though I suspect J might be holding out on me (some stuff isn't worth knowing. Monopoly has taught me the benefits of occasionally paying a ten-pound fine and staying well clear of the chance card). I remind myself of my plan to stay mute and then I pull my sweatshirt hood up around my face and look down, wishing I had a fat, smelly Cuban cigar.

'Terrible business,' he says. I carry on running my eyes over words without reading them. I drop the letter in my lap and slump the back of my head on to car fabric, giving him my attention, wanting to get it over with. 'Looting, petrol bombs, mayhem on the streets. There's no excuse for it. In the 1930s we had it all: unemployment, poverty, single parent families because of all the men killed in the First World War you know. But did we set fire to cars and steal from local businesses? No, we did not.' The words of the policeman who shot Cherry Groce are still fresh. *I just shot the first black shape I saw*. I lean forward in my seat and talk softly into his left ear.

'With all due respect, you *didn't* have it all. You might have been unemployed, but if you were smarter or better than the next man, they gave *you* the job. The local bobbies where you lived came singular, twos at the most. Special patrol groups didn't roam in vans looking for 1930s man to stop and search for no reason. White women didn't clutch their handbags when you walked past. PC Plod didn't raid your mother's house looking for an armed robber and accidentally shoot her as she slept and leave her a cripple in a wheelchair.'

I sit back. 'Nah, you *didn't* have it all.'

He looks at me in the rear-view mirror as if he didn't see me properly when I got in. He is eyeing me up, psyching me out, ready to identify me if necessary at a later date. 'A tall black fellow, had a lot to say for himself. He had a lazy eye.' I may as well give him a copy of my fingerprints. He is silent for all of thirty seconds. The pulse in my neck slows down, then speeds up when realize I've messed up. All I had to do was keep my lip buttoned and not make eye contact. If I was going to shoot my mouth off I coulda done that on the bus and saved money. So much for travelling incognito. Now he knows my voice and he's had a good old butchers.

'The way I see it,' says Blabbermouth, breaking the thirty-six seconds of silence. 'There can be no excuse for hacking a policeman to death the way those animals on that estate in Tottenham did.' He looks right at me when he says this. Presumably in the middle of nowhere it is fine to drive forward whilst looking backwards, because there are no other cars. I feel like I'm stuck in a lift between floors with a Radio 4 discussion being piped in.

He wants me to feel bad because most of 'those animals' look like me. I refuse. I've had this shit all my life, holding our collective black breath when an old white woman with a yellow and blue face, who was good to cats, whose husband had a line of ribbons on his chest from the war he fought to save thugs like us from Hitler, is knocked down and killed for 57p, breathing out when we see a mugshot in the *Evening Standard* and it isn't a picture of us. I'm having none of it. I am pretty sure white people aren't tossing and turning at night because they share the same pigmentation as the Yorkshire Ripper.

I think of telling Robin Day to *Shut the fuck up and drive*, but I have no idea where I am. There are no landmarks. No traffic lights to turn left or right at. Unless phone-boxes are a different colour out here I haven't seen one. Not even Ronald McDonald dares to venture this far. Left at this blade, right at that cluster of weeds? If an A–Z of dead grass exists I don't have one. The next time an old codger gives me left at the Rising Sun, right at the Prince of Wales, keep going until you get to the Fox and Grapes directions I won't laugh, I'll hug him.

Nobody knows I'm here. I think of the Moors Murderers burying their victims in the soulless earth. I'm inside out, back to front. I'm seeing myself instead of being myself. I remember when I was really young my grandfather telling me how easy it was to recapture a slave. They'd pull us all – the free men and entertainers, sea merchants, businessmen and slaves. *There was no point in running. We stood out because of this*, he'd said tapping the skin on the front of his hand. I take a deep breath and lean forward again. Polite as I can I ask, 'Is there any way you can cut the political debate and just drive the fucking car?'

In replying to this letter, please write on the envelope:

Number ...... K47P9602 ...... Name ...... *Johnson*

Wing ...... C ......

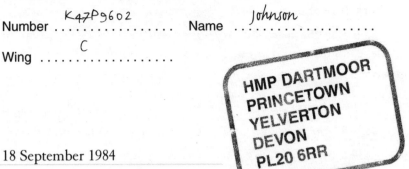

HMP DARTMOOR
PRINCETOWN
YELVERTON
DEVON
PL20 6RR

18 September 1984

Dear Son

Many happy returns of the day. Eighteen. As your birthday approaches I been thinking of the day you were born. Your real <u>birth</u> <u>day.</u>

Gordon Banks

George Cohen   Ray Wilson

Nobby Stiles   Jackie Charlton   Bobby Moore

Alan Ball   Bobby Charlton   Martin Peters

<u>Geoff Hurst</u>   Roger Hunt

Geoffhurst I been thinking about your name. My mother was pushing to christen you <u>Jeremiah</u> at the United Pentecostal Church of God. Your mother's father wanted Huey. He wasn't insisting. He understood if we didn't want to name you after a Black Panther. But what about Malcolm. Malcolm was our collective manhood he said. Surely no black man could object to Malcolm. Wasn't enough he called your mother after Marcus Garveys Sister. In the end he agreed it was our choice but pleaded for us not to name you after an English footballer. He said educated white people were happy to have us running around a cold muddy field chasing ball whilst their kid acted like Sensible Somebody going to university and studying books in the warm library. On your fourth birthday I bought you a football and he bought you a stethoscope.

I was in England with talent to burn and I had to hold on keep training and wait until I could put everything I had behind the ball and score before the whistle blew and the ref called time. It wasn't like now. You couldn't turn on the TV on a Saturday afternoon and watch Brendon Batson and Laurie Cunningham and Cyrille Regis dance the kind of music that their team mates could never make because The Three Degrees had the rhythm of the drum and their ancestors wore feathers on their feet and later they sang Negro spirituals and flew all the way home.

I am not good with dates your mother took care of that sort of thing but I remember 30 July 1966.

I'll tell you a story now.

It was a rainbow-making day. Hard rain and bright sunlight both. But the weather didn't matter. What mattered was I had a ticket to the World Cup final. I had bought the ticket on the gamble that Brazil would get through. The ticket cost ten shillings. If Pele had been playing the ticket would have seemed cheap but it was an England v Germany final and the ticket seemed pricey. I thought of selling it on for a profit but the buyers were offering me so much money I started thinking if this thing was so great why was I giving my ticket away. There were 93,000 fans. The Queen came. Germany took an early lead after thirteen minutes of play. No matter. What goes around comes around and Overath who had already tripped Ball now tripped Moore and Geoff Hurst scored with a header off a free kick from Bobby Moore and we were even. 1–1. Things were tight. Not that England couldn't handle the Germans. Charlton for instance he played smooth as Nat King Cole not a wrong note. It took until thirteen minutes before time was called for Martin Peters to score. 2–1. England had won every face around me told me so. But then fifteen seconds before full time the Germans powered the ball at close range past Gordon Banks. Shock. The referee called 2–2. We were in extra time. In the hundredth minute Hurst scored off an Alan Ball pass. Under the bar and in. The decision rested with the Soviet linesman and he called it in. What a fuss. World War Two come again. 3–2 to England. In the last few seconds it seemed like the game was done then Geoff Hurst ran on to a long ball from Bobby Moore and shot every hope and dream and ambition I carried to England past the German goalkeeper into the roof of the net. The Trafford crowd raised up from the dead hands held high cheering chanting Geoff Hurst Geoff Hurst and giving praise and magnifying his name and he was no more white than Pele was black because they had gone past colour. I was witnessing something future generations would ask about over and over. They would shake their heads in wonder and even if it meant they might never have met their wives or had their children they would secretly wish they were born earlier so they could have been there. Geoff

Hurst came through. He came through for me. And the greasy teddy boys in their winkle-pickers chasing me with knuckle dusters and the money dropped on the counter by the shopkeeper who had just taken a fat slice of my wages but still he couldn't bear to touch me and my arse always on the reserve bench and the fungus on the wall and freezing when the shilling ran out and all the other shit it was all worth it just for that one moment.

I'd always been a big shot on the island. I could dance up a storm and run faster than any man I met. From when I arrived I'd realized that English people were trapped inside their heads and even as they hated us for our loose-hipped walk and the ease we danced the mashed potato they were watching and copying and trying to break free. Martin Luther King was marching in Mississippi. The whole white world was watching Cassius Clay. Sophisticated people who were above hating put their hate into the boxing ring transferred it to men from different stables to act out. And they watched every move Cassius made scared of missing the fight when the cocksure uppity nigger got his comeuppance and falling head over heels while they watched him use every square inch of the ring to dance like Sammy Davis only he weren't ugly and he didn't need Frank Sinatra and his posse of rats because Cassius was a king whatever way they carved up the world. It wasn't all sweet. Enoch Powell's moustache twitched every now. We drank outside of pubs because the landlord wanted it that way and we walked in groups for safety. They killed Kelso

Cochrane a carpenter just come over not long from Antigua but for all that I believed I could make it here. We all did. You suckled blind at your mother but when she passed you to me you opened your eyes for the first time. You were no stranger to me. I was swell hearted same way as when the third goal came in the hundredth minute and first I couldn't speak. When I found my voice I started quiet and got louder and louder filling the ward with my chanting and scaring the nurses. Ge—oooo—ff Hurrr—st. Ge—oooo—ff Hurrr—st. Ge—oooo—ff Hurrr—st.

I remain your ever loving father.

Sonny

I wind the window halfway down and press my face against the hard rush of cold air. After a few minutes I wind the window back up and then I stuff the unread letters back in my rucksack.

♠

If I keep walking straight and don't turn my head the mishmash grey buildings with matchbox windows sprawl my whole horizon.

Even without the prison this moor wouldn't qualify as an area of outstanding natural beauty. I doubt people picnic out here. I could walk alone for ever, like a dusty cowboy with the wind uprooting dried grasses and blowing them away. Then all of a sudden the ground dips and swells and the grass turns spongy. I think of swamps and quicksand. I won't take concrete for granted again. I will notice the regular, dependable slabs holding me upright. Trips to the countryside are a long way off, but when I have a family and *have* to go, the wife, kids and golden Labrador will explore the countryside at thirty m.p.h – driving through with the windows open – past the flying insects and different types of stomach-turning shit – the hard pellets and stools and great wet rivers of cow dung.

A firework whizzes into the sky, breaks into a hundred pieces of jewelled light and spatters down in loud, silent colour. And that's when I see the silhouette of a man walking towards me. Then he is gone. Peek-a-boo. Alone again, with a menacing figure approaching, witches' chins, with the ground preparing to suck my body into a six-foot grave, with the pissed-off taxi driver at large, and if needs be I could call for help, but I'm no photo-fit victim. And one time a kid with National Health specs and freckles and a cute little white girl cried out, and still they were tortured, and after their dying pleas were tape-recorded, their bodies were buried. So what chance do I have? My eyes are adjusting to the dark. The shadow is growing. Keeping my head high I drop my gaze down in three-second bursts, searching out the nearest quarry stone. There is a sizeable rock a few paces ahead but if wrestling has taught me anything it is, 'don't lower your centre of gravity unnecessarily'. I fix my head straight, noticing birds' nests looking vulnerable, exposed to predators in leaf-less trees. I walk steadily pulling my rucksack off my back as I go. I unzip my bag and feel for the leather pouch of my knife, slip it in the side pocket of my jeans. A Catherine wheel splutters: 12-year old Susie showing off; cartwheeling, firing rockets of pink and purple in different directions.

A tall shadow is forty feet away. It drops its weight on a bent left knee and comes up fast on a straight-legged right; a cool, once-prac-tised swagger. *He*. His hands are thrust deep in his pockets. He hunches forward showing the crown of his head, protecting his face against the wind, hiding his identity. A firework sounds a gap-tooth whistle behind me and he looks up, then he jolts to a standstill as if he's walked slap-bang into a glass door. If I stop too, he is in charge. *Simple Simon Says* . . . I keep my pace even. My eyes are drying out from the wind and from trying not to blink. My lazy eye turns away, spinning out of control, useless; reminding me I can't rely on anyone, not even myself, because I am inside a body and all bodies let you down in the end. I squeeze my bad eye closed, willing my left vision to compensate, sharpen up. Loneliness grows into a blubbering embrace, traps me in its cleavage, and threatens to suffocate me. I think of Auntie Blossom. *Help and thank you. Most prayers are one or the other*. I pray silently, in time with my footsteps. 'Help' with my left foot, 'me' with my right. But it's not God I want. It's her palm on my forehead. Her pillow, imprint of her head still fresh, to flatten my nose into. A plaster for my knee – my name dragging through the air as her legs scramble to reach me – long wraparound arms.

My right hand hovers over my trouser pocket. He is close enough for me to see his face. I slow down, willing him to move, because I have the feeling I am on a train and he is in the carriage in front of me, and if I move too quickly and he stands still I will walk into my future. He is wearing a beret the French way, pulled down on one side over horizontal worry lines that cut into his fleshy forehead. He is a curious mixture of well presented and rough. A square, freshly shaven jaw juts out below a turned-up coat collar, above two rolls of fat. His skin is near-dead; a spider plant determined to stay alive in a dark corner of a doctor's surgery.

I look down at his shoes but they are blocked from view. I step back, confused by a two-foot bush blooming in November, by the Anchor-butter glow in front of his feet, protecting him with thorns and the hundreds of high-yellow flowers joined together, rolled into one, like a golden football. I watch my nose. Watch my lips curve as he gives me the scared smile. I think of movies where the sane slide into craziness after destroying their mirror image, of a mountaineer on the news who hacked away his own frostbitten arm to save himself. I don't know this man. *This guessing game you'll never win*. It isn't Rumpelstiltskin.

I stroke the surface of my grief and wince. I want his suffering to be taller, deeper, wider, and then he opens his arms close to his sides, revealing the palms of his hands, like Jesus showing his wounds.

Acknowledgements

For background information on witchcraft the author gratefully acknowledges *Hoodoo* by Harry Middleton Hyatt (Cambridge, 1978).

'Foolish Little Girl', The Shirelles, words and music by Helen Miller and Howard Greenfield © 1963, Screen Gems. Reproduced by permission of Screen Gems-EMI Music Publishing Ltd, London, WC2H 0QY.

'Sha-la-la', The Shirelles, words by Robert Mosley © Windswept Publishing. Reproduced by permission of Windswept Publishing-Music Sales Ltd, London, W1D 3JB.

'Mama Said', The Shirelles, words by Luther Dixon © Windswept Publishing. Reproduced by permission of Windswept Publishing-Music Sales Ltd, London, W1D 3JB.

'Don't Say Goodnight and Mean Goodbye' words by Partee/D'Angelis. Copyright © Maggie Music Company. All rights reserved. Used by permission.